CONVICTION

Also by Julia Dahl

Run You Down

Invisible City

CONVICTION

Julia Dahl

Minotaur Books
New York

CONVICTION. Copyright © 2017 by Julia Dahl. All rights reserved. Printed in the United States of America. For information, address St. Martin's Press, 175 Fifth Avenue, New York, N.Y. 10010.

www.minotaurbooks.com

Designed by Omar Chapa

Library of Congress Cataloging-in-Publication Data

Names: Dahl, Julia, 1977– author.
Title: Conviction : a novel / Julia Dahl.
Description: First edition. | New York : Minotaur Books, 2017. | Series: Rebekah Roberts novels ; 3
Identifiers: LCCN 2016047069| ISBN 9781250083692 (hardcover) | ISBN 9781250083715 (ebook)
Subjects: LCSH: Jewish women—Fiction. | Women journalists—Fiction. | Families—Crimes against—Fiction. | Cold cases (Criminal investigation)—Fiction. | BISAC: FICTION / Mystery & Detective / General. | FICTION / Mystery & Detective / Women Sleuths. | GSAFD: Suspense fiction. | Mystery fiction.
Classification: LCC PS3604.A339 C66 2017 | DDC 813/.6—dc23
LC record available at https://lccn.loc.gov/2016047069

Our books may be purchased in bulk for promotional, educational, or business use. Please contact your local bookseller or the Macmillan Corporate and Premium Sales Department at 800-221-7945, extension 5442, or by e-mail at Macmillan Special Markets@macmillan.com.

First Edition: March 2017

10 9 8 7 6 5 4 3 2 1

For Mick

PART 1

CHAPTER ONE

Morning
July 5, 1992
Crown Heights, Brooklyn

The little boy walked to the storefront church alone, with blood on his hands and face.

Dorothy Norris arrived early, as usual, to lift the gate and set out the worship programs she'd photocopied the night before. She found him standing on the sidewalk, eyes unfocused, feet bare.

She bent down. "Ontario, where are your parents?"

He didn't answer. It was already eighty degrees, but his teeth were chattering.

Dorothy used her key and ushered him inside, flipped the lights, and walked straight to the phone in the pastor's tiny office. She dialed Ontario's foster parents, but no one answered, so she called Pastor Green, and then she called her husband and told him to stay home with the girls until she knew what was going on.

Dorothy asked and asked and asked, but Ontario wouldn't say a word.

Redmond Green's wife, Barbara, answered the phone at his apartment. Red was in the bathroom scribbling last-minute sermon notes in a rare moment of solitude. Barbara sent fourteen-year-old Red Jr. to bang on the door and summon his father. Barbara hadn't asked for details—*Just go,* she told her husband—and as he walked the eleven blocks between their apartment and the church, he worked himself up, convinced the metal gate had been defaced again. Since opening Glorious Gospel on Easter morning 1982, Pastor Green had been losing a battle with vandals. He called the police often, but they rarely came to take a report. He knew that most of the officers in the precinct thought his crusade silly, given the many miseries plaguing the neighborhood, but he wasn't about to stop calling. In 1992, one year after the riots, Crown Heights was still a disaster. A battlefield and a garbage dump. It was getting hot again, and everyone seemed to hold their breath, waiting for the neighborhood to explode.

Pastor Green found the gate up when he arrived at Glorious Gospel. Dorothy Norris was inside with Malcolm and Sabrina Davises' foster son, Ontario. The pastor's first thought was that the boy had been attacked on his way to church. But Ontario was wearing sleep clothes, not church clothes.

"Something's happened at the Davises'," said Dorothy.

"What?"

"He won't say."

"Ontario? Are you hurt?"

Ontario stared at the pastor. Past him, really. Through him. Pastor Green kneeled down and touched his arm.

"He's freezing cold," he said, looking up.

"I think he's in shock," said Dorothy.

Ontario's face was smeared with red. If the pastor had to guess, he would say that the boy had rubbed his eyes with his bloody hands.

"Is this his blood?"

Dorothy lowered her voice. "I don't think so. But I don't know."

"Have you called the precinct?" asked Pastor Green.

"Yes," said Dorothy.

The pastor turned back to the boy.

"Ontario. Can I make sure you're not hurt?" He took the boy's right hand, turned it over, looked up and down his arm. He repeated the inspection on the boy's left arm. "Is it all right if I lift your shirt?" Ontario was still. "I just want to see if there are any scratches or cuts. . . . Good. Looks good. Ontario? Will you turn around for me? Just to check your back." As he turned, Pastor Green put his fingers on the boy's neck, and then his skull. "Good. Looks like you're okay."

He put his hand on his knee to straighten up, and as he did, Ontario vomited. Right on the pastor's Sunday wingtips. The boy's eyes widened and filled with tears.

"Oh, honey," said Dorothy, leaning down. "It's okay."

"It's all right, son," said Pastor Green. "Nothing a little water won't fix up."

Dorothy walked Ontario to the bathroom to wash out his mouth.

A voice came from the front door.

"NYPD."

CHAPTER TWO

Summer 2014
New York City

I know I didn't get the job when Gary, the *Trib*'s Sunday editor, calls and asks me to come in and chat.

"We decided to give the position to Jack," he says the next day. Jack, a Columbia Journalism School graduate, has been at the *Trib* six months to my two years. He is tall and blond and dresses like he grew up in Greenwich, Connecticut, even though he's from Queens. Tucked-in oxford, leather belt, blazer. He's one of those guys who walks on his toes; he bounces everywhere and so always seems as if he's excited to get where he's going, even if it's to the bathroom. Jack plays shortstop on the *Trib* softball team and is apparently a "big hitter." I've never been to a game.

"Honestly," says Gary, "we felt like he was a little more committed."

"Committed?"

Gary leans back in the creaky old chair, his arms folded over his stomach. I have no idea who this office belongs to. There are framed front pages of yore hanging crooked on the wall. Headlines from when the city was bankrupt, from the Son of Sam murders, from the first World Trade Center bombing.

"The whole Roseville thing," he says. "Those interviews you got were a real scoop. Nobody from the town has talked to a single reporter since the shooting. And you gave it to that magazine."

Of course. A couple months ago, a magazine called *American Voice* published a long article I wrote about the aftermath of a mass shooting in the ultra-Orthodox Jewish community of Roseville, New York, last year. It's not *The New Yorker*, but it's respected, and they paid me two thousand dollars, on top of the three-thousand-dollar fellowship I won from an organization called the Center on Culture, Crime and the Media to report the story. A Pulitzer Prize-winning reporter at *The Washington Post* tweeted that it was an "important" read, and I got invited to be a guest on a podcast out of Baltimore that focuses on healing after violence. I had fantasies that the article might lead to, say, a job offer from *The New York Times*.

So far, however, no go. I'm still working shifts at the *Trib*. I'm freelance, even though I work full-time, so I don't have any obligation to alert them if I've gotten work elsewhere—unless it's a competitor, like the *Ledger* or even *The Times*. When I finally told Gary and Mike, the city desk editor, about the fellowship, I said the Center had already set up publication with *American Voice*. But that wasn't completely true. The woman who approved my fellowship gave me the *American Voice* editor's e-mail address, but I spent weeks crafting a pitch, then had to write the entire draft on spec to convince the executive editor that a reporter from the *Trib* with "no feature experience" could produce something to meet "the standards of *American Voice*." I didn't tell Mike and Gary any of this, but they aren't stupid and they probably guessed the truth, which was that the *Trib* was my last choice for publication. I am prouder of what was printed in *American Voice* than anything else I've written—by far. It had context, depth, and even a little art in it. If I'd given the piece to the *Trib* it would have been a quarter as long and they would have played it like an exposé ("EXCLUSIVE! INSIDE THE ROSE-VILLE MASSACRE") instead of an essay ("After Roseville"). So I suppose I shouldn't be surprised they're passing me over for a staff position. I don't bother protesting to Gary that I didn't have control over the execution of the fellowship. Like I said, he's not stupid.

"We might not be *American Voice,* but we break news here. Evan Morris beat *The Times* on the name of the officer in the Kendra Yaris shooting, *and* his history of excessive force complaints."

"I know."

Kendra Yaris was shot and killed by police in the East Village last week. Kendra was a line cook at the Dallas BBQ on Second Avenue and was on her way to the 6 train at Bleecker Street when the two plainclothes officers mistook the twenty-two-year-old gay woman in a Brooklyn Nets hat and baggy shorts for the "young black man, slim build, ball cap" who had just held up a bodega on St. Mark's. Kendra, who had been attacked by three drunken frat boys two weeks earlier, was carrying a knife. She noticed the men following her and began to run. When the officers caught up, she whirled around with her knife—and took four bullets to the chest. The shooting occurred five days after two cops on Staten Island tried to arrest an asthmatic man named Eric Garner for selling loose cig-arettes, and ended up killing him in the process; and a month after a cop shot and killed eighteen-year-old Michael Brown in the middle of a Ferguson, Missouri, street. Within twenty-four hours, #Justice 4Kendra joined #ICantBreathe and #HandsUpDontShoot as an internationally trending hashtag. The NYPD withheld the name of the officer who killed her, but Evan Morris, who used to cover Manhattan courts for the *Trib* and recently moved to writing fea-tures for the Sunday section, got a tip that he recently cost the city

$150,000 after the family of a man whose arm he broke during an arrest on Avenue D in 2013 sued. Morris did a little digging and discovered that Detective James Womack had a long history of civilian complaints of excessive force. That, plus the fact that Womack and his partner chased and shot not just the wrong person, but a person of the wrong *gender*, made the story national news, and up until yesterday—when the NYPD finally confirmed Womack's name and the exact sum of the recent settlement—every news outlet in the country credited the *Trib* when they reported the story.

"So," says Gary, getting up, "we'd still like you to write for the section. Pitch me ideas anytime."

We walk out of the office, and before I head to Mike's desk to get my assignment for the day, I duck into the bathroom to call Iris. She picks up on the first ring.

"So?"

"Nope," I say.

"I'm sorry," she says. "You kind of expected it, right? And did you even really want that job?"

"It would have been better than what I'm doing now."

"Maybe. Or it would have kept you from looking for something at a better publication. Maybe you'll meet somebody tonight who's hiring."

Tonight I am attending a cocktail party hosted by the organization that gave me the fellowship. It'll be the first time I've met any of the other journalists who've gotten support from the Center, and, yes, I've been fantasizing that I'll make a connection that might provide a path out of the *Trib*.

"We'll see," I say.

"Don't get all down about this, okay? It's not like you lost out on your dream job."

In the past two years, Iris has been promoted twice at the fashion magazine where she works. She's humble about it; she says it was just lucky that she happened to be there when people left, but I know she's also proud of herself. And she should be. Iris wants to be the editor-in-chief of a magazine by the time she's forty. Her dream is *Vogue,* of course, but I doubt they could get Anna Wintour out of that job with a shovel.

"I know," I say.

"Good. Hey, did you call that guy yet? Is his friend having people out again?"

That guy is Wyatt Singer, a twenty-six-year-old assistant director—or director's assistant, I don't remember—that I made out with at a pool party in the Hamptons two weeks ago. Iris dragged me to the land of the Kardashians when one of her colleagues had to bail on a prepaid weekend "share." The house was a poorly maintained seven-bedroom monstrosity. There were more than twenty people sleeping there, and by the end of the weekend two of the bathrooms were unusable. All the female occupants were related to fashion in some way, and the males were mostly in TV or movies.

"I'm not calling the random guy I hooked up with in the Hamptons."

"Why not!"

"Because I hate people who go to the Hamptons."

"So does he!"

"He only said that because he knew that's what I wanted him to say."

"*How* is that not a good thing? He was being intuitive."

"Oh, please."

"How long has it been since you slept with anybody?"

Creeping up on a year. Van Keller, a ridiculously good-looking sheriff's deputy from Orange County, New York, came to the city for a friend's birthday last fall, and we ended up spending the night together. We met last spring when I was investigating the death of Pessie Goldin, a Hasidic women found dead in her bathtub in Roseville, and were together when we heard about the shooting. The sex was great—urgent but unhurried, lots of kissing and locking eyes— but when he called a couple days later he said he didn't think we should do it again. *I think I'm too old for you,* he said. What he meant, though, was *I think you're too young.* I think you're too immature. He's on Facebook, and in June someone tagged a photo of him with his arm around a beautiful black-haired woman with freckles. She has a kid, I think.

"A while," I say to Iris. "Too long."

"Exactly, so let's fix that. His friend has a share and I literally cannot spend another weekend in this city. I basically had to bathe in the bathroom sink when I got into work this morning."

"When did you become such a pussy? The humidity was worse in Florida."

"Yeah, but I didn't have to dress up in Florida. My thighs stick together under this skirt. And the subway is *so bad.* I one-hundred-percent had my face in this dude's armpit all the way over the Manhattan Bridge this morning. There wasn't even enough room to turn my head. I could see the white chunks of deodorant in his armpit hair."

"Gross."

"Oh, it was horrible."

I hang up and go into one of the stalls. I don't want to spend my entire career at the *Trib,* but alienating the editors at a paper with a million readers—the only place that offered me a job when I moved here two years ago—is a bad move. I probably could have found a way to turn at least one of the stories I found in the past year interviewing the people of Roseville into a piece for the *Trib.* It just wasn't

a priority. I started thinking of the fellowship as a way out the minute I got it. Does that make me a snob? The anxiety buzzing in my
stomach, making me sweat in the air conditioning, tells me I've
made a mistake. I've been in talk therapy, and taking daily antidepressants and the occasional antianxiety pill for a year now. The
regimen controls the worst of it. I'm not running to the bathroom
with the frequency I was last year, but my body still screams at me
sometimes. Interacting with my mother sets it off, as does, apparently, the kind of self-doubt (or, as Iris would probably call it, self-
flagellation) that losing a job I disdained ignites.

I pass Jack on my way toward the city desk and congratulate him.

"Thanks!" he says, chipper as always. "I read your piece in
American Voice. Wow! That's, like, the byline of the century!"

I smile. "Thanks. On to the next, I guess."

Mike, as usual, is bent over his computer at the city desk.

"Hey," I say.

He lifts his head before his eyes. "Oh, good, you're in a dress."

"Excuse me?"

"That's not . . . I mean, I can send you someplace *professional*,"
he stammers. Unlike some of the red-faced, thrice-divorced men
in the newsroom, Mike is not a flirt, and he's so clearly flustered by
my insinuation that I forgive him immediately. Plus, it *is* somewhat
remarkable that I am wearing a dress. I borrowed it from Iris this
morning for the party.

"Someplace professional?"

"Sandra Michaels is speaking at an event at the Plaza. We can
get you in." Sandra Michaels is a Brooklyn prosecutor and, according to a fawning cover story in last week's *New York* magazine, the
presumed next district attorney of Kings County. Her boss, seventy-
nine-year-old DA Stan Morrissey III, was diagnosed with stage two

melanoma last month and Michaels is the one running the office—which means she is the one deciding whether to indict James Womack for killing Kendra Yaris. But my guess is that neither of these things are what the *Trib* wants me to ask her about. "Did you see the story about her ex this morning?" Mike asks.

I did. I picked up a copy of the *Trib* at the bodega above my subway stop and went through it on the way to the office. On page five there was a story headlined "Exclusive: Next DA Is a 'Deadbeat' Mom." That article featured Michaels' ex-husband telling a *Trib* reporter that after their divorce in 2000, she missed three months of child support payments.

"I don't think she's qualified to be the DA if she didn't follow the law herself," said Tom McGinty.

"It's doing really well on the Web site," says Mike. "We want to get a response from Michaels for a follow."

It's the cheapest kind of tabloid story. If I'd gotten the Sunday job I might be able to spend a day or two working on a story about how much the city paid out each year to people who accused cops of misconduct, but as a runner on the city desk, I just have to go where they tell me.

At just before noon, I climb the red-carpeted steps to the Plaza Hotel where the New York Women's Law Coalition is holding its annual awards luncheon. I've never been here before, and it's less grand than I imagined. Wallpaper a little faded, lights a little too bright. But worst of all, the air conditioning seems to be on the fritz. It's easily eighty-five degrees in the lobby.

An easel displays a poster with the future DA's face on it: THE NEW YORK WOMEN'S LAW COALITION HONORS SANDRA MICHAELS. I approach the check-in table and say I am from the *Trib*. Both women manning the table look up from their clipboards aghast. Clearly, they've seen the article about her ex.

"ID please," says the one wearing a "J" necklace around her neck.

I show her my *Trib* badge. She looks at it longer than she needs to, hands it back, and says, "Table fourteen."

The room fills up quickly. Everyone is fanning themselves with their paper programs and motioning to the waiters for more ice water. My tablemates are three third-year law students on scholarships from the NYWLC, a reporter from the *East Coast Law Review*, and an intern in Michaels' office. Of the four, only the girl from the office had read the article about Michaels' ex.

"I didn't write it," I say.

"What a fucking asshole," says the intern. "Guy should be *embarrassed* his ex-wife had to give him money."

Well said.

While we wait for the program to begin, I grab the breadbasket and take two rolls and a pat of butter. Assignments involving free food are rare. Every once in a while I cover a press event with snacks, and last year I got sent to the annual chocolate show at the Javits Center; that was a highlight. But this is my first sit-down meal. After the waiters serve the entrée, the president of the NYWLC makes a speech and solicits donations for the organization's scholarships, gesturing to the girls at my table, who stand and smile to applause.

"And now," says the president, "it is my great pleasure to present this year's NYWLC Woman of the Year, soon to be the first female district attorney of Kings County, Sandra Michaels."

Everyone claps, and Sandra Michaels stands up from her seat at the table by the little stage. Sandra is wearing a stylish sky-blue and cream suit and low beige heels. She's had her well-cut blond hair blown out this morning. I'd guess she's in her late fifties. She

was in black-and-white on the cover of *New York* magazine. A
Hillary-style headshot and the coverline "The Next DA of Brooklyn." They ran the statement without a question mark, which caused
a fuss. When I saw it I wondered if she knew they were going to do
that, or if they pulled a reverse *Sex and the City* and surprised her.
According to the article, Sandra grew up in Brooklyn Heights, one
of two daughters of a history professor and a piano teacher. She
went to Fordham, then Columbia Law, and spent two years at the
Children's Defense Fund before taking a job in Morrissey's office in
the late 1980s. She started with drug cases, then got a chance at
homicide in 1992 and rose quickly, "prosecuting some of the most
complex cases of the crack era." Now, she teaches a course at NYU,
and when Morrissey retires next year, will likely run for—and win—
his position, making her just the second female district attorney in
New York City history. The *New York* magazine profile did not
mention her personal life at all. Not even a line about marriage or
children, but I know from the *Trib* that she's been married at least
once and has an adult son.

"I had a speech prepared, but honestly, it's too hot to listen to
me talk for long."

Everyone chuckles.

"This award is especially meaningful to me because when I
made the choice to leave advocacy law and begin prosecuting cases,
I worried that many of the women I admired in law school and
early in my career would think that I had abandoned those who
were most needy in order to become part of the big, ugly machine.
Don't get me wrong, the machine *can* be big and ugly. But I believed then and I believe even more strongly now that we cannot
surrender the functioning of our justice system to men. We need
women of substance, women with *backbone*, women with righteous
anger. We need them to go after the child killers and the rapists

and the stalkers and the abusers. As women, we *must* be present at the prosecutor's table, on the bench, and on the ballot."

She fans her face with her hand, and someone sitting at her table passes her a glass of ice water.

"God, it's bad in here. I'm going to cut it short so we can all escape. Thank you so much for recognizing the work prosecutors do. Thank you."

Everyone claps, and the president comes back, gives Sandra a hug, and reminds the audience to check the organization's Web site for upcoming events, job opportunities, and the mentorship program. People gather around Sandra at her table. I better just get this over with. I wait in a not-insignificant line of well-wishers, and a couple other reporters, who either congratulate, question, or take a photo with the honoree. Close-up, Sandra Michaels is wearing a little too much makeup. Her nails are French manicured and a tasteful emerald band encircles the ring finger of her right hand.

"My name is Rebekah Roberts," I say, when it is my turn. "I'm a reporter with the *Trib*, and I wondered if you have any response to what your ex-husband is saying about child support."

I speak quickly, assuming she read the article I'm referring to. The way you articulate a question as a reporter is very important. You often only have one chance before whomever you're talking to moves on to another reporter, hangs up, shouts you off the lawn, or, in this case, potentially chases you out of the room.

Sandra Michaels flinches, and the president of the NYWLC, who is standing beside her, gasps.

"Who let you in? You should be ashamed of yourself."

Sandra lifts her chin and shakes her head slowly: *tsk tsk.*

"It's hard to believe this is the best use of your time," she says, almost cordial in her condescension.

"I know . . . I'm just . . ."

"Oh, *please* don't even say you're just doing your job," says the young woman in line behind me.

I look at my notebook. All around me, women murmur their assent.

"Sandra *paved the way* for female prosecutors in the city. And *this* is what you want to write a story about? It's *so* anti-feminist!"

"As you would have known had you talked to a single source other than my former husband for your story," says Michaels, "the period of time during which I did not send child support checks to Tom was a period of time when my son was living with me, and Tom was hospitalized for depression. Feel free to call the Marymount Psychiatric Center in Roslyn for confirmation. And feel free to request the *rest* of the public documents on the situation, which tell the story quite clearly."

I don't bother protesting that I had nothing to do with the original story. All I want is out of there.

"Got it," I say, stepping back. "Thanks. Sorry."

I beeline out of the hotel, half expecting to be pelted with scones, and jog across Fifty-ninth Street to the sidewalk at the top of Central Park. The horseshit smell is practically visible, hovering at nose level as the carriages wait for tourists to spend thirty-five dollars for a fifteen-minute memory. I call the city desk and am routed to Marisa, who used to run with me but switched to rewrite after she got pregnant.

"This story is so gross," she says.

"Oh, it's worse than that," I say. "It's not even true."

I fill her in, she tells me to hold, and after about four minutes she comes back on to tell me I'm done for the day.

"Aren't you glad you majored in journalism?" asks Marisa. "We're really doing God's work."

Most of the people I know that work at the *Trib* have a love-hate relationship with the paper. They complain and talk shit and make jokes about the managing editor, Albert Morgan, "going for a Pulitzer" when there's a spread or a series on something borderline ridiculous—like a map of the venues where Shia LeBeouf has been arrested. But they also talk shit about *The New York Times*, and the ridiculous stories they do about rich people decorating their TriBeCa lofts with driftwood from Hurricane Sandy, or the home fermentation "craze" in Williamsburg. *Trib* reporters take pride in the fact that we cover the murders and trials and corruption and union disputes that *The Times* ignores. Still, we'd all jump if *The Times*—or just about any other news organization—came calling.

I kill the rest of the afternoon in the air conditioning of the Barnes & Noble at Union Square, then head to the Village for the Center's cocktail party. The bronze plaque on the door of the brick townhouse just off Washington Square Park reads: THE UNDERHILL CLUB, est. 1913. In the foyer there is an easel holding a poster that bears the Center's name and the phrase WELCOME FELLOWS! Two easels in one day. Printed around the greeting are the names of news organizations that, presumably, my fellow fellows work for: NPR, the *Guardian, ProPublica, Frontline, Mother Jones, The Marshall Project*. A piece of paper with an arrow printed on it directs me upstairs. There are probably twenty-five people in the room—that perfectly awkward size between intimate and anonymous. Iris's borrowed heels knock against the old wooden floor as I make my way to the bar: a card table set with bottles of wine, plastic glasses, and bowls of mixed nuts. I pour myself a glass of the chardonnay—it's too hot to even consider red wine—and scan the room for a familiar face. Valerie, the woman who gave me the fellowship and helped me place it with *American Voice*, appears deep in conversation with two women and a man. It's funny: I can walk up to a cranky stranger and bug them about why they're waiting in line for a pastry, or whether they'd be willing to share a memory of their just-murdered next-door neighbor, but the idea of starting a conversation with one of the people in this room terrifies me. If Iris were here, she'd drag me to Valerie. *Don't be lame,* she'd say. *Just because they have fancier jobs than you doesn't mean they're better than you.* I take a wide swallow of the lukewarm chardonnay and head over.

"The problem isn't space," says the older of the two women talking to Valerie. "It's not even will. Young editors have visions of Pulitzers, too. If they can get somebody else—somebody like the Center—to pay for the reporting, they'll run a big investigation. The problem is the readership. They don't fucking care! We exposed what agribusiness was doing to the California water supply five years ago! There were literally thousands of people who had *no water* all over the Central Valley—even back then. We're talking people—*working* people, people who own their homes—who ate exclusively microwave dinners so they didn't have to do dishes. But no one gave a shit. They held one hearing—one—in Sacramento. A couple CEOs got questioned, said they'd do better. It was utter bullshit. The only people who made the effort to come to the capitol and show support were four families who had been showering at a gym five miles from their home for literally *two years*. No one else cared enough to even, like, hold a fucking *sign* outside the hearing."

"That was at *The Chronicle*, right?" says the man. He's a little older than I am, possibly Filipino. He's wearing khakis and a seafoam polo shirt. "Didn't you guys win an IRE medal for that?"

"Sure. But do you know how many clicks the story got? Like, fifty. Seriously, the science page did better that week." She hikes up the soft briefcase she is carrying on one shoulder. "I mean, if people don't care, what the fuck are we doing? My sister says I should go into PR. I've got two kids about to take on huge student loan debt because I've been banging my head against a wall for fifty grand a year."

Valerie and the younger woman look mildly uncomfortable. Each nods and sneaks a look around them, which is good for me.

"Rebekah! So glad you could make it," says Valerie. "Kate, Domanick, Amanda, this is Rebekah Roberts. She wrote the piece for *American Voice* about the aftermath of the Roseville massacre."

"Great piece!" says Domanick. "I remember thinking when it happened that we were never really going to know what was going on. I learned *a lot*. And the writing was really beautiful."

"Thanks," I say, unable to suppress a smile. "You just made my day."

"Domanick was a fellow, what? Two years ago?"

"Four."

"*Four!* John Jay College had collected a ton of great data on people who confessed to a crime but were exonerated by DNA. Really groundbreaking stuff, but they needed personal stories to drive it home. We hooked them up with Domanick."

"And I am forever grateful," says Domanick. "I was freelancing doctor profiles for a medical newsletter out of Pennsylvania to make rent. All of a sudden I got the cover story in *The Atlantic*."

"Not all of a sudden," says Valerie. "It took you, what, nine months of reporting?"

"At least."

"I remember it," I say. "We read it in school, in my investigative reporting class."

"Yeah? Well, that makes me feel good—and old." Everyone laughs. "It got a good response. I don't know about the clicks. I try not to pay attention, honestly."

"I learned a lot," I say. "I mean, it's hard to imagine why somebody would say they committed a crime—especially something like murder—when they didn't. But you made it come alive. How it felt to be in that room. You know, scared and tired and just wanting to go home. I remember one guy you profiled said he actually *knew* the kid who had done the shooting. He said a bunch of people saw it, right? And he was like, they'll figure it out eventually so, yeah, sure, I did it."

"Marco King," says Domanick, nodding. "He was seventeen. Did twenty-six years inside."

"That's what you get for trusting the system," says the younger woman.

"Amanda, I've been meaning to introduce you and Rebekah," says Valerie. "You're both in Brooklyn. Amanda does the Homicide Blog."

"That's you?" I say.

"That's me," she says.

I've heard of the Homicide Blog—the *Trib* did a short piece on it last year. Basically, they track every single homicide in New York City. I think there were around 350 murders last year, but they don't all make the paper. And a lot of the ones that do only make the blotter, often without a name. Just: victim. Amanda's blog makes a new page for every person killed. She maps the deaths, too. And updates the pages if there's an arrest.

Amanda does not look like a gritty homicide reporter. She's wearing what is essentially a muumuu, and, if I had to guess, I'd say she is pregnant.

"I'm a big fan," I say.

"Thanks." She smiles and I see she's got something stuck in between her two front teeth. Part of a nut shell, probably.

"Where are you now?" asks Kate.

"I'm at the *Tribune*," I say.

"Oh, yeah? Chicago's a great news town. I was at the *Sun-Times* in the nineties. Couldn't take the fucking cold, though. Damn."

"Not Chicago. The *New York Tribune*."

"The *Trib*?" Kate doesn't even attempt to hide her disdain. "Really? *Tell* me you didn't work on that bullshit from Sandra Michaels' ex."

I shake my head.

"Fucking *bullshit*," she continues, raising her voice. "Did you guys see it?"

Head shakes all around. Now all three of them are looking to get out of this conversation.

"You read the profile in *New York*, right?" Kate doesn't wait for a response. "Sandra Michaels has the best record of convicting violent domestic offenders in the city. She's going to be the next Brooklyn DA. Anyway, the fucking *Trib* digs up her ex-husband—who she divorced fifteen years ago and who I happen to know hasn't been *employed* since—to talk shit on her."

I decide not to mention the Palm Court luncheon.

"Sounds awful," says Valerie. She puts her hand on my shoulder. "I think we need to get this started. Are you all coming to the panels tomorrow?" The Center is hosting a conference on criminal justice reporting.

"Of course," says Kate. "I'm moderating the environmental crime panel."

"I have to work," I say. "I'm really sorry."

"We'll miss you," she says. "Keep in touch. I'd love to fund something else from you. We've gotten really great feedback on the *American Voice* article. That peek behind the curtain of the Hasidic world was really powerful."

"Thank you," I say. "I'll definitely be in touch."

"I was telling these guys that we just got funding to dig into wrongful convictions. Thanks, in part, to Domanick. So let me know if you've got anything there."

"Definitely."

Valerie walks away. Kate follows her without saying good-bye.

"Great meeting you ladies," says Domanick. "I'll see you tomorrow, Amanda?"

Amanda nods.

"Good luck, Rebekah," he says, handing me his card. "Let me know if I can ever help you with anything."

"I will," I say. "Thanks."

Domanick heads to the bar, where he immediately starts chatting with another group of people.

"Kate's an asshole," says Amanda. "She's the perfect example of people stuck in the old media model. I mean, come on. What did you think when you got into public service reporting, that you were gonna be able to pay for your kids to go to Yale? Please."

I smile, then lean in and whisper, "You've got a little something in your teeth."

Her hand goes up to cover her mouth.

"Oh, Christ," she says. "Thanks for telling me."

"I'd want to know."

"Exactly." She pulls out her phone and grins at the screen, picks the nut shell out with her fingernail. "All good?"

"Gone."

"I hate these things. I wouldn't have come except that Valerie's been really supportive of the blog. She recommended us to a couple other organizations that give grants, and without those we would be under."

"How many people work for you?"

"It's just me," she says.

"You do all that yourself?"

"Well, my husband helps with the back end. But basically, I never leave the house. And when this one comes I will officially never leave." She puts her hand on her belly.

"When are you due?"

"September."

"Is it your first?"

"Ha! I wish. No, I'm kidding. This'll be my third."

"Whoa."

"I know. I'm insane. But I was an only child. My husband's from a big family and I always really wanted that."

"How old are the other two?"

"Two and four. The oldest one starts preschool next month, *thank God*. Having three at home at the same time might actually kill me." She laughs. "That would be hilarious. You could take over the blog and write about me! Amanda Button, insane person, was found dead in her home. Police suspect her children are at fault, but can't find the murder weapon."

I laugh, too, partly because Amanda's laugh is so funny. It's this grumbling cackle that sounds like a cross between Dr. Evil and Bette Davis. I like this girl.

"How do you take care of two kids and do the blog? There's, like, almost a murder every day, right?"

"Just about. I do a lot when they're asleep. I'm kind of an insomniac. My husband works from home, too, so we trade off. He does freelance web design and software stuff."

"You do everything from home?"

She nods. "I've got a police scanner so I get alerted when there's a body. Then I start trolling social media for keywords in that neighborhood. Now that people know about the blog they tweet at me and send me Facebook messages. But what about you? What are you working on?"

"Nothing, really," I say. Amanda doesn't seem like the judgmental type. "I'm kind of looking for something."

"Well, if you're interested in pitching Valerie's wrongful conviction project, I get letters all the time from prisoners who say they're innocent. I don't have time to go through them, but there might be something there."

CHAPTER THREE

Two days after the cocktail party, I take the F train to a neighborhood called Ditmas Park, which is south of where I live in Gowanus and north of Borough Park. Amanda and her brood live on the second floor of an enormous old house that was probably once elegant, but is now covered entirely in roofing shingles. An exterior staircase indicates the home has been partitioned into apartments. It's the biggest house on the block—and all the houses are suburban-style big—but hands down the ugliest.

There are four buzzers by the front door. I press the button marked "Button!" After about thirty seconds, Amanda opens the door, carrying a little boy on her hip.

"Welcome to the madhouse," she says.

"Who's this?" I ask. I'm not exactly a kid person, but it seems rude to ignore him.

"This is Liam," she says. "His brother is asleep and he's supposed to be asleep, too. Isn't he?"

Liam rests his head on his mommy's shoulder. Big eyes blink at me.

"Come on up. It's messy but we've got the AC cranking."

I follow her up the wide carpeted staircase to a landing with one door at either end.

"They split the house into apartments in the eighties, I think," says Amanda, pushing open one of the doors. The main room is enormous—someone must have knocked down a wall at some point. A bank of windows faces the backyard, and the space appears to function as a combination kitchen-office-playroom-living room-dining room. The floor is half-covered in foam tiles with a letter of the alphabet on each and strewn with toys. On one side is a playpen, a stationary tricycle, an easel, a plastic table and chairs set, and a tub full of more toys. On the other side is a flimsy IKEA desk with three computer monitors in a semicircle.

"This is mission control," says Amanda. "The bedrooms are tiny and there's only one bathroom, but this room makes it doable. I mean, it's insane. But doable. Do you want something to drink?" She opens the refrigerator. "I actually made lemonade last night. Do you want some?"

"I'd love some," I say. Liam has closed his eyes. "Looks like he's out."

Amanda looks down at him. "Sweet," she whispers. "Okay, give me a minute to see if I can put him down."

"I'm not in a hurry. Do what you gotta do."

Amanda smiles and disappears down the hall, waddling in bare feet, one baby in her belly, one on her hip. Before I got here, Iris and I had brunch. When I leave, I might take a nap. Tonight we're headed to Prospect Park for a free reggae concert. We'll take a blanket and a cooler and maybe stop at a bar on our way home.

That's a Saturday in my life. But for a mom like Amanda, the work never ends. Even leisure life is work. I'm not going to lie: it doesn't look fun.

The dining room table is a circle with four chairs, two of which have booster seats strapped to them. I sweep a couple Cheerios off one that doesn't and drop them in a trash can near the stove, then sit down. As I do, one of the dark computer screens comes to life. Amanda is getting an alert. I get up to look and see her coming back from the bedrooms.

"Your computer just lit up."

"Oh, yeah? There was a stabbing in Brownsville last night. Female. She wasn't dead when the cops found her, but she might be now."

Amanda sits down at her station and moves the mouse around, presses a few keys. "Yeah, looks like. Getting RIP tweets from the neighborhood." She points at the middle screen, which shows a map of Brooklyn, and every few seconds a red flag pops up. "I can search for hashtags, like RIP, in the neighborhood where the cops find the body. Then whenever anybody who's got their locator on tweets with that hashtag it maps it. Look." She clicks on one flag and a window opens with a tweet from BayBeGurl89: *too young too soon. I'll always love you @Jasmeen190. #RIP #lovekills #prayersplease*

"Love kills," says Amanda. "I bet it turns out to be her boy-friend. Or an ex." Amanda clicks into the profile of Jasmeen190, aka Jaz. Her profile picture shows her as a young dark-skinned black woman with neon pink and black cornrows and a silver stud in the space above her lips where Cindy Crawford has a mole. Her personal description reads: *sing from the heart.*

"Sad," I say.

"Yup," says Amanda, clicking around. She opens a window on the computer screen to her left. "I entered a dummy post last night when I heard the scanner call. Female and Brownsville. I'm gonna message this baby girl eighty-nine and ask her if she has a photo of Jasmeen I can use. And see if she can hook me up with family for a full name and DOB. See if they're taking donations. I can post a link to that."

"Should I get out of your hair?"

"No, no. It's nice to have company. Jonathan's out of town all weekend doing an on-site with a client in North Carolina. Bastard!" She giggles. "I haven't left the city in *years*! That cocktail party was the first time I'd been in Manhattan since there was *snow*. Literally. Okay. Let me just send a couple quick messages. . . ." She types and clicks and then swivels around in her chair.

"Lemonade?"

"Sure," I say. "Thanks."

She pops up and goes to the refrigerator, which is covered with children's drawings, wedding announcements, and coupons from CVS. She grabs a Tupperware pitcher from the top shelf and rights two glasses that appear to be part of a set from McDonald's from their upside-down perch in the dish rack on the counter.

"Hope you don't mind the Hulk," she says.

"Not at all," I say. "I love the Hulk."

"So," she says. "The letters. I realized after I mentioned them to you that I really have no idea if they're even worth looking at. I started getting them a couple months after the blog went live. At first I was going through them, but then they just piled up. Everybody says they're innocent, obviously. But a lot of the cases are from the eighties and nineties, which was ground zero for murders in the city. There were more than two thousand murders in 1991. That's what, six times as many as last year? And it's not like there were six times as many cops or prosecutors. It makes sense that they might have botched some of the cases. DNA technology didn't really exist. And all that stuff Domanick wrote about with false confessions. Not to mention how unreliable eyewitness testimony is. . . ."

"The Central Park Five case was around then, right?"

"Exactly! Those poor kids were totally railroaded. I was in elementary school in 1989. My mom used to run in Prospect Park and my dad made her stop after that. We lived in Park Slope, which was nicer than Harlem or Crown Heights, but there was still, like, broken glass from crack pipes all over the sidewalks. I remember I wasn't allowed to wear open-toed shoes at all until high school when things started getting a little better. My dad was convinced I'd step on glass or a needle and get AIDS.

"The tabloids had everybody scared, too. They made it seem even worse than it was. Now, everybody's all over the killer cops, but back then it was all about the scary black men terrorizing the city. Men and boys. Teen super-predators, shit like that. Did you know Donald Trump actually took out a full-page ad to declare that the Central Park Five should get the death penalty? I'm serious! And they were more than happy to take his money." She pauses. "Sorry, I'm rambling."

"It's okay," I say. "I didn't grow up here, so there's a lot I don't know."

"Where are you from?"

"Florida."

"Oh, yeah? What part?"

"Orlando."

"Near Disney World?"

"Yeah," I say. "My grandpa worked there for years. In the corporate offices."

"Did you get discounts?"

I nod. "I worked in the park the summer right after high school.

At one of the stores that sold Mickey hats and stuff. It was hell. Hell. That's sort of when I decided I wouldn't have kids."

"I should have worked at Disney World!" shouts Amanda, laughing that enormous laugh. Then she covers her mouth. "Shit. I really hope I didn't wake them." She shakes her head, smiling.

"Are you sure this isn't something you want to work on?" I ask.

"Oh my God, no. The whole fucking 'justice' process makes me crazy." She uses her fingers to put air quotes around the word *justice*. "I'm about the victims. I mean, if somebody got wrongfully convicted, they're a victim, too, obviously. But mostly I try to give the people who *literally* can't speak—the dead people—a voice. Make sure they aren't completely forgotten. And the people left behind. Have you ever known anybody who was murdered?"

"No one I was close to," I say.

"Good," she says. "I don't wish it on anyone. When I was fourteen, my aunt's husband came home and shot her and then himself. They lived a couple blocks from us. She was a lot younger than my dad, and he'd practically raised her after his mom died from cancer. It destroyed him. My parents got divorced a couple years later. He just gave up on everything. He started drinking too much, lost his job. I was really pissed at him for a long time. I mean, I loved her, too. So did my mom. But you can't predict how a violent death like that is going to affect someone. Some people can take it. But, I mean, some people can take *war,* too. When somebody you love is murdered, it's like a bomb goes off in your life. If you survive intact you're lucky. And the thing is, there are neighborhoods in this city where bombs like that are going off every night. The same families are getting hit over and over. The cops come in and *maybe* the reporters come in, and they ask questions so they can do their jobs, and then they're gone. Can you imagine if your brother, or your best friend, was shot to death and didn't even get his picture in the paper? For you, for everybody around you, it's front-page news. It's bigger than 9/11. But for the rest of the world, it's like nothing even happened. That disconnect fucks with people. What I do is mark the deaths. All of them. The rest of it, 'justice,' that's somebody else's job."

Amanda puts eight packets from various prisoners across New York State into a paper shopping bag from Trader Joe's and tells me she'd love to help if I find anything interesting. I walk a few blocks south to Cortelyou Road, order an iced coffee at a café with a sidewalk patio, and start opening the envelopes. Some are more than an inch thick, with photocopies of motions and statements and judgments, sentencing reports, witness lists, disciplinary records, medical histories. Some even include crime-scene photos. Each begins with a letter, addressed to Amanda. *Dear Ms. Button*. The handwriting breaks my heart: careful, neat and even as a grade school cursive test. I almost feel embarrassed for the men writing, imagining them hunched over in a cell with a pen, trying to imbue each letter with the sincerity of their plea. Thinking, if this *f* is upright, she will believe me and I will go free.

Michael Malone, writing from Otisville Correctional Facility, was convicted of rape and burglary in 1997: *The victim had bite marks on her and a doctor said they matched my teeth*. He includes an article from *Mother Jones* with the headline: "Everything You Think You Know About Forensics Is Wrong: How Prosecutors Sold Bite Mark, Bullet Casing and Fingerprint Analysis as Real Science." Timothy Whiting, an inmate at Attica, says he has been serving time since 1989 for a bank robbery in Queens where a guard was shot and killed: *Two of my friends testified I was in Manhattan that day, but the prosecutor said they were lying because we grew up together.* Timothy's packet has statements from his friends, a photograph of his daughter (she was eighteen months old when he went upstate) and grandson, and a photocopy of a certificate that congratulates him for completing an associate's degree through Genesee Community College. Elmira inmate Kenneth Deeds, convicted of hit-and-run homicide in 1990, says that his lawyer was incompetent: *The witness who swore it was me told the cops she saw a tall man running away. I'm 5' 6" and my lawyer didn't ask her a single question at trial.* Deeds includes the witness's original signed statement to police, as well as a photograph of him standing next to a wall height chart.

DeShawn Perkins, a prisoner at Coxsackie State Prison in Greene County has written in blue ink.

Dear Ms. Button,

My name is DeShawn Perkins. Every time I can get to a computer, I read your blog. I think you are doing a very good thing. My mama died by murder when I was little but nobody cared. I'm glad to see some things are different now.

I got in a lot of trouble when I was a teenager. I stole and I lied. But I didn't do the crime I was convicted of. I'm not a murderer. Malcolm and Sabrina Davis took me in when I was 6 years old and they were my family.

I was with my girlfriend, LaToya Marshall, that night of the murders, but the cops didn't believe her when she told them. And the detective tricked me into confessing.

Since I've been inside I've learned a lot. I got a high school diploma and I work in the kitchen. I know life isn't

fair. But somebody else killed my family and I'm paying
for his crime.

> Thank you. God bless.
> DeShawn

Along with the letter, DeShawn included the original incident
report on the murders, his signed confession, and a statement from
a woman named Henrietta Eubanks. I don't see anything about
physical evidence, but there are some administrative-looking documents identifying DeShawn's lawyers—for the trial and his appeal—
and a sentencing report. Sandra Michaels was the original prosecutor.
The confession and the witness statements are both just a few lines
long. The confession was signed and witnessed by Detective Pete
Olivetti on July 6, 1992, at 2:15 P.M. Henrietta Eubanks' statement
was signed and witnessed on July 5, 1992, at 8:45 P.M., by Officer
Saul Katz.

"Holy shit," I say, out loud.

The waitress and the couple she's seating all look at me.

"Sorry," I say.

I haven't even known Saul Katz for two years, and yet he has
become one of the central figures in my life. I met him one freezing
night last January outside the home of a murdered Hasidic woman
in Borough Park. He said I looked like my mother—the mother
who abandoned my father and me when I was an infant—and ushered me into the ultra-Orthodox world she had been born into. It
was a circuitous route, but Saul led me to Aviva. Now I know my
mother. Or rather, I have met her and learned some things about
her. I know, for example, that she didn't leave us because she wanted
to go back to Brooklyn and live the strict Hasidic life she'd been
raised in. Quite the opposite: getting knocked up was an accident,
and she fled because becoming a mother at nineteen years old was

the fate she thought she had escaped by running off to Florida with my dad. I know other, more human things, too. I know that when I hug her she feels fragile, but that she has endured shunning and homelessness and divorce and despair. I know that she cleans homes for a living, and I suspect it is partly because she never considered the idea that she could make money doing something she actually enjoyed. She didn't grow up being encouraged to strive for anything but motherhood, and she fucked that up early. I know that her sense of humor is limited. I know that, like me, she takes antidepressants. And I know that, until last year, she was mostly alone in the world. Now, she and Saul are together, which makes him almost like a stepdad. Saul owns a one-bedroom in Brighton Beach, but Aviva still lives up in New Paltz. They take turns driving to see each other every week.

I don't know much about Saul's life as a cop except that it ended badly. His son committed suicide a few years ago. As a boy, Binyamin had been sexually abused, and after he died Saul beat the man who helped cover it up into a coma, which got him suspended. When he pretended he was still on the job and convinced a rookie reporter (me) to use him as a source in the story of a murdered Hasidic woman, the NYPD finally fired him.

In 1992, when Saul witnessed this statement by Henrietta Eubanks, he would have been new to the force. I wonder if he even remembers the case.

CHAPTER FOUR

Morning
July 5, 1992
Crown Heights, Brooklyn

Olivetti knocked on the window of the unmarked sedan to get Saul's attention.

"Call the precinct," he said when the younger officer opened the door. "Tell them we need to transport a child, then meet me inside."

Saul did as he was told. It wasn't even ten o'clock, but when he stepped out of the air-conditioned vehicle, the wet July heat pressed back at him. Parishioners were beginning to arrive at Glorious Gospel, and he had to "excuse me" his way to the glass door of the church. The men and boys were dressed in suits and the women in jewel-colored dresses, stockings, matching hats. Some wore short gloves on their hands. The little girls had ribbons on their socks and the little boys wore bow ties. If you looked at it a certain way, Saul thought, you could find similarities in the attire of the Hasidim he had grown up among and these black church folk. Everyone in a costume signifying fellowship. A man in a certain hat was haredi. A woman in a certain hat was church-going. His wife, he knew, would call these people vain. *Do they think Hashem is impressed by sparkles?* Frieda's spirit had turned mean since Saul shaved off his peyes and enrolled in the police academy. He moved out of their little apartment three years ago, but she refused to grant him a divorce. If he wanted to see his son—which he did, desperately—Saul had to remain cordial, walking a fine line between respecting Frieda as his child's mother, and taking care not to give her hope for a reconciliation. He endured her venomous words against the people of Brooklyn whom he had sworn to protect, and only occasionally attempted to explain why he did the work he did. After the riots last year, he stopped bothering.

August 19, 1991, had been an unseasonably cool day. Barely eighty degrees. Saul was working patrol then, walking the beat in his blue uniform and the yarmulke the brass insisted he wear. Saul protested that he was no longer observant, but his captain didn't care. An obviously Jewish officer helped with "community relations." And Saul was not in a position to argue. He was working a four-to-twelve shift and was just two blocks away from the intersection of Utica and President when the 22-year-old Lubavitcher lost control of the big car he was driving and pinned the two black children against an iron window grate. He heard the long scrape of the car against the building; he heard the screams. He saw the twisted bicycle that the little boy had been fixing thrown into the street. And he saw, as the mêlée began: black men pulling the driver from his car and beating him; Jews taking him away in a Hatzolah ambulance; city workers trying to extricate seven-year-old Gavin Cato and his cousin Angela.

When he thought about it a year later, Saul supposed that what happened next was inevitable. Here they were, two communities with years of grievances against each other now face-to-face over the body of a child. Add a man like Al Sharpton, looking for attention, exploiting the anger and the timing (it was just a few months after America watched Los Angeles police officers beat Rodney King, after all), and cognizant of, indeed counting on, the fact that the longer the fires burned the more the TV and tabloid audiences would see his face and say his name. Saul sometimes wondered if the men and boys chanting "Heil Hitler!" and hurling rocks and smashing windows appreciated the awful symbolism of the boy being struck by a car in Rebbe Menachem Schneerson's motorcade: the power structure of one group literally colliding with the weakest members of the other. Saul knew it was just a terrible accident, but he couldn't help thinking that the neighborhood was being punished.

When the riots were over, the little boy beneath the car was dead, as was a Jewish student from Australia, set upon and stabbed in the street; and a salesman, maybe mistaken for a Jew because of his beard, dragged from his car and killed. An elderly Holocaust survivor was dead, too, but by her own hands—so distraught by the chants of "kill the Jews" that she leapt from her window.

It would be inaccurate to say that any "good" came from the riots, but there were people who saw the near destruction of the neighborhood as an opportunity to reset and rebuild, and even to reach out. Pastor Redmond Green was one of those people. Pastor Green was one of the first residents Saul met when he was assigned to the 77th precinct back in 1988. He and his then-patrol partner, Officer Kevin O'Connor, were driving past the storefront when Pastor Green flagged them down. Saul expected he was going to report being robbed—they'd just come from a stick-up at a Chinese food restaurant—but instead the pastor pointed to human feces at the doorstep of the church and demanded they write it up as vandalism. O'Connor didn't even want to take the report, but Saul admired Pastor Green for his commitment to his neighborhood.

Since being sworn in to the NYPD, Saul had found that there

were all kinds of cops. The kind of cop he was—or at least, the kind of cop he wanted to be—was the kind that worked hard for people who didn't break the law, people who wanted to live peacefully and with a little dignity in the middle of an ugly, dangerous place. His days were filled with people spun out by rage and shame, people with deep holes in their souls. Many of his fellow officers focused on those people. They called the residents animals and complained that they didn't sign up to be zookeepers. Why should they go out of their way, risk their lives, make their wives widows and their children orphans, to protect people who would kill their own mother for crack? Or shoot a teenager for sneakers? They considered themselves exterminators in a rat-infested building. Most did not believe the neighborhood would ever get better, and there were days when Saul felt that way, too. But he tried to focus on the people who called in the crimes. Without them the neighborhood *was* doomed. Saul saw it as part of his job to support people like Pastor Green. The more support they had, the more likely they were to lift Crown Heights out of the sticky hell it had fallen into.

Inside the church, Saul found the pastor kneeling beside a small boy with what looked like blood on his face and shirt. Olivetti and a black woman were standing beside him.

"Pastor Green," said Saul.

"Officer Katz," said the pastor, standing up. "Thank you for coming."

"You know each other?" asked Olivetti.

"I've taken some vandalism reports," said Saul. "What's going on?"

"The kid won't say," said Olivetti. "We'll go check at his house."

"I didn't clean him off," said the woman. "I thought perhaps there might be evidence."

"We're going to have him taken to the precinct," said Olivetti.

"I'd like to accompany him," said the woman.

"Fine."

Outside, the sidewalk was crowded with churchgoers.

"There a problem?" asked a man smoking a cigarette.

"Step back, please," said Olivetti.

"I'm a member here," he said. His tan suit was worn thin and shiny. "I got a right to know."

"Step back, please."

A squad car pulled up behind Olivetti's sedan.

"You *arresting* that little boy?"

"I'm not going to ask you again," said Olivetti.

"Go inside, Walter," said Dorothy. "Talk to Red."

"Where's Malcolm?" asked the man. "He know Ontario being taken away by the po-lice?"

"Walter, *please*," said Dorothy.

Walter flicked his cigarette toward the marked car. Saul saw it, but mercifully, Olivetti didn't. Saul was working with Olivetti as part of his training for Anti-Crime. They were grooming him for detective, and Olivetti was the precinct's prodigy. He worked Homicide, officially, but like everyone else, Olivetti caught what came in, because there was too much crime and not enough cops. If it turned out to be murder, Olivetti stayed on the case. If not, he usually kicked it down. He was just thirty-five then, not much older than Saul, who had come to policing late, but Olivetti was beloved—revered, even. He helped other cops work their cases. He had no children or wife—he told Saul he'd married once and wasn't the kind of man to make the same mistake twice—so his financial obligations were minimal, and he could always be counted on to buy a round or two. In the beginning of his time as a cop, Saul had been surprised how much the camaraderie among officers resembled the camaraderie among the men in shul. In the police academy classrooms and the precinct locker rooms and the bars and on the street, the men in blue uniforms—like the men in black hats—had a common language, a common purpose, a common set of rules and prejudices. They were misunderstood by outsiders, but outsiders were not important. What was important was the man beside you. Olivetti personified this ethic. At first, he rubbed Saul the wrong way. He was impatient; an adrenaline junkie. In the academy, Saul learned that police work required precision. Evidence must be collected and preserved. Witnesses listened to carefully, inconsistencies probed. It only took a few days with Olivetti to see that precision was not chief among the detective's talents. It was hard to argue with the solve rate, though. Since January, Olivetti had been lead on twenty-two homicides and made arrests in seventeen. So, by the time they pulled up at Glorious Gospel, Saul realized that there was a lot he could learn from the man. They were to ride together for one month, and for that month Saul would follow Olivetti's lead.

"Here we go," said Saul, opening the back door of the squad car for Ontario and Dorothy.

"Come on, honey," said Dorothy. She sat down in the car first and slid over, her church dress hiking up above her knee. She held out her arms to Ontario and he stepped inside. Saul shut the door, then leaned into the front window and handed the officer in the passenger seat a five-dollar bill.

"Pick up some breakfast from McDonald's for him. I don't know how long we'll be."

CHAPTER FIVE

Afternoon
July 5, 1992
Crown Heights, Brooklyn

There was no sign of forced entry on the front door to the Davises' ground-floor apartment. Olivetti knocked. Knocked again.

"NYPD," he shouted. The street was quiet, the sidewalks littered with detritus from the night before: popped bottle rockets, torn red, white, and blue streamers, and family-sized bags of chips, in addition to the usual cigarette butts and broken crack pipes and beer cans and dog shit.

Olivetti tried the knob and the door opened.

"NYPD. Anybody home?" He drew his weapon and motioned to Saul to draw his. "What was the name again?"

"Davis," said Saul.

"Mr. and Mrs. Davis?"

The house was still. They stepped into the front living room. A worn leather sectional sofa and a glass coffee table faced an old television set inside a wooden cabinet. Children's toys were put away neatly in one corner. Above the fireplace hung framed portraits of Malcolm X, Martin Luther King Jr., and Jesus. Olivetti called out again. Silence. They checked the kitchen—mismatched dishes stacked in the drying rack, a frying pan soaking in the sink—and then Saul followed Olivetti down the hallway. The first bedroom had bunk beds, both unmade. In the second, there was a toddler bed and a play kitchen. The bathroom was clear.

"Can you smell that?" asked Olivetti.

They found the bodies in the master bedroom. Saul saw the little girl first, twisted near the end of the bed. Her torso flopped sideways, face blown open to the ceiling. The man was facedown in the pillows, one bare foot hanging off the side of the bed. But for the back of his skull being gone he could have been fast asleep. The woman was slumped against the headboard, eyes wide open, a hole in her chest.

Olivetti spoke first. "I'll call it in."

Saul thought of the little boy at the church, and then of his own son. He would rather Binyamin blinded than see what Ontario saw this morning. "Do you think the boy saw what happened?"

"Could be," said Olivetti. "Though, if the perp killed the girl you'd think he'd kill the boy, too. Kid was probably hiding. Or maybe asleep. Stay here. I don't have to tell you not to touch anything, right?"

"No," said Saul. The iron scent from the blood and the bits of gunpowder in the air tickled the inside of his nose. The only sound was an air-conditioning unit humming somewhere, upstairs perhaps. There was blood spray up the wall behind the headboard. Blood spray on the carpet on both sides of the bed. Blood spray on the mirror of the woman's bureau. Blood spray on the pile of clothing in the laundry basket on the man's side of the bed. The sheets were soaked in blood. Saul tried not to look at the little girl who had lost her face. He tried not to look at the woman's bare chest, one breast gone, one exposed by a fallen nightdress. He tried to focus on the details of the room. There were no explicit signs of a robbery: no drawers pulled out, no overturned jewelry boxes or lamps on the floor. He looked at the carpet beneath his feet. The evidence team might be able to find footprints or hair. He wondered about drugs. The Davises wouldn't be the first straight-looking family to have a connection to the trade. Theirs could be a holding house. Perhaps one of the Davises had a past: maybe the husband left a gang years ago, or testified against someone. Maybe one of them was having an affair. The child was what threw him. A girl this young would never remember, let alone be able to describe or testify to the killer's face. He could have left her alive.

Olivetti returned with his camera and began taking pictures.

"I'll wait here for the techs," he said. "You knock upstairs. See what they know. Fucker picked a great night to shoot people. Nobody's gonna remember gunshots on the Fourth of July."

Saul left the bedroom. He stepped into the bathroom and glanced around. There was a child's training toilet and smears of finger paint on the inside of the plastic bathtub-shower insert. A black Barbie doll in an evening gown lay inside the tub. A cup held three toothbrushes. Saul looked into the bedroom with the bunk beds. Both appeared to have been slept in recently. The room was spare: one poster of Spider-Man, one of Michael Jordan; a bin full of sports equipment, and a row of sneakers along the wall. Two pairs appeared likely to be Ontario's, but two others belonged to a bigger boy. An older boy.

Saul rang the bell for the upstairs apartment, and after about a minute, he saw legs on the stairs. An old woman making her way down. He held up his badge and she opened the door.

"Good morning, Officer," said the woman. He could smell liquor on her breath.

"Good morning, ma'am. My name is Saul Katz; I'm with the 77th precinct. Do you mind if I ask you a few questions?"

"Is everything all right?"

"Perhaps we can talk inside."

"Is it Monique? Oh, dear God, what's she done now? I have done *everything* I can for that girl."

"No, ma'am," said Saul. "I just have a few questions. It's about your neighbors. The Davises."

"Sabrina and Malcolm? Oh, they're probably at church. If you come back in an hour or two . . . Though they might take the kids to the park. Sometimes they pack a picnic on Sunday."

"Do you mind if I come inside, ma'am? It shouldn't take too long."

"Well, I suppose that's all right." He followed her up the green-and-blue carpeted staircase. Her back was bent and her heels cracked to white in her slippers. She wore a pink housedress that zipped up the front.

"Can I offer you some coffee, Officer. . . ?"

"Katz. No, thank you, ma'am."

"Like I said, Sabrina and Malcolm should be home this afternoon. They usually cook out on Sunday evenings."

Saul took out his notebook. "May I ask your name?"

"Mrs. Treble," she said. "Virginia Treble."

"When was the last time you saw your neighbors, Mrs. Treble?" asked Saul.

Mrs. Treble set a mug of coffee on the oilcloth covering the table. Her hands trembled, and she plopped down, barely bending her knees.

"The last time? What do you mean?"

"Did you see them last night?"

"I don't understand. Has something happened?"

"If you could just stay with me a minute, ma'am."

"Well, I suppose I saw them yesterday afternoon sometime. I don't stay up for all the hoopla." Saul imagined Virginia Treble passing out in the La-Z-Boy chair with a folding dinner tray beside her, ice melting in a glass. He imagined the television turned up loud. He wondered what her drink of choice was. Saul had a brother, Ira, who drank. He kept little bottles of gin in coat pockets and poured them into coffee mugs and plastic cups and water bottles. Mrs. Treble didn't seem drunk, but with a longtime drinker you often couldn't tell. Drunks were difficult to interview and made terrible witnesses. Saul needed her to focus her mind into the past and re-call small details. If the case ever got to trial, she would drink before she got on the stand, and even if she managed to testify coherently, all the defense attorney would have to do to discredit her entirely is ask, *Have you been drinking today, ma'am?*

"Did you hear anything unusual last night? Shouting? Or . . . anything?"

"No. Not that I can recall. I'm a pretty sound sleeper. My hus-band snored something awful. Woke the kids up down the hall. Never bothered me, though. What's this about?"

"I'm sorry to have to tell you this," said Saul, "but the Davises were victims of a crime last night." He told Mrs. Treble that her neighbors were dead. He told her that Ontario appeared to have discovered them this morning, and walked to church to report what he'd seen. She listened, her hand over her mouth. When he finished, she put her shaking hands on the table.

"Honey," she said. "I've got a bottle in the cabinet above the sink. Bring it to me, would you? I need a steady."

Saul got her the bottle: vodka. She pointed to the dish drying rack, and he brought her a glass. She poured herself two fingers-full and drank it. She poured again and lifted it to her mouth, then set it down.

"What about DeShawn?"

"DeShawn?"

"DeShawn been with Sabrina and Malcolm for years."

"He's their son?"

"Foster son. Been with them longer than any of the others. Is he dead, too?"

"No," said Saul. "Do you know where I might find him?"

She shook her head. "Sabrina and Malcolm have been having trouble with him."

"What kind of trouble?"

"Skipping school. Smoking dope."

"How old is he?"

"Sixteen, I think."

"What's his full name?"

Mrs. Treble thought a moment. "Perkins. DeShawn Perkins."

"Do you know if he has a criminal record?"

"I know he was arrested once. But I don't know the details. Sabrina was ashamed. She and Malcolm are good people. The best kind. When they couldn't have children of their own they started taking in strays. That's what I called them. Sabrina didn't like that." Mrs. Treble took another drink from her vodka. Saul got up and filled a glass with water, set it beside her vodka. She acknowledged this gesture with a nod, but didn't take a drink.

"So the Davises had three foster children? The little girl . . ."

"Kenya. They'd just taken her around Christmas. Poor bird was born addicted to crack. She's little for her age." She drained the rest of the vodka glass.

"Can you think of anyone who might want to hurt them? Anyone who might have a grudge against them?"

"No one," she said.

"What about the parents of the children? Was there any trouble there?"

"Not that they mentioned."

"What sort of work did they do?"

"Malcolm works at the YMCA in Bedford-Stuyvesant. He runs athletic programs and after-school. Sabrina works for the city. Secretarial. She's very organized. She helps me with my taxes every year."

"Do you know if they were involved in drugs?"

"Absolutely not."

Saul knew she wouldn't necessarily know, or say, but his first read of her response was that she was telling the truth as she understood it.

"What about their relationship? Did you know about any problems?"

Mrs. Treble shook her head. "No. They love each other. They were a team." Saul noticed that Mrs. Treble vacillated between referring to her neighbors in the past and present tense.

"Most marriages have some troubles," said Saul.

"Of course. Lord knows. But nothing out of the ordinary. I never heard them arguing, if that's what you mean. Only time I ever heard shouting was between Malcolm and DeShawn."

"They argued?"

"Yes."

"Did you ever see him act out? Or get violent?"

"DeShawn? Oh, no, no, nothing like that." She looked at Saul. "You don't think he could have done this? He's practically a child!"

"I'm just gathering information, ma'am," said Saul. "Just asking questions."

"Well, I can't imagine that. He was going through a difficult period, but so many are now. It's *hard* to be a young man today. So much violence. Drugs everywhere. It wasn't always like this. Well, you must know. Did you grow up in Crown Heights?"

"Borough Park," said Saul.

"You know, you are the first Jewish police officer I've ever met. I remember when our folks used to get along just fine. My husband worked for a Jew once and he was good to him. Always paid on time. It's too bad the way things are now."

Saul nodded. That was putting it mildly.

"Have you seen anyone strange hanging around lately?" he asked. "Any strange cars?"

Mrs. Treble shook her head. Saul didn't think she would notice either way. Downstairs, he heard bootsteps and voices. He pulled a business card out of his shirt pocket. Saul didn't have his own cards—even detectives routinely waited years for cards with their personal information on them; the card listed the phone number and address for the precinct. Saul wrote his name on the back.

"Please call me if you think of anything else, or if you have any trouble at all. Until we find out who did this, you should keep your doors locked. Be on the lookout."

Mrs. Treble almost smiled. She tipped the vodka bottle and poured another drink. She hadn't touched the water. "In this neighborhood, I'm always on the lookout."

Saul showed himself out. Two uniforms were unrolling yellow crime-scene tape across the front porch, and neighbors were starting to gawk. Olivetti was on the porch, instructing two more uniforms to check the perimeter of the house and start talking to neighbors.

"There's an older son," said Saul, once the officers were off. "DeShawn Perkins. Sixteen. Been in some trouble before, apparently. We should pull his sheet."

Olivetti nodded. "Looks like the back door was locked, but one of the bedroom windows was open. The one with the bunk beds. And the screen was popped out. Certain kind of people, living on the ground floor in this neighborhood without bars on the window."

Saul relayed what Mrs. Treble told him about the Davises.

"They had straight jobs," he said. "Probably worth checking those out. If the husband worked with troubled kids he might have pissed somebody off."

"We need to talk to the little boy," said Olivetti. "I doubt he's going to be much help, but he might know where the brother is. Why don't you head back to the station and do that. I'll watch the techs and call if the uniforms pick up anything on the canvas. You want one of them to drive you?"

"I'll walk," said Saul. The precinct was eleven blocks away, and Saul tried to walk fifty blocks each day. It wasn't scenic, by any means—past piles of garbage baking in the sun, past men and women nodding against buildings and sleeping half naked on benches, past empty storefronts with torn, faded canvas awnings advertising shops and restaurants gone for years. He walked over broken sidewalks, dodging gum and glass and all other manner of human and animal discharge. Saul didn't want to stop being appalled at the condition of the neighborhood he policed; if he wasn't angry he wouldn't work as hard to save it.

Dorothy Norris and the boy were sitting together in the lobby. When Saul entered, Dorothy stood up; her eyes searched Saul's face for a glint of good news. He squinted at her, drew a shallow breath.

"May I speak to you a minute, Mrs. Norris," asked Saul.

Dorothy tucked her purse beneath her arm. She put her hand on Ontario's shoulder and said, "I'll be right back, honey."

Saul motioned to the officer behind the reception desk. "Keep an eye on him." The officer looked up at Saul and nodded, looked at the boy, then looked back down, flipped a page on the *New York Tribune* in front of him.

Saul took Dorothy into a small hallway off the main lobby, and then into an interrogation room.

"Were you close with the Davises?"

Dorothy nodded.

"I'm sorry to have to tell you that they've been killed."

"Malcolm *and* Sabrina?"

"And the little girl."

"Sweet Jesus." Dorothy made a fist and clutched the neck of her dress. She shook her head no. "What happened?"

"They were all shot."

Dorothy kept shaking her head.

"Do you have any idea who could have done this? Anyone who didn't like the Davises?"

More shaking. Her eyes began to turn red.

"I'm told the Davises had an older son. DeShawn? Do you know where I might find him?"

"No," she said. "Oh, Jesus, those poor boys."

"Do you know if the Davises have family in Brooklyn?"

"Sabrina's parents are dead. I think Malcolm's mother is still in Harlem where he grew up, but I don't think she's capable of taking care of two boys. . . ."

"We need to find DeShawn," said Saul. "And I need to interview Ontario."

"I'm not sure Ontario is going to be able to help you much," said Dorothy. "He hasn't said a word since I found him."

"We're going to need to take his clothing as evidence. Do you think you might be able to find a change for him?"

"I have two girls. But if I can use your phone, I'll call Pastor Green and have him bring something."

"Thank you," said Saul. "The Davises were fostering Ontario, am I correct?" Dorothy nodded. "I'll contact CPS about another placement. If you, or someone from the church, is willing . . . it might keep him from having to go to a group home."

"My husband and I will take him. At least for now. I don't know about DeShawn, though. With my two girls . . ." She trailed off, realizing belatedly, perhaps, that she didn't want to actually speak what she was thinking.

"I understand. What can you tell me about DeShawn?"

"Well, he's been hard lately. Sabrina told me she caught him stealing from her purse near the end of the school year. Malcolm wanted to file a police report but she begged him not to. He had some trouble this spring, and she didn't want him to get in any more. DeShawn has been with them since he was younger than Ontario. He's never been easy, but none of them are."

"Do you think he could have killed them?"

Dorothy shook her head. "I don't *think* so. He's never been violent, that I know. Just . . . restless. Angry. I really can't imagine him . . ." She squeezed the fabric of her dress again, making a fist so tight Saul saw the muscles in her arm tense. "Shooting his parents. Shooting that baby girl."

"You don't think he's the type?"

"Lord, I don't know. I just don't know! I can't believe this is happening. I just don't know!"

"Do you have any idea where we might find him?"

Dorothy furrowed her brow. "Maybe St. John's Park," she said. "I think he plays basketball there sometimes."

CHAPTER SIX

I call in for my shift Monday, and while I'm waiting for an assignment, I e-mail the library and ask them to run checks on LaToya Marshall, the girl DeShawn claims was with him the night of the murders, and Henrietta Eubanks, the eyewitness who picked him out of a lineup. The library is one of the perks of working at the *Trib*. They'll run a backgrounder on anyone and the information they get is vast: phone numbers and street addresses going back decades, criminal records, liens, even contact information for relatives and "possible" relatives. I also ask them to pull articles mentioning DeShawn Perkins and anything on the murders.

At nine thirty, Mike calls and tells me to go to Kendra Yaris's house in Crown Heights.

"Al Sharpton's supposed to be meeting with the mom before the march against police violence in Union Square tonight. Ask him what he'll do if they don't indict Womack."

"What time?"

"Afternoon. But go there now. We can't miss it."

I take my time in the cool shower, and after drying off I apply baby powder over the skin on my thighs that rubbed together all yesterday beneath my sundress, trying to soothe the raw bumps of a heat rash. I don't complain about the heat because I like it a lot better than the cold, but damn, summer in the city ain't pretty. Before I moved here, I basically lived my entire life in air conditioning. School, car, home, work—I don't think I was ever without central air in Florida. Here, I work outside half the time, and although we got a unit at Lowe's in June, lugging it up three flights of stairs and installing it, precariously, in our living room window, was so harrowing we haven't been able to bring ourselves to repeat the endeavor for our bedrooms. So, we sweat.

I'm waiting for an iced coffee at the bodega above my subway station when I get an e-mail from Jim, the librarian on duty:

> *LaToya's address is in Crown Heights. Got some clips on her being All-American in track in the early 90s, too. Found a criminal record for Henrietta Eubanks going back to 1982—drugs, prostitution, theft—the last address is from 1999. The articles I pulled mentioned a survivor, kid named Ontario Amos. He's in his 20s now, address in Bed-Stuy.*

Attached is a document with contact information for LaToya, Henrietta, and Ontario, as well as five *Trib* articles: DeShawn's arrest on July 6, 1992 ("Psycho Son: Cops Nab Foster Kid in Brutal Triple Murder"); the Davises' funeral three days later ("Slain Family Mourned"); a fund-raiser for Ontario Amos ("Crown Heights Supports Survivor of Family Massacre"); DeShawn's conviction on October 19, 1992 ("2 Hours to Guilty! Jury Convicts Teen Murderer in Record Time"); and, in early 1993, DeShawn is the anecdotal lede in a story about new protocols for screening violent youth in the city's foster care system ("CPS Tries to Spot Killer Kids"). Then twenty years of nothing.

I decide to door-knock at LaToya's before heading to wait for Al Sharpton at the Yaris family home. Her address is in the Albany Houses, a collection of six fourteen-story brick buildings on a plot of grassy park that's slightly elevated from the street. I'm often self-conscious walking into public housing. There must be white people who live there, but I never seem to encounter them, and as much as I try to walk with purpose, I feel like an intruder.

The entryway door is propped open and a handwritten paper sign taped to the elevator reads *Broke*. Others have scribbled beside it: . . . *ass nigga!* and *Fuck deBlasio.* Two pieces of gum are also stuck to the sign. LaToya lives on the twelfth floor. I start the climb and am immediately overwhelmed by the smell of urine. There are no windows in the stairwell, and the overhead bulbs are either burnt out or flickering a weak orange. I try not to look in the corners, but there are definitely puddles. The *Trib* has done articles about how dangerous the stairwells in public housing are, and by the fifth floor I'm thinking that I should have at least called LaToya's number to make sure someone was at home. I pause at the landing of the ninth floor and text Iris:

> *I'm door-knocking in the Albany Houses. If you don't hear from me in two hours, call the cops* ☺

On the eleventh-floor landing, Iris calls.

"What the fuck?" she says.

"It just occurred to me I should leave a record of where I am."

"Dude, *why* doesn't the *Trib* send a photog with you to places like that?"

"I'm here for that wrongful conviction story I'm researching for the Center."

"You're killing me, Roberts. I'm going to text you every ten minutes. I'm calling the cops if you don't text back."

"Give me an hour. I will definitely text you in an hour."

"Sixty-one minutes and I call the cops."

"Fine."

"You're a fucking nutball."

I knock at the door of 12G and after about thirty seconds someone comes to the peephole.

"Who is it?" a woman asks.

"My name's Rebekah," I say. "I'm a reporter. I'm looking for LaToya Marshall."

The woman flips the dead bolt and opens the door. She is wearing a scarf around her hair and a baggy T-shirt and workout shorts. Paper towels are woven between her toes: she's giving herself a pedicure.

"A reporter? Who you work for?"

"Um, the *Trib*," I say. I could have said I was from the Center, but it seemed like a shortcut to legitimacy to name a publication she was certain to recognize. It's a decision that could backfire, though. New Yorkers have strong opinions about the *Trib*, and they aren't always good. In April, I got sent to cover the opening night red carpet of the TriBeCa Film Festival, and one marginally famous actor (the ex-husband of a legitimately famous actress) saw my badge and refused to speak with me. "I don't talk to the *Trib*," he sneered.

"What you looking for?" asks the woman at the door.

"I'm researching a story about DeShawn Perkins."

"DeShawn? He out now?"

"No. I'm looking into wrongful convictions. . . ."

She puts a hand on her hip, raises a skeptical eyebrow. "That's a long time ago."

"Right," I say. "He just wrote me a letter, actually."

"Toya's sleeping," she says. "She works nights. I could see if she wants to get up."

"Yeah? That would be great."

"Come on back."

The woman walks on her heels down a narrow linoleum hallway, and I follow her, pulling out my phone to text Iris while her back is turned.

all good

We walk past two closed doors and a bathroom and into a back room that serves as a living room-laundry room-kitchen. Half-dry clothing is hanging over every chair and two foldout drying racks. There is a three-foot stack of magazines and newspapers in one corner and a pile of shoes in another. It is mercilessly hot inside. An elaborate series of fans keeps the air moving, although the one near the window is black with whatever it's pulling from outside.

The woman points to a piece of wicker porch furniture.

"Move something if you want," she says. "I'll see if Toya wants to get up."

I take a pair of black pants off the seat and set it gently over the T-shirts, then sit down. As I wait, I try to identify the smell coming from the kitchen. Cheap cleaning liquid over very spicy food, if I had to guess. I can't imagine turning on the stove in this heat. Every square inch of my body is sweating. My skin is covered in a thick film, like the layer of grease raw chicken leaves on your fingers.

"Sorry it's so hot," says the woman as she comes back into the main room. "You know they charge you for having AC?"

"You mean Con Edison?"

"No, NYCHA." The New York City Housing Authority. "You gotta buy the thing, pay the electric, *and* pay them a couple hundred bucks for the right to put it in. And they strict, too. I seen a woman down there with a clipboard counting up all the ACs. They'll fine your ass if you got one you didn't tell them about."

"Wow," I say, thinking, maybe that's a story.

"So, what'd DeShawn do?"

"Nothing. I mean, he says he didn't. He says he's innocent. So I'm kind of looking into the case."

"Why?"

Because I'm hoping to get a fellowship, seems crass. So I repeat: "He wrote me a letter."

"That shit messed Toya up bad," she says.

"Yeah? So, are you her . . ."

"She's my baby sister."

"You guys live together?"

"I been here my whole life. Toya been back, like, ten years at least."

"She wasn't here for a while?"

"After DeShawn got arrested my mama sent Toya down to Atlanta. She stayed there for a while. Then Mama died and she came back."

"I'm sorry," I say.

"Lung cancer."

"Ugh."

"Runs in the family," she says. I wait for her to explain, but she doesn't.

"So, LaToya was in Atlanta?"

"With cousins, yeah. My mama wouldn't have sent her there if it wasn't for Winston. That was mama's boyfriend back then. He was real strict with Toya. He tried to play like he was all watching out for her 'cause she was smart and she was good at running and wanted to go to college. But he wanted to fuck her. So there was no way she could have a boyfriend. Said she'd end up with a baby like Mama and me."

"Did you know DeShawn?"

"She kept him away from us. She was worried I'd snitch on her."

"You woulda," says a voice behind me. Toya. She's taller than her sister, and thinner. There are freckles across her cheeks and nose, and her hair is in a messy, slept-on ponytail. Beneath her eyes are the most intense circles I've ever seen. Four shades darker than the rest of her face and ashy, like powdered cocoa. She is otherwise quite beautiful. Strong jaw, sharp cheekbones, amber eyes.

I stand up. "Hi. I'm sorry I woke you up. If it's better for me to come back . . ." I trail off; Toya doesn't respond. She rubs her eyes and plops on the sofa next to her sister.

"You writing about DeShawn?" she says.

"Yeah. Are you guys in touch?"

She shakes her head.

"He says he was with you the night his family died. Is that true?"

LaToya nods.

"But he still got convicted."

She shrugs. It's a gesture of resignation, not indifference.

"Did the jury not believe you?"

"I didn't go to the trial."

"You didn't testify?"

She shakes her head.

"Why not?"

LaToya bends forward, looks at her sister.

"I just turned fifteen. I wasn't supposed to be with DeShawn. We spent the night together at this kid's apartment. His mama nannied for a family in Manhattan and on weekends they kept her overnight a lot. People went there to drink and mess around. It wasn't a big deal. Some weed, but nothing crazy. Anyway, when the cops first asked I said we weren't together. Then later they didn't believe me when I said we were. They had me all confused. The detective kept asking, are you *sure* he never left? How could you be sure, you were asleep? And he said DeShawn confessed. He said somebody saw him. That got me doubting. I mean, I *was* asleep part of the night. What if he did do it? What if he murdered three people and then crawled back in bed with me? How did I not know?

"I was really scared. And Mama and Winston were pissed. They sent me down to Atlanta for the next school year. Winston was on and on about how I had to concentrate and that I'd blow my scholarship chances if I was distracted and no college would want me if they knew I was mixed up with a murderer."

She rubs her eyes and pulls her legs up, tucks her long feet beneath her.

"I blew it anyway. There wasn't no Facebook or whatever but people found out why I'd moved down there and they looked at me funny. I was a good girl, okay? I mean, me and DeShawn had sex once. For real. One time. And then all of a sudden I'm this girl whose boyfriend is a killer. Anyway, I wanted to fit in and I got drunk one night and fell down some stairs at somebody's apartment. Broke my foot. I couldn't run that year and I just kinda gave up. Got into drugs. Ended up dropping out. It was all shit from there. I finally got locked up for bad checks and got clean inside, got my GED and a certificate in Exercise Science. But when I got out they told me I couldn't coach kids 'cause of my record."

"It's not like she's a fucking *child molester* or some shit," says her sister.

"That sucks," I say.

Toya raises her eyebrows, picks up a magazine and fans herself.

"And you never heard from any of DeShawn's lawyers or anything?" I ask.

Toya shakes her head.

"So, like I told your sister, DeShawn wrote me a letter. He says he's innocent."

I wait for a response, but don't get one.

"What do you think? Do you think he did it?"

Toya shakes her head. "I thought maybe for a while. But he was with me all night. I'm sure of it. He just . . . he wasn't that kind of person. I mean he acted tough sometimes, but when you got him alone he was really sweet. He would have done anything for me. He didn't care if he looked cool or not. I know he fought with his foster parents, but he loved them. I remember once I was telling him how our bathroom sink was all backed up and we'd been waiting days for somebody to come fix it. He said his dad could probably do it. He was, like, Malcolm—that was his name, right?"

I nod.

"Yeah, I remember. He was, like, Malcolm can fix anything. He said he put in a whole new shower—or maybe it was something in the kitchen? Anyway, he admired him. They fought and shit, sure, but we was teenagers. And the mom. He was all proud that she taught him to cook. I remember he came over one night when we knew Mama and Winston was gonna be out. He made this fancy pasta thing with some special cheese. And bread and salad and everything. That was the night we had sex. I was all bragging to people, like, my boyfriend is so *sweet*. . . ." She almost smiles, then looks at the ceiling, and I can see she's trying to roll back tears. "Ain't no man every cooked for me since."

For a few moments, none of us speak. LaToya's sister stares at the floor, her hands folded between her legs. I wonder if she's thinking the same thing I am, which is that no man has ever cooked for me. Toya was just fifteen, but she had something lovely. Something special. Until it was gone.

"Is Toya gonna be in the paper?" asks her sister, finally.

"Maybe," I say, looking at Toya to gauge her reaction. I haven't been writing anything down. "I'm only starting to look into the case. I mean, would you be willing to be quoted saying he was with you?"

"Yeah," says Toya. "But they didn't believe me then. Why they gonna believe me now?"

Before she was shot on her way home from work, Kendra Yaris lived with her mom and two siblings on the second floor of a brick house just off the Nostrand stop in Crown Heights, about a twenty-minute walk from LaToya's. I can see the signs on the lawn and the crowd on the sidewalk from a block away. I spot a reporter from the *Ledger*, a guy named Sebastian, and wave.

"You here for Sharpton?" he asks me.

"Yeah. Did I miss him?" It's just after noon.

"I don't think he's coming. Somebody inside said he canceled last minute."

"How come you're still here?"

"My desk wants me to follow the family to the march."

"I guess I better go knock," I say.

The front door on the side of the house where the Yarises live is open, just a screen door separating inside from out. I press the buzzer marked #2 and after a moment a male voice calls out, "Who is it?"

"My name's Rebekah," I say into the empty hall. "I'm a reporter for the *Trib*."

The man appears at the top of the stairs.

"You looking for Sharpton?"

"We were told he was going to be visiting before the march."

"He ain't here."

"Did he cancel?"

"So what? Why everybody so worried about Sharpton? This ain't about him. This about Kendra. And the fucking NYPD."

I scribble what he's said into my notebook.

"Do you think they'll indict Womack?" I ask.

"They better or we gonna shut this city down! My niece ain't even got a *record*. Fucking killer cops got to be stopped."

"You're Kendra's uncle?"

"Her mama's my half sister."

I get his name and call Mike from outside.

"'We're gonna shut this city down.' Great shit," he says. "Stick around in case Sharpton shows."

I sit on a curb across the street and Google Ontario Amos, who, I discover, is the sous chef at a new restaurant in Clinton Hill. Eater described it as "an inventive mix of Afro-Caribbean flavors expertly curated for new Brooklyn's tastes." A *New York Times* profile of his boss, a Haitian native and James Beard Award nominee named Jean-Phillippe Dade, mentions Ontario by name, saying that Dade passed over applicants who'd soused for Marcus Samuelsson and Dan Barber for the unknown whose food he tasted at a *Village Voice* showcase.

"I have never met anyone with a palate as refined as Ontario's," Dade told the *Times*. "His ideas are reflected in every dish at Dade."

At three thirty, Mike calls to tell me Sharpton is doing a live spot on CNN and I can cut out for the day. I hop on the B43 bus up

Kingston Avenue to Bed-Stuy and knock at the address the library gave me for Ontario. From the landing, I can hear children. After about a minute, a woman opens the door. She is barefoot, wearing a jersey sundress that looks like it accidentally got thrown in the wash with some bleach. There is food—possibly banana—in her hair.

"Hi," I say. "I'm looking for Ontario Amos."

"He's at work."

"Oh, okay," I say. "Do you know when might be a good time to find him?"

"What you want?"

"I'm a reporter," I say, "from the *Trib*."

"You gonna do another story about how great J. P. Dade is? How about you do a story about how he work his people so hard they don't see their families no more? How about that?"

"I'm actually working on a story about Ontario's foster brother."

"James?"

"No," I say. "DeShawn."

"*DeShawn?* Shit. What'd he do now?"

"Nothing," I say. "I'm just looking into a couple of old cases."

"Well, Ontario ain't gonna want to talk about DeShawn. *I* don't want him talking about DeShawn. You know he still won't take the girls to the fireworks. It's been twenty years. He won't go. Stays home with his headphones on all night so he can't hear nothing. Won't take 'em off till the next day."

"So, he hasn't been in touch with him all this time?"

"Hell no," she says.

A little girl with half a dozen pigtails in her hair comes to hang on the woman's leg. "Mommy, I want some ice cream."

"Not till you finish your fish sticks."

"I don't want fish sticks!"

"Then you don't get ice cream."

"Nooooooooo!"

"I'm not gonna say it again, Kenya," says the woman. "If they're not gone when I get back your sister gonna get ice cream and you're not. I ain't playing. Go!"

The girl looks at me, then back at her mom, lip stuck out dramatically, arms crossed, and stomps away.

"Mommy being *mean*," I hear her say.

The woman angles her voice back into the house. "You think I can't hear you? You have three minutes. Three minutes. I'm counting." She turns back to me.

"Kenya," I say. "Isn't that the name. . . ?"

"I shoulda said no when he wanted to name her that."

"I'm Rebekah," I say. But she doesn't offer her name in return.

"I gotta go," she says.

"I might try stopping by the restaurant."

"We really don't need this shit right now. He working like a dog and we never see him. You go asking him about DeShawn and . . ." She sighs. "What's he gonna help you with? He was just a little boy."

Dade is a tiny sliver of a restaurant on Lafayette Avenue. There are no diners inside. Two men in chef whites and caps do a controlled dance in an open kitchen at the back of the dining room while a woman in a short black jumper folds napkins at the bar.

I open the door and walk in. The woman turns, smiles, and slides off her barstool.

"Can I help you?"

"Hi," I say. "I'm looking for Ontario Amos."

She turns to the men in white.

"He must be out back. Can I ask your name?"

"My name's Rebekah. I'm a reporter from the *Trib*."

"Oh, cool! Are you guys gonna write about him?"

I decide not to elaborate on the nature of my visit.

"We might," I say.

"Hold on. I'll get him."

She scurries off and returns a few minutes later with Ontario. He is six-foot-something and close to three hundred pounds.

"Hi," I say. "I'm sorry to bug you at work." I wait for him to say something like, it's okay, but he doesn't. His wife, I'm guessing, has texted.

"Do you have a minute? I promise not to take up too much time."

"Even Dade hasn't been in the *Trib*," says the woman. Her earrings are bronze knives hanging to her chin. "I think it's great. Maybe more of the neighborhood people will get to know the place. Did you know we do BYOB? That really helps cut the price. Plus they're working on a fifteen-dollar lunch special for the fall."

"She ain't here to talk about food," says Ontario.

The woman looks at him, then me. She shrugs, and makes a face, like, sorry he's so grumpy.

"I got five minutes," he says. "Then I gotta get back to prep."

I follow him outside and he lights up. He doesn't offer me a smoke and he doesn't look at me.

"I guess your wife said I was by."

He nods, pulls off his white cap and stuffs it in the back pocket of his black-and-white–checked pants.

"I'm looking into some old cases," I say. "For a . . . project on wrongful convictions." He doesn't respond, so I prattle on, trying to connect. "Things were really different back then. Cops were, you know, really rushed and under the gun. . . ." Fuck. Wrong cliché. "And the standards of evidence were different. No DNA, that sort of thing. Plus now we know a lot more about how teenagers, like, sometimes make false confessions."

"What you saying? You saying DeShawn didn't do it?"

"I don't know," I say. "He wrote me a letter saying he didn't."

"So? What else he got to do up in there?"

"Do you think it's possible?"

"That he's innocent? Not really. He was always mad at Malcolm and Sabrina. He stole from them. He used to sneak out of the house, smoke weed in the bathroom. It got worse when they brought Kenya home. We had our own rooms before but they thought since she was a girl—and none of us was really related—she should get one. That pissed him off. I know Malcolm and Sabrina talked about putting him back into the system. Maybe a group home."

"You remember that?"

Ontario nods. "They should have. But they was good people. They didn't think they had a psycho murderer in their house."

"Do you remember anything about that night?"

"I remember hearing Kenya scream. But she screamed a lot. She had nightmares and she'd go into bed with them."

"What about the gunshots? Did you hear those?"

He nods almost imperceptibly.

"Did you think they were fireworks?"

He shakes his head, flicks his cigarette into the street. Wipes his nose.

"Did you hear anything else? Anybody coming or going?"

"I don't remember."

He's already told me more than I expected he would. I've interviewed dozens, maybe even hundreds of people who've been victims—or survivors—of crime in the two years since starting as a stringer for the *Trib,* and it never fails to surprise me how bad I am at guessing who's going to bury me in details and who's going to slam the door in my face. It doesn't break down by age or race or neighborhood or gender or religion or class. I once knocked on the door of a giant Frank Lloyd Wright rip-off in Westchester to try and get a quote from the daughter of a seventy-five-year-old who'd been arrested at JFK after getting drunk on a flight from Miami and screaming that the passenger sitting behind her, who happened to be wearing a hijab, was a terrorist. I figured the woman wouldn't even come to the door, but she invited me in, gave me a photo of the old lady, and said she'd had enough and hoped this whole thing shamed her mom into finally going to AA.

"Had DeShawn been with you guys that night?" I ask.

"Nah. He wasn't around much. And he definitely wasn't doing family things like fireworks and picnics."

"He says he was with a girl all night."

Ontario shrugs. "What's she say?"

"She says she was with him. But that nobody believed her."

This surprises Ontario, I think. He looks me in the eye for the first time since we've met.

"Where did you go . . . after?" I ask.

"You mean where'd I go live? I stayed with a church family for a little bit, then a group home in Brownsville. Then some different fosters. When I aged out, I moved in with some guys I knew from work. Me and Tammy been in Bed-Stuy a while now."

"Where'd you learn to cook?"

"Sabrina. She didn't cook fancy but she was real good at making cheap food taste great. Spices and stuff. She got me comfortable in the kitchen, and it was a good way to, like, get in with my other foster moms. They was always happy to have help. I got my first job at a takeout taco place when I was fifteen."

"I met one of your daughters," I say. "Kenya."

"Yeah. I don't know. Maybe it was bad luck to name her that. I barely knew her. But she had no chance, you know? No life at all. I remember it felt cool to be a big brother. And I always thought about her after. I thought about her a lot. I thought about how if she'd come sleep with me when she got them nightmares she'd be alive. I'd wonder what she'd be doing now. Then when Tammy had a girl . . ." He rubs his eyes. "You really listening to DeShawn?"

"I don't know," I say. "I'm trying to track down the witness who said she saw him leaving the house. Other than that—and the confession—it doesn't seem like the police had much." When I hear myself say it, I realize it sounds a little silly: *just* an eyewitness and a confession. Not exactly nothing. "These days, they'd need more to get a jury to convict, I think."

"That doesn't mean he didn't do it. It wasn't no robbery. Malcolm and Sabrina didn't have nothing to steal. Everybody loved them."

"What about Kenya's mom and dad? Or even yours? Might somebody have been mad they were raising their kids?"

"I doubt it. Not my mama anyway. She gave me up when I was three. I don't think she knew who my dad was."

"Oh," I say, thinking, I wonder if it would have been better or worse if my mom had stuck around long enough for me to have a couple memories. "I'm sorry."

"I better get back."

"Thanks for talking," I say. I give him my card, which is a generic New York *Tribune* card with my name and cell number handwritten on the back. "If you think of anything, call me."

•   •   •

That night, Iris and I order Indian food from the new place across the street. We eat and watch an episode of *The Real Housewives* of Somewhere. At 10:00 P.M I go into my room and start drafting a letter to DeShawn.

CHAPTER SEVEN

Evening
July 5, 1992
Crown Heights, Brooklyn

Saul and Olivetti found DeShawn at St. John's Park at dusk. He'd been arrested that spring for shoplifting, so they had a recent photo, and as the park started to empty out—families home for bath-time and bed, good kids to do the homework they'd neglected over the holiday weekend—DeShawn and his buddies were still fooling around on the court. Saul and Olivetti approached, and Olivetti called out.

"DeShawn Perkins."

The boys turned. "Who's asking?" said one, but DeShawn was already running. He was fast, but Saul was faster. He'd taken up running when he got into the academy, afraid of how far behind his classmates he would be in physical conditioning. Yeshiva boys didn't take gym, and exercise—beyond a Shabbos walk—wasn't thought worth pursuing. The mind, not the body, was important to Hashem. The running helped as things fell apart with Frieda. Last year, Saul placed ninth in the department's 5K. He caught De-Shawn by the collar less than two blocks away, on the street in front of the precinct. Dumb kid had practically run through the station's doors. They stumbled forward together, DeShawn crashing to his knees on the sidewalk. Olivetti came jogging behind, chuckling.

"Bad move, bro. Bad move."

"Why did you run, DeShawn?" asked Saul, bringing him to his feet.

DeShawn's knees were bleeding. Olivetti took out his handcuffs.

"What'd I do?" asked DeShawn.

"You ran."

"That ain't against the law."

"Fuck it ain't," said Olivetti. "Resisting arrest."

"You arresting me for that? Running?"

Olivetti closed the cuffs around DeShawn's wrists.

"You got needles in here?" he asked as he patted the teenager down. "Am I gonna poke myself?"

"Nah, man. I ain't no junkie."

"Oh, you ain't, ain't you?" said Olivetti, pulling a dime bag of weed out of DeShawn's front pocket.

"I want a lawyer," said the boy.

Olivetti laughed.

"Where were you last night, DeShawn?" asked Saul.

"What you care?"

"Answer his question, asshole."

"With some a' my peeps. Watching the fireworks. Hanging out."

"What time you get home?"

"Why?"

"Answer the question," said Olivetti.

"I don't know, man. Right around midnight."

"You sure?"

"Yeah, I'm fucking sure."

"Whoa, watch your mouth there, boy. Officer Katz is being real nice to you."

"Whatever."

Olivetti grabbed DeShawn's cuffed arms and shoved him through the front door of the 77th precinct, right past the witness.

She had come in alone two hours before. *Wait here,* they told her when she said she wanted to talk to whoever was in charge of the Troy Avenue murder case. She sat on the bench across from the desk sergeant, skinny arms and legs braided together, leaning forward and tearing at her cuticles with burnt fingertips. Her flip-flops were two sizes too big, and looking down she decided she'd buy some new shoes—sexy shoes—with the money he was paying. A hundred dollars when she agreed, and nine hundred more when it was done. It would take months to earn that tricking.

After an hour, she went outside and found a cigarette on the sidewalk, smoked what was left. She found another. An officer walking in tossed a copy of the *Trib* in the garbage can just outside the doors. She picked it up and brought it inside. Sure was a lot of shit going down. She read about a big fire at a warehouse in Williamsburg, and a shoot-out in McCarren Park. She read that the saxophone-playing man trying to be president was coming to town and planned to eat at a Harlem restaurant. She read about Rodney King getting out of the hospital. Poor bastard. A cop shot her daddy in 1979. He was stealing a car, and when they rolled up behind him with their lights he jumped out and ran. He died in the street, her mama said. Like the dog he was. She has only a handful of memories: the time he brought a red tin bucket of popcorn for Christmas—or maybe it was Valentine's Day—and her mama let him stay for supper. The time she saw him passed out in the alleyway off Myrtle Avenue and kept on walking. His big white socks and his long arms. The time he carried her on his shoulders all the way up the stairs and she brushed her hands along the hallway ceiling like she was a giant.

Her mama said it wasn't the cops that killed him, it was the heroin. But Henrietta blamed the cops. And now, here she was, waiting to help them out. But really she was helping herself. That was what she had to remember.

A cop with a little Jewish hat came to get her.

"My name is Officer Katz," he said. "Come on back."

In the interview room he asked if she wanted something to drink.

"You got Dr Pepper?"

He brought her a Dr Pepper. She opened it and drank, waited for him to ask a question.

"What can I do for you?" he said finally.

"You working that case then?"

"Which case?"

"Those people that got killed on Troy."

He nodded.

"I saw somebody running out a' they house last night. Running fast. And I saw a gun in his hand."

"You know the family?"

She shook her head.

"How did you know it was their house?"

"I didn't. But this morning I saw all them cops. I asked around."

"You live in the neighborhood?"

Again, she shook her head.

"But you just happened to be on Troy Avenue?"

She nodded.

"What time was this?"

"One or two." She wasn't supposed to be too specific.

"And what did this person you saw running out of the house look like?"

"He was a black guy."

"Tall? Short? Skinny? Fat?"

"He was going pretty fast. Not fat, though. Not too tall."

"What about the gun?"

"What about it?"

"What kind of gun was it?"

"I don't know guns. The kind you can carry in your hand."

"What hand was he holding it in?"

"Right. His right hand."

"You're sure it was a gun?"

She nodded.

"You remember what he was wearing?"

She squinted, looked at the ceiling like she was thinking. "Basketball shorts. And a T-shirt."

"What color?"

"Like I said, he was running."

"Which way did he run?"

"Away from me."

"Toward Atlantic or Eastern Parkway?"

She picked one. "Atlantic."

"Where do you live?"

Pause. Was this a trick? She decided to tell the truth. "Bushwick."

"But you stayed in Crown Heights all night?"

"I was with some friends."

"Names?"

"We ain't close. We just hang sometimes."

"And you hung all night?"

"Huh?"

"You said you saw the police this morning."

"Yeah. Right. Yeah."

"This person you saw. Do you think you could identify him?"

"Maybe."

"Anything else you want to tell me?"

"Like what?"

"I'm asking you."

"No."

He stood up. "Wait here." She waited, and when he returned he asked her to write down what she saw on a yellow notepad and sign it.

"I need your full name and address and phone number," he said. "When I run you, am I gonna find a record?"

"Yeah. So?"

Hunny couldn't remember the last time she'd had a pen in her hand. In school they made her write with her right hand and she was terrible at it. She leaned over the notepad and wrote: *I saw a black man run out of the house on Troy Avenue after the fireworks. He was carrying a gun. He ran toward Atlantic.*

She gave him the piece of paper, and he disappeared again. While she waited, she thought about that hit her roommate, Gina, had waiting. Soon she'd have enough money to buy rock for months and months and months. She imagined a backpack full of rock. Imagined pouring it onto the bed and rolling around in it.

The officer came back with the typed statement.

"Read it over. Make sure it's right. Make sure the address and phone number are right."

She looked at the paper, nodded.

"Sign here," he said. "We'll be in touch."

CHAPTER EIGHT

Night
July 5, 1992
Crown Heights, Brooklyn

After three hours in the interview room, DeShawn started to get nervous. Maybe this wasn't about his curfew. The pot was bad, but they ran after him before they found it in his pocket. He rolled back through the last few days in his mind. Had he done anything else they could violate him for? LaToya. Was it statutory rape if they were both underage? Toya wouldn't tell her mom's boyfriend she was with him—she'd be in for worse than him if she did—but maybe Winston followed her or something. Maybe he saw them leaving Michael's apartment this morning together. They should have walked out separately. He was just so sleepy and happy that he didn't think of it. Neither did she. He'd never actually spoken to Winston Lawrence, but he saw him around the Albany Houses sometimes. Before they were a couple, DeShawn used to hang out in one of the courtyards, hoping to catch Toya coming or going; bump into her casual-like. Winston was the kind of man Malcolm was afraid DeShawn would turn into: entitled and mean; a hustler with kids by who knows how many different women. Living off his girlfriend's welfare checks and whatever cash he could make selling dope or loosies or stolen electronics. Toya told him once she thought Winston had been a pimp when he was younger. She said he commented about her body constantly, "joking" that if she didn't make it as a runner she could make good money stripping. DeShawn asked her why she didn't tell her mom about it, but Toya said she did. *She doesn't believe me,* she said. *She thinks I'm just trying to make trouble because Winston's strict.* DeShawn wanted to introduce Toya to Malcolm and Sabrina, but he hadn't found the right time. He knew they'd like her—everybody liked her. He hoped if they saw a girl like her wanted to be with him, maybe they'd see that he wasn't so bad after all. That he was worth keeping.

DeShawn leaned forward in the hard metal chair, shoulders bowed over and arms crossed at the elbows, pressed between his legs. Malcolm and Sabrina had talked to him about his rights and stuff, but he never really absorbed the details. He knew he was supposed to be polite, and he knew he wasn't supposed to run. He remembered the part about asking for a lawyer. But he'd have to call Malcolm to get a lawyer. And he was already in deep shit with Malcolm. He shouldn't have said those things about Sabrina. Being a mom was the most important thing in the world to her. But the way she looked at him when the school called and said he'd been suspended for stealing money from a teacher's desk drawer (Five dollars! So he could buy LaToya a fucking slice after school!) made him so mad he started spewing ugliness he knew would hurt her.

"Why are you so surprised?" he yelled that night at home. "God didn't want you to be a mom. But you go taking other people's kids anyway thinking you gonna save us? Fuck that. Look what you done."

Malcolm didn't hit him—he never hit him—but for a second

DeShawn thought he might. That was more than a month ago but the words he said still sat in every seat in the apartment. It was as if they were stenciled on the walls. *God didn't want you to be a mom.* He heard Malcolm and Sabrina whispering about him at night. Heard them saying maybe taking Kenya in was a mistake. Maybe DeShawn was too volatile. Maybe she was unsafe around him. That pissed him off, too. They thought he was gonna hurt a little girl? What did they think he was? He might be a fuck-up but he wasn't a *monster*. Where were they even getting that from? He'd never hurt anybody in his life.

After he got booked for the petty theft at school there were a whole bunch of new rules. He had a curfew, and was subject to random drug tests. But it had been weeks and he hadn't heard a thing. Now all of a sudden they come chase him down? Had Malcolm and Sabrina called his juvenile probation officer because he didn't come home last night? Sabrina was always talking about how important it was for DeShawn to stay out of "the system"; would they really have dropped a dime like that? It had to be Toya's stepdad. Had to be.

After another hour, the cop who cuffed him entered the room.

"What's this all about?" asked DeShawn, trying to sound tough, like he knew his rights and was ready to assert them.

"My name is Detective Pete Olivetti, son. I'm gonna ask you a few simple questions and you're going to tell me the truth. Got it?"

DeShawn didn't answer.

"I didn't hear you."

"Yeah, whatever."

"Where were you last night, DeShawn?"

"Home."

"Home on Troy Avenue?"

"I only got one home."

The cop smirked.

"What? Somebody saying something different?" What was the worst that could happen for a curfew violation? It wasn't worth getting Toya in trouble.

"Nope," he said.

"Can I go now?"

The cop laughed. "Nah, son," he said, affecting a slight accent he probably thought was funny. "We just getting started."

CHAPTER NINE

Night
July 5, 1992
Crown Heights, Brooklyn

"She's left three messages since six," said the desk sergeant, handing Saul three slips of paper with the words *Katz* and *wife* written on them.

"Thank you," said Saul.

It was almost 11:00 P.M. when he finished with the witness. The 4-to-12 was starting to trickle in with collars of their own, and Olivetti had his feet up on his desk, finishing a sandwich from the filthy bodega across the street. Saul wouldn't buy a coffee there, let alone allow the sweaty workers to touch his food. He didn't keep kosher anymore, but he wasn't stupid. Olivetti was fresh-eyed; as animate as if it was the first twenty minutes of his shift, not six hours after he should've gone home. He was keeping the kid in an interview room. With no parents to complain, Saul wouldn't be surprised if DeShawn was still there when he came back in the morning. Olivetti liked to let them sit and stew; get angry and scared and hungry and generally as uncomfortable as possible. Olivetti was popular with everyone in the precinct except the maintenance staff, who had to clean up the urine when the detective wouldn't let his suspects use the bathroom. One kid he picked up for stealing cars took a shit in the corner of Interview Two last year. Olivetti made him stay in the room with it for nine hours until he finally gave up two buddies.

"What'd the crackhead have to say?" asked Olivetti.

"She says she saw a black man with a gun run out of the Davis house last night around one."

"Really." Olivetti kicked his legs down to the floor, wiped the crumbs off his shirt.

"She a neighborhood girl?"

Saul shook his head. "Address in Bushwick. Said she was with friends but wouldn't give me names."

"She got a record?"

Saul nodded.

"Let's bring her in for a lineup. She still here?"

"I let her go."

The desk sergeant came back.

"It's your wife again," he said. "Line two. Can you pick up? She kinda scares me."

Olivetti chuckled. Most of the men in the precinct complained about their wives and ex-wives. But as miserable as Fraidy made him, Saul felt even more miserable when he spoke about their troubles. The failure of his marriage was a failure he was responsible for; he understood that. He had been a different man—barely a man at nineteen, but nonetheless—when she was sanctified to him before Hashem and the community. It was his loss of faith that had turned her desperate and petty. He could not fault her for wanting to keep her family together, but as the years went by and she made no concessions to reality, it was clear to him that her behavior was at least as damaging to Binyamin as his own. He was beginning to lose patience.

Saul picked up a phone as close to the far end of the room as possible and pressed the blinking white button.

"Fraidy," he said.

"Your son has something he wants to tell you."

"Has something happened?"

"What kind of question is that?"

"You left three messages," he said. "Is everything all right? Is he hurt?"

"He is suffering! He has no father!"

Saul closed his eyes.

"He wants you to come speak to him right now."

"He has school tomorrow, yes? He should be asleep by now."

"What do you know!"

"May I speak with him, please?"

"You may speak with him when you get here."

She hung up the phone. His ears felt hot and his breath was shallow. He would go to her. He always did.

"Don't sweat it," said Olivetti. He was up from his desk now, folding a strip of gum into his mouth. "Patrol just called in a body on Pacific. I'll be here all night. The lineup'll have to wait. I'll keep the kid till the morning. Maybe he'll wise up and tell us what we already know."

"You think he's the shooter?"

"He ran. That shows a guilty conscience. And something like this you always look close to home. Shit was personal. I'll run checks on the mom and dad—see if they have any past we need to know about, but my money's on the kid. Call it intuition. I'll tell him this witness is coming and send some uniforms for her in the morning. Give him some time to decide if he's gonna cooperate or not."

"Does he have a lawyer coming?" Saul asked.

"He hasn't asked for one."

He had, of course. They'd both heard it. But Saul was following Olivetti's lead. And his son was waiting.

The apartment Saul once shared with his wife and son was just off New Utrect Avenue in Borough Park. The building was relatively new and the construction astonishingly shoddy. The concrete balconies jutting from the living rooms of every other unit were declared unsafe within six months; they were poured improperly and had begun to crack. Kitchen cabinets and the Formica counters laid atop them didn't meet at right angles; the prominently advertised individual laundry hookups ended up being nonfunctional because of improper plumbing; and paper-thin walls made an already gossip-prone community increasingly wary of—and entertained by—their neighbors. Saul hated the place the moment they moved in. Fraidy used the fact that the families on either side of them could hear every argument to try to shame him back into observance. During their arguments she took to addressing their neighbors: "Batya Levine, do you hear this? My husband has brought a radio into our home! A radio! He does not care what sort of poison goes into my poor Binyamin's ears!" Saul brought the radio home to break the silence of the apartment. He tuned it to the public station after his wife and son had gone to bed. He closed his eyes and listened to the wordless music—jazz, he knew now—and imagined himself with other people, people so full of life that they could blow into an object and make it sing. People so in sync with one another that they could create something together out of nothing at all. Their hearts, he felt, must be connected by some powerful force. Was it the music? Or was it something else and music came from that? Saul had never been in sync with anyone. He had only recently

even considered what lived inside his own heart, and he certainly never imagined that anyone else could know what he was discovering there.

He felt like a prowler each time he visited Fraidy. The men and women who had been his friends, had attended his wedding and his son's bris, hurried past as if they did not know him. He understood, to an extent: if they were seen talking to him they, too, might be the subject of rumors. It was simply the way of the community. But knowing it was the way did nothing to dull the resentment and despair he felt when someone he once shared hours of conversation with no longer acknowledged him on the street. At the mailboxes just inside the downstairs entrance, two men—Aron Finkel and Yossi Gold—stood chatting. They saw him approach the glass door. It was nearly midnight; if Binyamin had fallen asleep, the bell would wake him. (Another problem with the building: the buzzers were firehouse-loud, announcing a friendly visit with a heart-stopping blast.) Saul put his hand up and waved; he had known these men his entire life. But they turned their backs on him.

Fraidy buzzed him in. She did not greet him at the apartment door, just left it ajar. Binyamin was sitting at their kitchen table, dressed in his pajamas. The boy had never been particularly hearty; he was born six weeks premature, with a tiny hole in his kidney that kept him in the hospital for a month. But Saul could not deny the clear effect that the breakup of his family had on his ten-year-old son. Binyamin was underweight, with the posture of an old woman and the eyes of an old man. He barely looked up when his father entered the room. Fraidy, too, had changed physically since Saul left their home three years ago. She was uglier, her face pinched. She stood in front of the refrigerator, arms crossed over her chest, the heel of her slipper knocking against the linoleum floor. He imagined the fury inside her exploding. Resentments and disappointments and fears spewed across the room, turning to monsters in the oxygen. Growing large enough to devour them all.

"Binyamin has something he wants to tell you."

Saul looked at the boy.

"Binyamin?" said Saul. He pulled out a chair and sat, leaned toward his son, but the boy said nothing. "Would you like to talk in your bedroom?"

"Absolutely not."

"Fraidy . . ."

"Rabbi Zelman warned me not to let you alone with him."

"What. . . ?"

"I will give you your divorce."

"Fraidy, I don't think this is the right time. . . ."

She picked up a folder from the kitchen counter and tossed it in front of him.

"Everything is signed. Just like you wanted."

"Binyamin, would you please go to your bedroom."

"You cannot tell him what to do! You are not my husband and you are not his father. No more."

Saul put his hand on his son's back, and his son flinched. It had been months since Saul wept over his estrangement from Binyamin. He missed everything about the boy. The way he smelled, the dirt under his fingernails, the sound of his sneeze. When Binyamin was an infant, Saul held him constantly. For weeks after he came home from the hospital, he would only fall asleep when he was lying on his father's chest. Saul used to close his eyes and smile, enjoying the weight of the tiny body pressed against his heart. He kissed the top of his head, inhaled, and thanked Hashem for the opportunity to learn how to love. Now the mere touch of his hand frightened Binyamin. It didn't matter that the source of the fear was not Saul but Fraidy, and Rabbi Zelman, and all the neighbors. All that mattered was that his boy felt unsafe around him. Was it cruel to force him to endure that?

"Tell him, Binyamin," said Fraidy. "Tell him what you told me."

"I don't want to see you anymore," he whispered.

What was the good of asking him to explain? Or asking if he was certain? Saul's heart was already so broken that he barely felt the blow. For now, he decided, it was best to leave it alone. The boy did not need to be pressured; certainly not this late at night. There was time, he thought. Time enough to show his son he was a good man, even if he was no longer religious.

CHAPTER TEN

I spend most of Tuesday standing outside a fancy TriBeCa apartment building waiting for a woman TMZ claims is the mistress of a movie mogul whose wife is pregnant with their third child. She never comes outside (smart woman), and when my shift is over I hop on the L train to Bushwick and Henrietta Eubanks' last address. It's a three-story building with ugly blue vinyl siding and six buzzers. I press #1 and after a moment, the door buzzes open. I push into the tiny hallway and a mop-haired kid about my age peeks his head out.

"Hi," I say. "I'm looking for someone who used to live here a long time ago. In the nineties."

"Ask Ronald," says the kid. "He's been here forever. If he's not sitting out front he's at the bar on the corner. Maria's."

"Thanks," I say.

The door to Maria's is propped open. It is gratuitously dark inside and the bartender sports the most impressive Mohawk I have ever seen: easily eight inches high, dyed pink with snow-white tips.

It looks more like concrete, or maybe papier-mâché, than hair. I can't imagine how she sleeps. At the bar are a black man and two Latino women, all of whom are roughly fifty—emphasis on the rough. The jukebox is low, and instead of conversation, the patrons appear deeply engaged in watching NY1—muted, but with closed captioning—on the TV above the bar.

I slide into a barstool and the bartender comes over.

"Just a Bud Light," I say.

She bends down and slides open a cooler, twists off the cap, and sets the bottle in front of me.

"I'm looking for someone named Ronald," I say. "Do you know him?"

"Who's asking?" says the man at the bar.

"Ronald?" I ask. He nods. "My name's Rebekah. I'm a reporter for the *Trib*. I'm looking for a woman who lived here back in the early nineties. Henrietta Eubanks. Any chance you remember her?"

"Hunny Eubanks? *Damn*. I ain't heard that name in forever. She long gone."

"Yeah?"

"Ten years at least. Actually, shit. More like fifteen. She was gone before 9/11. Yeah, I'm sure she was."

"Do you have any idea where she went?"

"Nope."

"You're not still in touch?"

He shakes his head. "We was neighbors but not really friends. We came up together. Same year in school. She had it tough. I guess we all did. We was both on the streets by sixteen."

"On the streets?"

"Up to no good. I did stick-ups. She was trickin'. Rock was turning folks into zombies. We was all just living one hit to the next. And AIDS. Shit. I got clean in prison." He lifts up his glass. "Club soda. She'll tell you."

The bartender nods. There is a tattoo of a tiger on the left side of her shaved head.

"I just like her company so much." Ronald chuckles, then coughs. The cough doesn't sound healthy. "So what you want Hunny for?"

"She was a witness in a murder case back in 1992. In Crown Heights."

"Oh, yeah?"

"You didn't know?"

"Nah, but that don't mean nothing. Hunny had her life and I had mine. We was all keeping our secrets as best we could."

CHAPTER ELEVEN

Overnight
July 5–6, 1992
Bushwick, Brooklyn

He came to her at strange times. She wasn't sure how he made his living, only that it seemed like some kind of hustle. Definitely not a nine-to-five. Once he hinted that he was paid to hurt people. He said he ran with a gang, but it wasn't one she knew about.

Gina thought he was full of shit. But Gina didn't know him like Hunny did.

She probably should have guessed he'd be waiting for her when she arrived home from the precinct. Gina was on the street in front of their building, pacing.

"I don't like how he just comes up when you're not here," she said. The glue holding Gina's magenta hairpiece in place was losing its grip on her forehead, the adhesive melting in the heat.

"You smoke it?" asked Hunny.

"I said I'd wait! But I ain't waiting all night."

"Just give me a couple minutes," she said. "An hour most."

"Fuck, Hunny."

He was standing at the window upstairs, his hands behind his back. He turned when she entered but did not speak.

"I done what you said," she told him.

"Good."

He pulled two fifty-dollar bills out of his pocket and gave them to her. His hands were steady; his gaze direct.

"You said a thousand."

"After they make an arrest."

She didn't argue. He left and Gina came back up.

"You get the money?"

Hunny didn't want to talk about it.

Two uniforms came for her early the next morning, just as she was coming down, getting ready to take a cold shower and maybe find some breakfast. The bell rang and when she went to the window she saw the cruiser. She put on her wig and went downstairs.

"Ms. Eubanks?" asked the young officer. He was blond with a military haircut. Sunglasses like the California motorcycle cops on TV. "We need to bring you down to the precinct to look at some photos."

She nodded and the second officer opened the back door to the cruiser.

"Your chariot, my lady," said sunglasses.

His partner snickered.

When they arrived at the precinct, sunglasses pointed to the same bench where she'd sat the evening before and told her to wait. There was a copy of the *Trib* at the far end, and she scooted down to pick it up. On page three there was a photo of a couple and the headline "Massacred! Mom, Dad, Toddler Murdered in Bed." The black letters swelled. She squinted her eyes and tried to focus. The first floor of a house on Troy Avenue. Neighbors thought the gunshots were firecrackers. The victims were church folk who took in foster kids. How was he mixed up in this?

"Henrietta Eubanks?"

She looked up. The newspaper slid off her lap. The cop standing over her bent to pick it up. It wasn't the Jewish cop who interviewed her last night. This one was Italian, maybe. Hair on his knuckles and a gold cross around his neck. He smiled at her. The Jewish cop didn't smile.

"Thanks for coming in," he said. "Come on back."

She followed him toward the interview rooms, but instead of talking inside one of the boxes, the cop motioned for her to sit in a chair next to a desk in the big open room.

"Can I get you something while you wait?"

"Dr Pepper?"

He disappeared for a minute, returned with a can of Dr Pepper. She opened it and sipped. The woman in the newspaper photo was beautiful. Like a movie star.

"We're gonna take you into a room, and you'll see a group of men. You tell us which one you saw running out of the house last night. That's it. Easy as pie."

She nodded.

"You know it was real brave of you to come in and say what you saw," he said. "I don't know if my colleague, Officer Katz, adequately related that to you. He's new. But I've been around a while. I get the sense you been around, too. Am I right?"

She sipped.

"I know it wasn't easy for you to walk in here. I know some cops make life real hard for girls like you. I want you to know I think that's bullshit. Everybody gotta make a living, am I right? No shame in that. I tell you what, the cops I know go hardest at working girls, they're the same ones cruising 'round the point after shift. Shit,

I know I don't have to tell you. But listen, I want you to know, we take care of people here at the 77. You help us, we help you. That goes from here on. You're in a jam, you call me. You got information, we got money for that. People like you, people willing to come forward, you are going to keep this community from destroying itself. Not the politicians. Not the cops, even. People like you."

He was a real talker. And she didn't quite know what to make of his speech. He was trying to convince her of something, that much she could see. But what? Maybe he was working up to it. Maybe he was about to tell her he knew she wasn't anywhere near Troy Avenue the night before last. He leaned forward, looked at her hard. She waited, ready with a story about watching the fireworks from the roof of a friend of a friend's apartment building. But he didn't ask anything. He just tapped his palm on the desk.

"You need anything else?"

She shook her head.

"All right, then. Just hang tight."

She finished her soda and watched the other cops move in and out of the room, helping themselves to coffee and donuts from a station in the corner, click-clicking on typewriters, ignoring her entirely.

The Italian cop came back and asked her to follow him into a little hallway with a window that looked into another room. After a minute, the men walked in, each carrying a number. She knew one by sight. Quentin Something. He used to hang in Williamsburg, but she hadn't seen him in a while. He didn't ever seem like a killer. She looked at them all. Number four was the kid she'd seen the detectives bring in in cuffs last night. Maybe he was involved in some way. Made sense.

"Number four," she said. "That's him."

CHAPTER TWELVE

Morning
July 6, 1992
Crown Heights, Brooklyn

After the lineup, DeShawn asked to use the bathroom, but the Italian cop told him to sit in the interview room again and wait. The clock on the wall said it was 10:00 A.M. He'd been in the precinct almost fifteen hours. His head ached. It felt as though the nerves behind his eyes were exploding. They shot pain into his neck, his ears, his jaw. If they didn't let him go soon he was gonna piss himself. The night before last, with Toya, felt like weeks ago. He had barely slept then, either, but that happy exhaustion was animating. When they'd emerged together from Michael's building into the late-morning sun and walked the three blocks to Lou's Diner for pancakes, DeShawn felt ready to run a marathon. Even hours later, he was playing great when the cops yelled for him. Now that energy was gone entirely. He wanted to put his head on his arms and fall asleep for a day—two days. They still hadn't said why he was even in this windowless hole.

Another hour went by. And then two. He hadn't eaten in a whole day. Wild, empty waves of nausea rolled through him. He squeezed his eyes shut and crossed his arms over his stomach. When the feeling passed he opened his eyes, but the darkness was still there, in blotches popping against the air. He'd seen enough TV to know the mirror opposite him was a window. Was someone watching? And what was that lineup all about?

Finally the door opened and the Italian cop entered the room.

"I want to call my dad," said DeShawn.

The cop chuckled. "Your dad?"

"Yeah. I know my rights. I'm a minor."

"I think we both know your dad isn't gonna be able to help you, DeShawn."

"What are you talking about?"

"Did he hit you?"

"What?"

"If he hit you, or touched you. He's not your biological dad, right? Maybe he was coming into your room at night. Maybe you couldn't take it anymore. Maybe he started doing it to your brother."

"What are you talking about? Malcolm didn't touch me! I want to call him. I know I get a phone call."

"You get a phone call when you get to jail, son."

DeShawn blinked. He put the heel of his hand into his right eye and pressed hard.

"I gotta use the bathroom."

"Too bad," said the cop. "So what was it, then?"

"What was what?"

"What pissed you off so bad? Did they threaten to kick you out?"

"What are you talking about, man?"

"Why'd you shoot them, DeShawn!"

Suddenly the cop was screaming at him. Standing up, spitting. He slapped his hands on the table and DeShawn jumped in his chair. His bladder gave way. Warm then cold down his leg, soaking his shorts. He'd peed the bed until he was in junior high. Sabrina said it was normal for someone who had been through trauma, but it embarrassed him. Made him remember that they weren't blood and that she and Malcolm could let him go anytime they wanted. But they never did let him go, and Sabrina saw that it pained him to bother her at night. She put extra sheets in his closet so he could change them himself.

"What? Shoot? I didn't shoot . . . what are you *talking* about?"

"You fucking shot your mama and daddy and that baby girl dead. I know you did it. You know you did it. And the woman who just picked you out of that lineup knows you did it."

DeShawn doesn't remember a lot about the rest of the conversation with the cop. He knows he said he didn't shoot them. He knows he said it over and over and over again. He knows he said he wasn't at home. And he knows he said LaToya's name. He didn't want to but he did. None of it felt real. He has no idea how long he was in the little room crying, screaming, pleading, explaining, but he does remember the way the cop looked at him. Like the words he was saying weren't even English. After a while, the cop, disgusted, apparently, with DeShawn's unwillingness to confess to the slaughter of his parents and little Kenya, rose and left the room. While he was gone, DeShawn, his lower body sticky and cold with urine, tried to focus his mind. Could Malcolm and Sabrina really be dead? Where was Ontario? The cop hadn't said a word about his little brother. Maybe it was all some sort of test. Like that *Scared Straight* program on TV. Maybe Malcolm thought the only way to get De-Shawn's attention, to get him back to right, was to do something dramatic. That had to be it. His foster parents weren't gang members. They didn't sell drugs. They weren't the kind of people who got gunned down in their home. This cop was fucking with him. He'd open the door and Malcolm and Sabrina would be there to take him home. He had to hand it to them—it wasn't the worst plan in the world. He imagined his bedroom, how he'd been complaining that since Kenya came he had to share with Ontario. Shit. He'd sleep on the floor for a month after this. All he wanted was a pillow.

But when the cop came back, he was alone, carrying a tape recorder.

"We've got your brother in the next room, DeShawn."

"Ontario?"

"You got another brother?"

DeShawn shook his head.

"Both of you are starting to piss me off. The only fingerprints on your parents' doorknob are yours and Ontario's. That's just a fact. If you're saying you weren't there, that you didn't do this, we're looking at him."

"He's nine years old!"

The cop shrugged, put the tape recorder on the table. "You think a nine-year-old can't pull a trigger on three sleeping people? I've seen kids younger than that kill their abusers."

"He wasn't abused!"

"Then why did you do it?!" The cop's voice cracked. A high-pitched blast blowing at his face. DeShawn's chest felt like an empty tin drum. His heart a solid rock rattling around. He wanted to stand, to leave, to run, but he could barely feel his legs. Did they even work anymore?

"I . . ."

"You already told us you were there last night, DeShawn. We know you ran out of your house. Did you run out because you'd just shot your family? Or did you run out because your little brother did? Did you run out because you were afraid? Tell me now. If he did it, you can't protect him. We'll break him sooner or later. Probably sooner. He doesn't look too tough."

DeShawn squinted. He was dehydrated. His eyes burning, his stomach in turmoil. He farted loudly. The detective looked disgusted. This man couldn't possibly think Ontario had murdered Malcolm and Sabrina and Kenya. This *had* to be some sort of test. Maybe Malcolm wanted to see if he was loyal to the family before he decided to kick him out. Malcolm was always bothering him about spending more time with Ontario. He said DeShawn had a chance to be a role model, to stand up for Ontario, to make his life better.

"Ontario didn't do nothing."

"So it was you."

"I'm not saying . . ."

"Which was it?"

"Ontario is a good kid!"

The detective glared at DeShawn and for a moment the teenager readied himself for a smack across the face. But then the man's expression changed. He sat down and pulled his chair up close to the table. Instead of looking menacing, he looked weary. He leaned toward DeShawn like he was about to tell him a secret. DeShawn prepared for the truth of the ruse to come out.

"Just admit you did it, DeShawn. You admit it, you make everything better for yourself. You'll feel better. I promise. You're still a minor. You show remorse, tell the judge Malcolm Davis was touching you, hitting you, whatever. You'll only get a few years. Ten, tops. You'll be out in your twenties. You'll be a young man. You're a strong kid. You'll survive inside. Ontario? You keep saying it wasn't you, and he's going away. And let me tell you—kids like him don't do well inside. He'll never be the same. They'll eat him alive. The guards in juvi got reps. They like to play with the young ones. . . ."

"Stop it!"

"I'm telling you how it is, son. How it's gonna be for your brother if you don't man up here."

"I know what you're doing," DeShawn said, his voice a whine, a plea.

"What am I doing?"

"You're trying to . . . you're trying to scare me. I get it." The cop pressed a button on the tape recorder. "I'm sorry. I'm sorry I fucked up."

"It's okay, son. Everybody makes mistakes. You're sorry?"

"Yeah."

"I need you to say it, DeShawn. Then this will all be over."

"It wasn't Ontario."

"It was you that killed your parents?"

DeShawn let his head nod. Any second now, he thought. He imagined Sabrina enfolding him in her soft arms. He imagined the cocoa scent of the buttery yellow cream she put on her skin. He imagined drifting off to sleep in his bottom bunk, the sounds of her and Ontario cooking in the kitchen. Pots and pans and the little radio playing Stevie Wonder.

"I need you to say it, DeShawn. It was you that killed your parents."

"It was me."

CHAPTER THIRTEEN

I am outside City Hall waiting for a press conference about asbestos in schools to begin when my phone rings showing a blocked number.

"You have a call from an inmate at Coxsackie Correctional Facility," says an automated voice.

I accept the charges, pull out my notebook, and find half a bench beneath a tree just away from the crowd.

"Hello?"

"Rebekah? This is DeShawn Perkins. I got your letter."

"Hi, DeShawn. How are you?"

"Doing good, thanks. And yourself?"

His voice is so upbeat I almost laugh.

"I'm okay. Thanks for calling."

"Thank *you*. You said you saw Ontario? How's he doing? He doing okay?"

"He seems good," I say. "He's married. They have two little girls. And he's a chef."

"*Man*, that makes me feel good. He was a sweet kid, but you never know. Every once in a while I'd see somebody in here that looked like him. *Pheew.* Did a number on me, you know? I was really hoping he'd stay outside. Give him my best, will you? Tell him I'm always thinking about him."

"Sure," I say. I decide not to tell him Ontario seems pretty convinced he killed their family.

"So you think you might write about my case?" he asks.

"I'd like to try." Do I say I know one of the cops who arrested him? "I talked to LaToya and she was pretty adamant that you were together the night they died. But she said she never testified. Did you tell your lawyer about her?"

"I told everybody. But they just thought I was trying to cover my ass. At first I didn't want to get her involved. They had me all turned around. I didn't know what I was saying. I just wanted to go home."

"Did they tell you if they ever interviewed her?"

"The cops didn't tell me shit. I asked my lawyer about it a bunch of times before the trial. He kept putting me off, and then he was like, oh yeah, she changed her story so she's some kind of 'unreliable witness.'"

"In your letter you said the detective tricked you into confessing. Was anyone else there? Did they record the interview?"

"He pressed record right at the very end. All he got on tape was me saying, yeah, I did it."

"And no one was there with you?"

"Nah," says DeShawn.

"I'd love to talk to your lawyers," I say. "You said in your letter they weren't very effective."

"My first one was like a hundred years old. He dropped dead, and I got a young guy. We only met one time before the trial. And the prosecutor lady, the one that's all up in the news now, she was really good. My guy was bush league compared to her. My appeals lawyer was better. She tried to argue I had ineffective counsel, but the judge was focused on the confession. And the witness."

"What do you remember about the witness?"

"She was a crackhead," he says. "She must have been confused. But she stuck with her story."

"Is there anything else I should know? Anything that might, I don't know, point to someone else who could have done it?"

"Someone was threatening Malcolm and Sabrina."

"How do you know?"

"For a couple weeks before they died somebody kept calling the house. Calling and hanging up. And there was some graffiti, too. Malcolm never figured out what that was about. Then one day I came home from school before anybody else was home. The mail lady used to drop the letters through the slot in the door and there was one that didn't have a stamp on it. I remember thinking it was weird, so I opened it and it had cutout letters. You know like a ransom note in the movies? It said something like 'I'm watching you.' I asked Malcolm later but he wouldn't tell me anything. He tried to play it off like it was a prank from his kids at the Y, but I know Sabrina was scared."

"And you told your lawyers about it?"

"Yeah. But they said the cops didn't find anything."

"Did you testify?"

"I wanted to, but my lawyers both said it was a bad idea. They said the DA would trip me up and make me look even more guilty."

An automated voice breaks in: "You have one minute left on your call."

"I'll call your old lawyers," I say, rushing. "Maybe call me back in a couple days? Is what you sent me all you have on the case?"

"There's a couple more things, motions and stuff."

"Great, send that."

He agrees, and I give him the address for the *Trib*.

"You didn't ask if I did it," he says.

He's right. Somehow it seems . . . inappropriate. But that's ridiculous.

"Did you?" I ask.

"No. I swear. They offered me twenty years if I pleaded guilty. They were like, you'll be out before you're forty. I'd be free now. But I wouldn't do it. I'm not a killer. I would never hurt Sabrina and Malcolm. They were the only family I had."

I don't necessarily believe him and I don't necessarily not believe him. The uncertainty, I realize, is both totally unacceptable and totally unavoidable. No attorney, no judge, no juror can ever really know if the person they are dooming to prison—or releasing onto the streets—did the crime they are accused of. I suppose one of the nice things about being a reporter is that you don't have to make that decision in the same way. You find facts, you reveal them, others take action (or don't). It's a potent but limited position. Our power comes in the choice of focus. I picked DeShawn because of Saul, not the merits of his plea. I have to remember not to let that cloud my judgment, either way.

The automated voice comes back. "Your call has been terminated."

According to the file DeShawn sent Amanda, a lawyer named Bob Haverford was the man who originally defended him in court. I search around on LinkedIn and find that the Bob Haverford who worked at Brooklyn's Legal Aid Society from 1990–1993 is now a "principle" at Haverford & Haverford Associates, a real estate company on Long Island. According to his profile, Haverford attended Hofstra University, then CUNY Law. He is the vice president of the Suffolk County chapter of the New York Real Estate Professionals Association and was voted "Broker of the Year" by the same chapter in 2006.

The Haverford & Haverford Web site lists his office and cell number. There is still no sign of anyone official at the asbestos press conference, so I try the cell and he picks up on the first ring.

"Haverford!"

"Hi," I say. "Is this Bob Haverford?"

"Sure is. What can I do for you?"

"My name is Rebekah Roberts. I'm a reporter with the *New York Tribune*."

"Love the *Trib*! Only paper worth reading."

I've lost respect for him already.

"Thanks," I say. "I'm actually calling about an old client of yours. DeShawn Perkins?"

"Shawn what?"

"DeShawn. You defended him on a triple murder back in 1992."

Silence.

"Hello?"

"I'm here," says Haverford. "Hold on." I hear a car door slam. "Okay. What can I help you with?"

"Well, I was hoping I could talk to you a little about the case."

"That was more than twenty years ago."

"I know," I say. "Are you practicing law anymore?"

"No."

"I spoke with DeShawn earlier today, and he said you only met once before his trial. Is that right?"

"Are you really writing an article about this?"

"Maybe," I say.

"Well, I don't want to be quoted."

"Right now I'm just looking for information. DeShawn says

he's innocent, and I talked to a woman who says she was with him that night but that the cops didn't believe her."

"You're asking me to remember one case twenty years ago."

"It was a pretty big case. Three people shot in their bed. A three-year-old."

He sighs. "I know. I'm sorry. I'm on my way to a showing. This isn't a good time."

"Fine. I'll call you back. Or we can meet. Whatever works."

"I've got your number now," he says. "I'll be in touch."

He hangs up just as the Schools Chancellor and half a dozen Department of Education staffers make their way to the podium. *Yadda yadda* we will investigate *yadda yadda* we will mitigate *yadda yadda yadda*. I call Mike with the relevant *yaddas*, and while I wait for another assignment, I get on Google and discover that I actually know DeShawn's appeals attorney, Theresa Sanchez. Or rather, I've interviewed her. Now a judge, Sanchez worked as a prosecutor in the Kings County DA's office after her time as a public defense attorney. Since 2008 she's presided over the Brooklyn Community Justice Center, which is where I met her last year when I was helping one of the Sunday reporters get information for a story about alternative courts. Usually, when I am sent to cover trials or observe hearings around the city, it is a sobering assignment. The people waiting outside the courtroom are curled over nervous legs on benches, huddled in corners, whispering into cell phones, snapping at children, biting their nails, adjusting ill-fitting suits, and scrutinizing the contents of thin folders as if inside they might find the solution to the predicament that landed them there. The muffled weeping and strained conversations echo along the wide, mirthless hallways.

The Justice Center, by contrast, felt more like a YMCA than a courthouse. They have a day care center for people appearing before the court, and my tour guide let me peek into one of the classrooms

used for GED prep, computer literacy, and various other educational opportunities that defendants are "sentenced" to take part in.
The halls are decorated with framed children's drawings and thank-
you letters from people who passed through the court. Photographs
of smiling men and women with their arms draped around Judge
Sanchez, giving the thumbs-up sign as they pose picking up trash
or delivering food or painting over graffiti while wearing "Brooklyn
Community Justice Center" T-shirts.

When I called to schedule an interview, Judge Sanchez invited
me not just to observe an hour of the court's session, but to sit with
her behind the bench, so she could chat with me about the various
cases before her. The Center didn't handle felonies, she told me, so
most of what she saw were drug cases, plus some theft, prostitution,
and "quality of life" violations like urinating in public and bicycling
on the sidewalk. I remember being astonished by Judge Sanchez's
demeanor; she spoke to the people who appeared before her like a
social worker. She asked them what they needed to stay out of trouble, and when they spoke—even when they rambled a bit—she listened. She was no pushover, though. Near the end of my hour, a man
with a star tattooed on his nose was called to stand.

"This guy is a regular," she said, swiveling back toward me,
pointing to his file. "Usually it's drugs, but today it's misdemeanor
assault. He served time for attempted murder in the nineties. And
he hasn't shown up to any of the interventions we set up for him."

She swiveled back and, despite the wild-haired man's twitchy
pleas, sentenced him to three months in jail and two years probation, adding drug counseling as part of his post-release plan.

"It can take ten, twenty times for some people to get clean," she
told me after a guard escorted the man out. "Not everybody can do it.
We've lost people. But you can't stop giving them chances."

I call the main number for the Justice Center and introduce

myself, reminding the woman on the phone that I visited last year and saying I'm interested in talking to the judge about an old murder case.

"Just a minute. I'll check if she's available."

Less than a minute later, Judge Theresa Sanchez picks up.

"Rebekah, how are you?"

"I'm good," I say.

"One of my staff gave me your piece on Roseville in *American Voice*," she says. "You write beautifully."

"Thanks. That means a lot."

"Still at the *Trib*?"

"I am," I say. "I'm actually researching a story about a case you worked on back in 1993. DeShawn Perkins."

"Remind me."

"He was sixteen, from Crown Heights. Convicted of murdering his foster parents and sister . . ."

"Oh, yes," she says, her voice lower. "Really horrible crime. The girl was, what, three?"

"Yeah," I say. "Did anything about the case strike you as odd?"

"Odd?"

"DeShawn insists he didn't do it. He says the detective coerced his confession. And I talked to his girlfriend at the time. She says she was with him all night."

"If I'm remembering it right, the case always felt weak to me. That confession was a big hurdle, though. We raised that he didn't have an adult present, but his voice on tape saying he did it—that's hard to argue with. At least back then. And they had a witness, I think."

"Do you remember anything about her?"

"I remember thinking that she didn't seem particularly trustworthy, but that doesn't mean she wasn't telling the truth. Or at least what she thought was the truth."

"You worked on his appeal, right?"

"Right. It was one of my last cases before I went to the DA's office."

"He sent me some of the documents in his file but I'm wondering if there's anything more."

"After the appeal we send everything we have to the defendant. What are you looking to write about?"

"I'm working with the Center on Culture, Crime and Media on a wrongful conviction project. All the stuff that's come out lately about eyewitness testimony and false confessions made me think there could be something there."

"Like I said, the case felt thin. It was such a heinous crime. Shooting a toddler in the face? DeShawn didn't strike me as the kind of person who would do that. And I don't think the cops did much investigating after they honed in on him. Try calling the precinct's administrative lieutenant to ask if they can help you track down their file. I'll make a call to my old office and see if I can locate what we had. I've still got some friends at the courthouse, too. They might have an old copy somewhere."

"Thanks. I really appreciate that."

"Are you looking to try and get the case reopened?"

"I don't know," I say. "Maybe?"

"You should know, unless that witness recants, there's probably not much you can do."

I almost add that I know one of the two original officers on the case and could seek his advice, but instead I just say thanks and tell her I'll call her tomorrow. Why haven't I called Saul yet? Typically, if you have a personal contact that might be able to illuminate something about a story you go straight to them. But going to Saul means going to my mother now, and I am not myself around my mother.

We hang up, and since I still haven't heard about a new assignment from Mike, I call the 77th precinct and ask for the administrative lieutenant.

"Lieutenant Graves," says a female voice.

"Hi," I say. "My name is Rebekah Roberts. I'm a reporter with the *New York Tribune* and I'm trying to get a copy of a homicide file from 1992."

"1992?"

"Yes."

"That's a long time ago."

"Yeah, I know."

"Hold on."

I hold. She comes back.

"You're going to have to call the Department of Records down at One PP."

"Okay. Thanks."

I Google "NYPD Department of Records" and find a Web site with instructions for mailing in a request for documents, but no phone number. There are few things more obnoxious than government agencies and corporations that don't list their direct contacts on their Web sites. I bet I've lost a week of my life searching online for phone numbers for city departments and public relations officers. I'm always clicking around, grumbling, thinking, I'm *going* to find the fucking number, you assholes, and when I do, I'll be pissed and less sympathetic to your point of view than I would have if you hadn't tried to hide it from me. After a few minutes, I give up and I dial the main NYPD switchboard to ask for the Department of Records. I am transferred.

"Goooood morning, Records!" trills a man's voice.

"Hi," I say, almost laughing. "How are you?"

"I'm just great, how are you?"

"Pretty good," I say, thinking, happy people are almost always more helpful than unhappy ones. I introduce myself and tell him I'm looking for a homicide file from 1992.

"Ah," he says. "You got the wrong records room." Shit. "You should probably call the legal bureau. They handle FOIL requests."

FOIL, the Freedom of Information Law, is wonderful in theory, but often useless in practice. There aren't enforced rules about how long a department can take to "process" your request for information, and if they deny it, they don't really have to explain why. You can appeal, but good luck with that. One thing I miss about Florida is the fact that my home state has some of the best open records laws in the country. Pretty much every government document is fair game. Even as a college reporter, I could call the Gainsville PD and get an incident report or arrest warrant e-mailed to me the day after it was filed, and often police departments would just post the documents on their Web sites as a matter of course. It's paradise for a reporter. New York City, on the other hand, makes it as difficult as possible to get information as simple as whether a person was arrested or not.

The nice man at Personnel Records transfers me to the FOIL office, where a less nice woman answers.

"Legal."

"Hi," I say. "I'm a reporter with the *New York Tribune* and I'm looking to get information about a 1992 homicide case. I'm hoping to get a copy of the original police file."

"The file? You mean the incident report?"

"That," I say, "and anything else that's available. Witness statements. Evidence inventory."

"We won't provide the report."

"Okay," I say. "So, the file isn't available?"

"I didn't say it wasn't available. I said we won't provide the report."

Shoot me now.

"What about the rest of the documents in the file?"

"You need to talk to DCPI for that."

Fuck. The Deputy Commissioner for Public Information is the NYPD's media relations arm and it is a complete black hole. At crime scenes, the DCPI officers stand sentry, blocking access instead of providing it. E-mailing a request to the office—which you are always asked to do—yields a response only about 50 percent of the time. And only about 50 percent of those responses actually include the information you've requested.

The FOIL woman gives me DCPI's e-mail address, which I already know by heart. I e-mail my request into the abyss.

At two o'clock, Mike calls and tells me to come into the office to help with rewrite for the rest of the day. Three hours later, I get an e-mail from DCPI:

You need to contact the FOIL office.

I e-mail back: *Already did—they directed me to you.*

Almost immediately, DCPI emails back: *DCPI is the media office that focuses on breaking news. We are unable to accommodate requests for historic files.*

DeShawn wouldn't call his case historic. He's living it every day.

CHAPTER FOURTEEN

July 6–14, 1992
Rikers Island

It wasn't until he saw the newspaper article that DeShawn actually believed Malcolm and Sabrina and Kenya were dead. He signed the piece of paper the cop gave him, but instead of his foster parents walking through the door to take him home, two men in uniform appeared, slapped cuffs on his wrists, and walked him out the side door of the precinct and onto a bus bound for Rikers. Even that first night, awake in his cell, the screams and cries of hundreds of boys bouncing off the walls, echoing through the bars, he thought maybe it was all part of a plan to frighten him into straightening up. He shuffled through the line with a tray at breakfast and threw his entire meal in the trash. At lunch, he spotted a copy of the *Tribune* lying open on the floor by a garbage can: "Psycho Son: Cops Nab Foster Kid in Brutal Triple Murder." His knees buckled and he stayed there, kneeling, as he read the article that told him his family was gone.

He used his phone privileges to call Toya, and by some miracle she picked up and accepted the charges.

"You know I didn't do it, right? I was with you all night."

"I know," she said. But she didn't sound sure.

"I didn't wanna get you in trouble, but I had to tell them I was with you. I'm sorry. I don't know if they believed me, though. Can you call the police and say we were together? Can you call Michael? He was high but he knows we were there. I don't remember the cop's name but it was the precinct on Utica."

"I'm scared," she said.

"Me, too." He wanted to ask her to come visit, but how could he? Some girls bragged about their boyfriends in lockup, but Toya didn't date thugs. She respected herself. It was one of the things he loved about her.

"Who do you think did it?" she asked.

"I don't know. The paper said Ontario is okay, though. Can you ask around about where he is?"

"Okay," she said.

A male voice broke in on the line. "Who's this?"

"I'm on the phone," says Toya.

"Who is this!"

"Winston . . ."

The line went dead. He called her back the next day. The recording announced a call from Rikers Island: "Will you accept the call?"

"Fuck no!" said Winston. "Toya don't want nothing to do with you. Call here again and I'll report you for harassment. Add some rape charges to your murder rap, motherfucker."

For a week he waited, certain she'd sneak away and come see him, assure him she'd gone to the police and provided an alibi. He moved from his bunk to the cafeteria to the yard and back to his bunk with his head down, the bewilderment turning to fear, the fear like a fist in his throat, turning his blood thin, his muscles soft, his bones brittle. Where was Ontario? His brother was a mama's boy, glued to Sabrina's legs since the day he joined the family. Was he getting picked on—or worse—in a group home somewhere? Could they have put him back with his mother? The one who gave him the burn on his arm?

And then, one afternoon, someone called his name.

"DeShawn!"

It was Freddie Anthony, the son of two parishioners at Glorious Gospel. Like DeShawn, Freddie had stopped going to church, but his mother and father were diehards. DeShawn hadn't seen Freddie in probably two years. They were a year apart in school, and Freddie dropped out when DeShawn was a freshman. DeShawn didn't know for sure, but he thought Freddie had gotten mixed up in a gang—one of the local crews affiliated with the Bloods.

"Fuck, man," said Freddie. "You look like shit."

DeShawn had been avoiding the metal plates that served as mirrors in the bathrooms.

"What are you in for?" DeShawn asked.

Freddie shrugged. "Possession with intent. But what the *fuck*, man? What even happened? Was Malcolm, like, *doing* something?"

"No! I didn't do it, Freddie. No fucking way."

"I heard you confessed."

"*Bullshit*," said DeShawn, almost shouting. "That cop lied to me. Got me all mixed up. I got an alibi! I was with my girl."

"Fucking cops will do anything to close a case," said Freddie. "But you up a creek, man. You got a lawyer?"

"No."

"They'll appoint one, but you gotta get your alibi together. They're not gonna play around on a triple murder. You should call Pastor

Green. He helped me out some the first couple times I was in here. He might could help you get a better lawyer. Your girl talk to the cops yet?"

"I don't know. Her stepdad won't let her talk to me."

"You gotta get on that shit. Fast. Longer you stay in here, the easier it is for everybody outside to forget you. They all thinking you blew your family away! If you didn't do it, you need to call everybody you ever known. Get them to go to the cops. Get them to talk to your lawyer. Otherwise you'll just be another murderin' nigger that deserves the needle. You feel me?"

DeShawn felt him. And Freddie's talk woke him up. He called Glorious Gospel, and two days later, Pastor Redmond Green made the trip to Rikers.

"I didn't do it, Pastor Green," said DeShawn as soon as they sat down. "You believe me, right? You gotta help me."

"The police have told me you confessed, DeShawn," said Pastor Green. "They've told me they have a witness who saw you running from the apartment, carrying a gun, late that night."

"They're lying!"

"You didn't confess?"

"No . . . I mean, that cop, he tricked me. I thought . . . he said they were gonna charge Ontario. He said . . ."

"Ontario? I don't think so, DeShawn. I think the best thing for you to do now is plead guilty and try to focus on getting right with the Lord. You can still be forgiven. You can still do some good. . . ."

"I didn't do it, Pastor Green. You gotta believe me. I *couldn't* do it. I love Malcolm and Sabrina. They've been nothing but good to me. . . ."

"I know *exactly* how good they were to you, DeShawn. And how good they were to Ontario, and Kenya, and anyone else who needed anything from them."

DeShawn remembers that Pastor Green's voice shook as he spoke, and that he had trouble making eye contact across the hard plastic table. The pastor had been part of DeShawn's life for more than a decade. DeShawn knew the inside of the little storefront that Glorious Gospel occupied as well as he knew his home. He knew the mop bucket and cleaning supplies tucked behind the plastic curtain in the shower stall; the art supplies in plastic bins in the storage closet; prayer books and hymnals stacked neatly atop the folding wooden shelves along the far wall of the pastor's tiny office. He knew that on Sunday morning, the sanctuary—which Malcolm told him had previously been a men's clothing store—would smell like coffee and cologne, until it began to smell like the sweat the worshipers leaked as they swayed and sang, rejoicing in Jesus Christ, the saving of their souls, the forgiveness of their sins.

"What about forgiveness," whispered DeShawn.

"Jesus forgives those who repent," said the pastor. "Are you ready to tell the truth?"

"I *am* telling the truth!" DeShawn slammed his hand down on the table, frustration and misery rising as rage inside him. How could Pastor Green think he was capable of murdering his family? What had he ever done but smoke some weed and swipe some cash? "I was with my girl! LaToya Marshall. Ask her! Please! I'm not lying!"

Pastor Green stood up.

"I'm sorry, Pastor Green . . ."

"You need to be a man now, DeShawn. You made your choices and now you need to live with them. Though, Lord knows I don't know how you will. Your church family will be here for you if you repent, but there is nothing we can do for you until you do."

·   ·   ·

When he got back to Brooklyn after visiting DeShawn, Pastor
Green called his wife from the church office and told her he would
not be home for dinner. For two hours, he sat in the creaky leather
swivel chair and cried like a child. Redmond Green had been sur-
rounded by violence his entire life. He had seen his father choke his
mother into unconsciousness in the kitchen of their apartment on
Throop Avenue. Had heard her head slam into walls and her arms
and legs tumble over furniture behind the door of his parents' bedroom. He had watched his brothers and cousins join gangs and attack other boys in the neighborhood for walking on the wrong side
of the street, collecting bats and chains and knives from school storage rooms and empty lots and kitchen drawers, suiting up for battle
like soldiers before they could properly grow a mustache. Uprising
and anger was everywhere: on the streets, in the schoolyard, on the
news. Assassinations, riots, war. Redmond avoided it all as best he
could. Enduring taunts about being bookish or a Goody Two-Shoes
was nothing compared to the terror that the violence—its perpetra-
tors and its victims—conjured inside him. Once, when he was nine
or ten years old, he saw a man stab a woman on a street corner, just
blocks from where he would later open Glorious Gospel. Other
people saw it, too. He remembers the groan the woman emitted when
the knife went into her stomach a second time. He remembers the
blood; that it ran down her bare leg and onto the sidewalk. He remembers the way the people walking by barely paused as the man
tore the life from her. And he remembers that once he got home,
out of breath from the fear and the running, his mother told him to
mind his own business, and that the woman probably deserved what
she got.

When he was thirteen, Redmond's oldest brother was shot to
death in Manhattan. At twenty-one, he watched his mother die
of stomach cancer, coughing blood into handkerchiefs and water

glasses at home because she refused to "be anybody's science ex-
periment" in the hospital. Yet, after all of this, Redmond Green
was not prepared for his best friend's murder. Malcolm Davis, the
only son of a city bus driver and a homemaker, moved from Harlem
to Crown Heights in 1970. He'd earned a scholarship to Hunter
College and graduated with a degree in psychology, then found a
job at the Boys & Girls Club in Flatbush. Redmond Green, who
was working at the program and attending seminary at night, was
the one who hired him. Malcolm was single, and at a Labor Day
BBQ in Prospect Park, Redmond's then-fiancée, Barbara, introduced him to her childhood friend, Sabrina Carlyle. Sabrina was,
as Barbara put it, "a prize," and Redmond knew he'd be in hot water
if he encouraged an introduction to anyone who would break her
heart or treat her wrong. But after a few months of working together, Redmond was convinced of Malcolm's good character. And
he wasn't surprised when Malcolm and Sabrina were married less
than a year after meeting. It was as close to love at first sight as
he'd ever seen. Sabrina was confident and beautiful. Tall and slim
and stylish, she did some modeling in high school but quit, Barbara
told him, after one-too-many photographers asked her to model
nude. Sabrina put herself through secretarial school and got a job
with the city, hoping the stable profession would put her in a position to meet a reliable man. Because all Sabrina Carlyle had ever
really wanted was a family of her own. Her father, a barber, died of
a heart attack when she was eight. Her mother began drinking and
didn't stop until her liver failed when Sabrina was seventeen. She
lived alone in their Flatbush apartment for most of her senior year,
skirting child welfare authorities until her eighteenth birthday. The
money from modeling paid the rent, and she ate lunch at school and
dinner at friends' houses. Sabrina used to tell Barbara how much she
envied her noisy, full life, sharing two bedrooms with four siblings

and two engaged, if harried, parents. When she wasn't pregnant a year after their wedding, Sabrina began to worry. After two years, she went to the doctor and discovered that she had an abnormally shaped uterus and would never bear children.

It was Redmond who suggested they apply to become foster parents.

"You don't have to make any long-term commitments," he said to Malcolm one Sunday after church service. The tiny flock he was assembling met in Red and Barbara's living room then. They didn't need much. Everyone had their own Bible, of course, and Barbara led songs on a Casio keyboard. Worship led to Bible study, which led to what Pastor Green called "community action." The congregation was mostly couples with young children looking for a church that preached a living gospel, a gospel that encouraged civic engagement. Pastor Green's parishioners weren't going to leave the fate of their community to the drug dealers or the police officers. They knew that they had to be organized and active to make a difference, and as they sipped Maxwell House and nibbled baked goods while the children napped, they discussed how to best focus their efforts. Everyone had a bugaboo: graffiti, prostitution, substandard housing, crumbing school buildings, easy access to drugs. They started small. One Sunday afternoon in May 1974, Pastor Green led about a dozen people with garbage bags and gardening gloves and sandwiches through St. John's Park, and together they picked up trash and passed out peanut butter and jelly to the men on benches and beneath trees. They repeated their mission each week, and the work brought the congregation closer to each other and to God. As the months and years passed, they named themselves Glorious Gospel and focused their efforts on improving the physical environment around their homes, and supporting and educating the next generation.

"I don't say this lightly, Malcolm," Redmond said. "But perhaps God has chosen you and Sabrina to be caretakers for children who are not your own. For children whose own parents cannot be parents."

Malcolm shook his head. "I don't know," he said. "Sabrina adores every child she sees. And they adore her. But I don't know if I can love somebody else's kid."

"I'm not saying it wouldn't be a challenge," said Redmond. "But I wouldn't suggest it if I didn't think you were capable. Think about it, will you? There are so many children in need, Malcolm. It would be a sin for two people as righteous and strong as you and Sabrina not to share your love."

Six months later, the Davises brought home their first foster child, a seven-year-old boy named Philip who was taken away from his mother when he arrived on the first day of first grade weighing less than a child half his age. The school called child welfare, and when social workers went to the boy's apartment they found bare cupboards, rat droppings, and three people packaging heroin into baggies in the kitchen. When they were approved as foster parents, Sabrina painted the spare bedroom mint green—suitable for boys or girls—and Malcolm assembled a bunk bed. But the Davises soon found that many of the children they opened their home to ended up sleeping in their bed, driven from sleep by nightmares and unable to soothe themselves. DeShawn had done the same when the Davises first took him in. And Kenya, of course.

Sitting in his office after visiting DeShawn at Rikers, Pastor Green couldn't help but wonder if he wasn't to blame for what happened to Malcolm and Sabrina and that beautiful, innocent little girl. He knew becoming foster parents would be difficult, but it never occurred to him that it would be dangerous. The Davises had been fostering for more than a decade when they brought DeShawn home.

He was six, and had been in a group home since watching his mother's boyfriend crush her skull with a cast-iron frying pan. The poor boy stayed with her body for three days before finally knocking on the neighbor's door when he ran out of food. Sabrina and Malcolm found him a therapist, and by fifth grade, he was reading at two years above grade level and playing third base for the neighborhood youth league. It took a while, but DeShawn blossomed into the kind of funny, caring kid Pastor Green imagined Malcolm and Sabrina would have created had God blessed them with their own children. But when DeShawn turned fifteen, things began to change. Malcolm and Sabrina had never parented a teenager. Most of the children they fostered were young and ended up back with their parents or a relative appointed by the courts. They decided to begin adoption proceedings when DeShawn was twelve. It took two years to find his father, and when they did, the man put up a stink. He wanted to see the boy, but missed every scheduled appointment. Finally, he demanded money to sign over parental rights. DeShawn pretended the man's machinations didn't bother him, but when his grades started dropping, Malcolm and Sabrina knew they were taking a toll. And this time, DeShawn was old enough to refuse the therapy they arranged for him.

Pastor Green blew his nose and filled a big glass of water in the church's bathroom, drank it down in front of the mirror. He had gone to the precinct and spoken with the Italian detective as soon as he learned they arrested DeShawn. He listened, mute, as the man told him a witness picked the boy he had known for ten years out of a lineup and that DeShawn had changed his story multiple times before finally confessing. When he got home that night, Barbara was in the living room with Abel and Dorothy Norris. They were planning the funeral, making lists of people to call, arranging for burial and flowers and agonizing over what would happen to

Ontario. Redmond relayed what the detective told him, and they all held hands to pray. As they lay in bed that night, he and Barbara whispered in the dark. Should they have seen this coming? It wasn't unusual for teens to break away from the church—and their parents—as they struggled to forge their own identity. And it wasn't unusual for teens in Crown Heights to do some of the things DeShawn had been doing: smoking pot, skipping school, even stealing. But Malcolm hadn't said anything about DeShawn getting into fights. Where could this violence have come from? What could possibly have sparked such an insane slaughter? He knew Malcolm was frustrated with DeShawn, and concerned, but had he been afraid of the boy in his home? And would he have said anything if he was?

Pastor Green wasn't sure what he expected, seeing DeShawn at Rikers. He felt obligated to visit the boy, of course. He owed him that. And yes, perhaps he was hoping for some sort of explanation—as if there could be any reason to do what he had done. He expected, at least, that DeShawn would show remorse. Beg forgiveness. Weep and shake and repent and wail that he'd smoked some of that crack that was everywhere and just gone crazy. What he really wanted was for DeShawn *not* to have done what the detective said he did. And yet, when the boy professed his innocence, Pastor Green could not believe him. Who else could have done this? Malcolm and Sabrina had no enemies.

CHAPTER FIFTEEN

At a little after noon on Saturday, my phone rings with a 917 number I don't recognize.

"Hi, it's Rebekah," I say.

"Rebekah, it's Ontario Amos. You came by my work a couple days ago."

"Hi, Ontario. How are you?"

"Tired. Listen, if you want to know what was going on with Malcolm and Sabrina, you should talk to the people at Glorious Gospel. Pastor Green's retired but he's still around. His son, Red Jr., is the pastor now. Him and Dorothy Norris probably knew them better than anybody."

I grab a pen. "Dorothy Norris?"

"She was the church secretary. She took me in for a little while, after."

"Are you in touch?"

"Not really," he says. "But I think she still lives in the same place."

"Would you mind giving me her address?"

"I'll give you her phone number," he says. "If you talk to her, tell her I said hello. Tell her I been meaning to call."

"I will."

"I been thinking a lot about that night since you came by. We spent the day in the park and I got a stomachache because I'd eaten a bunch of junk food. Cotton candy and popcorn and soda and stuff. Sabrina always read to me before bed, and that night I remember she sat with me and rubbed my belly, too. She was a real good mom. She was always patient. And we weren't easy, you know? I told you about Kenya. She would have these screaming nightmares. Wake everybody up. And I was really hyper. And DeShawn. I mean, he was always in a bad mood. Always saying mean stuff about Sabrina's cooking or something. Now that I got my own kids, I don't know how she put up with some of the shit we did when we weren't her blood."

"Was Malcolm that way, too?"

"Yeah. I remember feeling like I was really important 'cause I was in their family. Like, they'd picked me so I must be pretty, I don't know, almost special. I don't remember a lot. But I remember feeling that way."

I scribble what he's saying into my notebook.

"Have you thought any more about whether you think De-Shawn might not have done it?" I ask.

"Yeah, but . . . I don't know. I didn't like him. I mean, I did at first. But by the time I was starting school he was making things real hard in the house. I remember I tried to be really good. Helping Sabrina in the kitchen and cleaning up my room. I see it in my kids, too. When me and Tammy fight, they get all sweet. They just want calm, you know?"

"When we talked at your restaurant, you said DeShawn scared

you. Did he ever threaten you? Did you ever see him, like, get violent?"

"No. He was just . . . unpredictable. Like I said, always in a bad mood."

Sounds like a teenager, I think. Or, I suppose, a murderer.

"Thanks for calling," I say. "I'll reach out to Pastor Green and Dorothy Norris."

"You really think DeShawn didn't do it?"

"I don't know," I say. I can't tell Ontario that half the reason I'm looking into his family's murders is that I need a project—and that my mother happens to be dating one of the cops who actually saw their bodies. "I think it's worth asking some questions."

The Web site for Glorious Gospel is impressive, with video elements and tabs for worship and Sunday school, events, prayer, and a newsletter. I click into the August newsletter and scan. At the corner of the second page is an advertisement for The Davis-Gregory Activism Fund. A short paragraph below reads:

> *The Fund in honor of Malcolm and Sabrina Davis, and Kenya Gregory, seeks donations and volunteers to further Glorious Gospel's mission of peace and social justice in our community. For more information on the Fund's current projects, contact Pastor Green.*

I call the main number for the church and a woman answers. "Glorious Gospel."

"Hi," I say. "My name is Rebekah Roberts and I am a reporter with . . . the Center on Culture, Crime and the Media. I'm working on an article about Malcolm and Sabrina Davis and I was wondering if I could speak with Pastor Green."

"The Center on what?"

"Culture, Crime and the Media," I say. "It's a non-profit organ-ization. I'm a freelancer. I also work for the *Trib*."

"All right. Let me see if I can find him. Can you hold?"

"Sure," I say.

Two minutes later: "This is Pastor Green. How can I help you?"

"Hi, Pastor Green, thanks for taking my call. I'm working on an article about the deaths of Malcolm and Sabrina Davis, and their foster daughter." I decide not to go into detail about my specific angle. "I was hoping maybe I could speak to you—or your father, if he's available. Ontario Amos, the Davises' foster son, told me that he and a woman named Dorothy Norris were close with the Davises and that they were very kind to him after their deaths."

"How is Ontario?"

"He's good," I say. "I don't know if you've read about it, but the restaurant where he cooks has gotten a lot of praise. And he's a dad."

"That's wonderful."

I wait. After a moment, he continues.

"What sort of information are you looking for?"

"I just wanted to get a sense of what kind of people they were. What things they were involved in. I saw the church has a memo-rial fund in their name. I'd love to learn about that."

"And you say you'd like to talk to my father and Dorothy Norris?"

"That's who Ontario suggested."

"Would your article make mention of the Davis Fund?"

"Um, sure," I say. "I could probably do that."

"It's not essential. But we're doing a lot of positive things. Your readers might be interested in getting involved."

"Totally," I say.

"I'll contact Mrs. Norris and my father to see if they're willing to talk to you. Of course, I can't promise anything."

"Of course," I say. "I really appreciate it."

Two hours later, Pastor Green calls and invites me to come to Glorious Gospel tomorrow at noon, after worship.

I take the R train from my apartment and transfer to the 3 at Atlantic Terminal. At the Kingston Avenue station I climb the stairs up to the street and find myself at the corner of Eastern Parkway, and on the sidewalk in front of the World Headquarters of the Chabad-Lubavitch movement. I've spent almost two years reporting in the Hasidic world, but I don't know much about Chabad. I've heard them described as the evangelicals of the Jewish world. They wear the black hats and wigs like my mom's family in Borough Park, but aren't quite as insular or as contemptful of modern life. Their mission is to bring non-practicing Jews back into observance, so they routinely interact with people outside their sect. I actually follow a Chabad PR guy on Twitter. He posts a lot of inspirational quotes from Rebbe Menachem Schneerson—who died in the 1990s but is still their spiritual leader—and articles about the gentrification of Crown Heights. Apparently, just as the black and Latino and Chinese residents of Bushwick and Bed-Stuy and Sunset Park are being pushed out, the Jews of Crown Heights are finding it harder and harder to rent apartments in "their" neighborhood, too.

And indeed, here at the intersection of Eastern Parkway and Kingston Avenue, it's like an advertisement for the new Brooklyn melting pot: women in long skirts and flat shoes pushing strollers outside the Jewish Children's Museum; construction workers carrying drywall from a brownstone undergoing renovation (and, according to the sign out front, being offered for sale "exclusively" by Corcoran); a skinny white boy in pristine high-top sneakers carrying a leather satchel and sporting Beats by Dre headphones over his CROWN HEIGHTS ball cap; a black man with waist-length, half-gray dreadlocks selling water bottles out of a cooler; yeshiva students in black hats and pants, walking in packs; a modern Orthodox businessman talking into his Bluetooth headset; a light brown-skinned woman, bra-less and stunning in a maxi dress and gold jewelry, looking around and then down at her phone, lost apparently, hand over her eyes to shade the brutal sun. Bakeries and banks, cafés, cell phone stores, taquerías. I fucking love it, but living here doesn't come cheap. Iris and I looked at listings in Crown Heights last year when we were deciding whether to renew the lease on our shitty place in Gowanus: $2,500 for a two-bedroom walk-up; no laundry.

North of Eastern Parkway the black hats all but disappear. The bodegas advertise lottery tickets and beer instead of kosher food, and the rowhouses are far less pristine than those just a few blocks south. Glorious Gospel is a stone building on a corner lot. There is a gated playground on one side and a handful of parking spaces on the other. At my dad's church in Orlando, people wear flip-flops and shorts to Sunday service, but the men and women filing out here have put real effort into their appearance. Dresses, hats, heels, even suits on a day that's forecasted to reach a hundred degrees. I enter the door marked OFFICE and a woman behind a desk tells me to wait.

"Pastor Green should be here shortly," she says. "He always has a little coffee and some cookies after worship."

About ten minutes later the office door opens again and an impeccably dressed thirty-something man enters, followed by an older man and an older couple.

The youngest man extends his hand.

"You must be Rebekah," he says. "Pastor Redmond Green Jr."

"Nice to meet you," I say.

He takes out a key ring and unlocks an unmarked door, motions for us to enter. Inside is a small conference room: blue carpet, a dining room table and chairs.

We all sit down and Pastor Green makes the introductions.

"This is Dorothy and Abel Norris," he says. "And my father, Pastor Redmond Green Sr."

"Thank you all so much for taking the time to meet with me," I say. "As Pastor Green probably told you, I'm working on a possible article about Malcolm and Sabrina Davis. I spoke with Ontario Amos recently, and he said that if I wanted to know what was going on in their lives, you were the people to talk to."

Dorothy Norris is sitting up very straight at the edge of her chair, her elbows tucked to her chest and her hands folded on the table in front of her. Her gray-and-black hair is swept up from her face and cut short. I can picture her sleeping in pink foam curlers beneath a scarf like my grandma does, combing and fluffing each morning. Her dress is a tan-and-blue flower print with tiny buttons running from the prim collar to her shins. She wears a gold cross around her neck and small gold hoops in her ears. Pastor Green Sr. is in a gray striped suit with a blue tie. His hair is thinning, and mostly gray.

"I noticed you have a fund in memory of the Davises," I continue. "Maybe you could tell me a little about that?"

"The anniversary has just past," says Dorothy. "Is there some specific reason you're interested in this now?"

So much for my plan to ease in.

"Well," I say, "DeShawn Perkins wrote me a letter." Dorothy raises her eyebrows. Pastor Green Jr. makes a sniffing sound. "I'm sure you know that he says he didn't kill them."

"I believe the boy confessed," says Pastor Green Sr.

"Right," I say. "But he says he was coerced. He says the detective threatened him and that he was kept in the interrogation room for hours without an adult. He says he signed the paper because he just wanted to go home."

No response.

"What did you all think when you heard he'd been arrested?"

The people at the table exchange glances. After a few moments, Pastor Green Sr. speaks. "I think we were all surprised. But you have to understand, there was a lot of violence in our community then. It was a terrible time. People like Malcolm and Sabrina, they were working hard to provide stability and positivity for young people, but especially when the weather got hot and school let out, there was a lot of temptation to run wild."

"And how could you blame them, really," says Dorothy. "Most of the adults in the community were no better. Smoking crack in the middle of the street, shooting each other over nothing. Our little girl, Shirley. That same summer some woman mugged her on the way to summer camp. Stole an eleven-year-old's backpack! How can you even explain that to a child?"

"Had DeShawn been in trouble with the law before?"

"I believe he was arrested once or maybe twice," says Pastor Green Sr. "Marijuana, I think. Or it might have been stealing."

"I spoke with him over the phone a few days ago and he mentioned that his parents were getting threats."

"Threats?" says Pastor Green Jr.

"He said people—or someone—had been calling the house and hanging up. And he said he found a letter that said something like, 'I'm watching you.' He said that when he asked Malcolm about it he told him it was nothing, but that Sabrina was worried."

"Come to think of it," says Abel, "I think Malcolm did mention something about hang-ups. He was considering changing their number."

"You didn't tell me that," says Dorothy.

"Didn't I?"

"No!"

Abel turns his head toward his wife but doesn't make eye

contact. He is picking at his fingernails, leaning forward, legs spread wide. He wears a silver Medic Alert bracelet around one wrist.

"Did he say anything about who he thought might be doing it?" I ask.

"No," says Abel.

"What did the police say? About the phone calls."

Abel scratches his throat. "What do you mean?"

"You didn't tell the police?" asks Dorothy.

Abel looks down at his hands, plays with his wedding ring. "You were the only one they interviewed, Dorothy. I'm sure you remember I was taking care of the girls. And then Ontario came to stay. . . ."

He trails off, avoiding his wife's glare.

"So you weren't interviewed?" I ask, looking at Abel and the elder pastor. They shake their heads. "Did that seem odd? That the police didn't talk to people who were close with the victims?"

"Yes and no," says Pastor Green Sr. "They arrested DeShawn very quickly. And once they had a confession, and that witness, I suppose they thought—we all thought—they had their man."

"Did any of you know the witness?"

Head shakes all around.

"Were you at the trial?"

"We all went," says Pastor Green Sr. "We felt it was important to represent the victims in the courtroom."

"Do you think DeShawn got an adequate defense?"

There is a pause, then Dorothy speaks up. "I'm not sure we're qualified to say. We were mostly concerned with Ontario, to be honest. I'm just speaking for myself here, but when word got around that he confessed, and that there was a witness . . . well, that's pretty convincing, isn't it? I never thought of DeShawn as violent, but what happened to Malcolm and Sabrina and little Kenya was just so shocking. I remember thinking that if he was really innocent he would have asked for our help. He would have shouted it to the rooftops."

"He told me he wanted to testify but that his lawyer said it was a bad idea."

I wait for a response but there is none. Every person in the room is grimacing.

"Was there anything else Malcolm and Sabrina were involved in that might have made people angry?"

"They were involved in a lot," says Pastor Green Sr. "We all were. Trying to keep the community safe. Turn it back into a place people might actually be proud to call home. It's hard to say it now, but I voted for Giuliani the first time he ran. I thought his idea about cracking down on the so-called 'quality of life' crimes was a good one. Public urination and turnstile jumping and what have you. If we don't show our children that we respect our neighborhood, how can we expect them to behave? Malcolm and Sabrina helped with sweep-up Sundays. After worship we'd take brooms and garbage bags and try to clean things up a little. If a business had a broken window or some graffiti they wanted help with, we'd make that the day's mission.

"Of course there were bigger things, too. We worked against the gangs. We had midnight marches through some of the nearby housing projects that used to make some people angry. And the Crown Heights Alliance."

"What was that?"

"I'm sure you've read about the riots?"

I nod. I've heard the term "Crown Heights Riots," of course, but

I really only have a vague sense that it involved a clash between black and Jewish neighbors and took place around the same time as the Rodney King riots in Los Angeles.

"It was an ugly time," continues Pastor Green Sr. "There was a lot of hatred. A lot of misunderstanding. Glorious Gospel and a few other congregations began a monthly dialogue session with some of the Lubavitchers. It was informal. We were trying to find common cause."

"How did that work out?"

"It wasn't particularly well-attended, on either side," he says, looking at Abel. "But it was very important to me. It's so easy for people to forget their history. All Christians were once Jews. And the Jews were on our side during the civil rights struggles."

"Different kinds of Jews," says Abel quietly.

Pastor Green Sr. runs his hands over his pants and inhales through his nose.

"No one came out of those riots looking good," he says. "It was a black eye for everyone. And I was not going to sit by and watch my community burn to the ground because grown people were too stupid and angry to see common humanity in someone who looks different from them."

"It's not just that they look different . . ." begins Abel.

"Abel, I'm not getting into this with you."

Dorothy puts her hand on her husband's leg.

"Many of us thought it was important to channel the anger everyone was feeling into something positive," says the senior pastor.

"But not everyone agreed," I say.

"That's not unusual," says Pastor Green Jr., scooting up toward the table. "And frankly, this isn't the time for airing these past squabbles. Even today, there are disagreements about the priorities of the Davis Fund, as there are with many church priorities. Dad, I don't

think Malcolm was even particularly involved in the dialogue sessions, was he?"

"Well, he wasn't opposed."

"Red," says Dorothy, "Abel wasn't opposed, either."

"He could have fooled me."

"Okay," says the current pastor. "Let's move on, shall we? Ms.
Roberts, is there anything else we can help you with?"

I want to keep on friendly terms with these people, so I decide
it's probably time to go.

"I think I'm good for now," I say. "I'm not certain where this
story is going to lead, but I really appreciate your time."

I write my name and phone number on two pieces of paper and
give one to Dorothy and one to the senior pastor. His son stands
and walks me out.

"My father and the Norrises were very close to Malcolm and
Sabrina," he says. "The murders really devastated them. Off the
record, I think they feel some guilt for not seeing what DeShawn
was capable of."

"Did you know him at all?"

"A little," he says. "He's a couple years older than me, and he
stopped coming to church about a year before they died. Malcolm
and Sabrina used to drag him along, but he made a scene during
one of the Sunday sweep-ups and I think they decided it wasn't
worth it anymore."

"What kind of scene?"

"We were picking up trash and he threw an empty beer bottle
at Sabrina. I think he just meant to have her put it in her trash bag,
but he threw it hard. She ducked and it shattered on somebody's car."

"Do you think he was actually aiming at her?"

"I have no idea," he says. "I just remember everybody was
really upset and DeShawn got all defensive and ran off. We went

to different schools, so I didn't see him much after that. My mom thought he was a bad influence."

"What did you think when you heard they'd arrested him?"

"It scared me. There were a lot of rumors about him being in a gang, and I got the idea that the gang might go after my dad. I don't know why. I don't think I slept for a month."

"What gang was this?"

"I don't know. I don't think he actually was in a gang. I think people were just trying to make sense of how a kid—I mean, he was sixteen—a kid could do something that horrible. Later on, I heard he was angry because they'd taken in another child. And then I heard he'd gotten kicked out of school and Malcolm was going to send him to a group home. I have no idea what was really true. But none of it explained why he'd murder them all."

"Do you think it's possible that maybe he didn't do it?"

Redmond Jr. takes off his glasses and rubs his eyes. "It's not something I've thought much about. But yes, of course it's possible." He puts his glasses back on. "Lord knows we've see a lot of young black men falsely accused, even now. We had a parishioner whose son was arrested for allegedly stealing an iPhone last year. Fortunately, the congregation was able to raise the money for his bail, but so many others just get stuck in Rikers. The DA dropped the charges. It makes me sick to think that DeShawn's been in prison all this time if he didn't do it. And if it wasn't him, there's someone out there who shot an entire family in their bed. What else has he done?"

CHAPTER SIXTEEN

Afternoon
July 6, 1992
Crown Heights, Brooklyn

Saul found out about the lineup from one of the officers at the precinct.

"Your witness ID'd the son," said Officer Kevin Whitlock. "Kid confessed."

It was 3:00 P.M. Saul was scheduled for a 4–12. He could have come in early for the lineup, but no one called.

"When did this happen?"

"Just a couple hours ago." Whitlock was on desk duty because he had failed to secure his weapon properly and it went clattering to the ground as he ran after a robbery suspect last week. He lost the suspect, his dignity—a group of kids on lunch break from the nearby junior high saw the whole thing—and got demoted to desk work.

"Who took it?" asked Saul.

"Olivetti. I think that's his second confession this week. I should start a pool to see if he can top April. What was that? Six?"

"I don't keep track," said Saul. They'd done it all without him.

He felt himself going sour with anger, as if curdled milk were running through his veins. There had been so many days of feeling so utterly unmoored since he left the community. And yet he had almost always managed to maintain a kind of distance from what he knew his family and former friends were thinking of him, saying about him. He saw the other former Hasids he met at Coney Island come and go, sorrow and bitterness their only guide as they wandered lost and alone through a world they did not understand. Saul once told a group that had gathered for a Shabbos meal that holding on to anger and sadness was like building their new life upon sand. It could only crumble and be washed away. He took pride in re-creating his own life on the solid bedrock of police work; he was a peace officer, a guardian, a problem solver. His new identity gave him self-worth and that—not the hole in his heart that Binyamin's absence created; not the holidays and weekends and nights spent alone; not the weeping phone calls from his mother or the difficulty finding camaraderie with his colleagues—was what would forge the foundation of his future. But if his fellow officers didn't even respect him enough to loop him in on a lineup with his own witness, what kind of foundation was it, really? He walked past Whitlock and the detectives' desks, seeing the family photos of smiling wives and children looking at their uniformed fathers as if they were superheroes. He'd missed a significant morning in a significant case, and it was difficult not to dive headfirst into resentment and animus. So difficult it made him shiver.

"The rabbi returns!" said Olivetti when Saul found him in the precinct's break room with another detective, Paul Amodino. Saul knew some of his colleagues called him "rabbi" behind his back. He tried not to hate them for it.

"DeShawn confessed?"

"Sure did," said Olivetti. "Didn't have much of a choice after your witness fingered him."

"Where is he now?"

"The kid? Rikers."

"Have you talked to the ADA?"

"She's on her way."

"She?" Saul had only ever encountered male prosecutors.

"The new star," said Olivetti, not even trying to hide his disdain. "Sandra Michaels. She's one of those feminists they brought in for sex crimes. Affirmative action hire. One hundred percent."

"You want me to set up the chair?" asked Amodino.

"Perfect."

The "chair" was how some in the precinct referred to a seat beside a particular desk along the far wall and just below the one air-conditioning vent in the squad room. The vent blew cold air straight down, and some of the men thought it was amusing to sit an attractive woman there on hot days and hope her nipples made an appearance. Almost to a man, his colleagues spoke openly, and crassly, about sex, something Saul was unaccustomed to. Frum couples had sex, of course, but he never spoke about his body, or his wife's body, with anyone. As a child, in yeshiva, there was some talk, and yes, he had more than once encountered the gauzy, baffling photographs in a friend's stolen skin magazine. But it was all surreptitious; undoubtedly forbidden. At the precinct, officers taped naked and half-naked photographs of women inside their lockers. Even when female officers were around, the men bragged and teased constantly. He never joined in, and people noticed. It was yet another way he stood out.

While he waited for the ADA, Saul went outside to smoke, something he had begun doing occasionally. Half the time he didn't inhale, but he liked the way he felt holding a cigarette: serious, perhaps even a little dangerous. If the yarmulke set him apart from his fellow cops, the cigarette, he imagined, helped him blend in.

He was about to go back inside when he saw Naftali Rothstein get out of a cab across the street. Rothstein and Saul had not known each other growing up. Rothstein was a Lubavitcher, while Saul's family was Belz and lived in Borough Park. Like many haredi, Saul found the Lubavitchers odd. They wore short jackets, spoke English instead of Yiddish, and stood around the city on street corners asking clearly unobservant people if they are Jewish. He had to give them credit, however, for their tenacity. And since working in Crown Heights alongside members of the Chabad movement, he'd come to admire their general willingness to extend themselves for those outside their community—a trait Saul believed was in too short supply among haredi.

Saul also admired their practicality. Since the 1960s, the ballooning Lubavitch population—made up of survivors of the Holocaust and Soviet oppression, and their offspring—understood the importance of cultivating trust with the police. Most officers and even the top brass had little love for their ways, but because the sect wanted to keep their people safe from the street violence that had become as commonplace as gum on the sidewalk—and keep official eyes averted from issues they wished to handle inside the fold—a hand was extended, and relationships formed. Rothstein worked in the Crown Heights Jewish Council's nascent media office crafting press releases about events major and minor—the beating of two yeshiva students from Israel by "neighborhood thugs"; the dedication of a child-care center. He completed the Citizens Police Academy and signed up for a monthly ride-along, usually to the chagrin of those tasked with having him in their backseat. He was also one of those pressuring the NYPD's recruitment officers to invite Jews to the academy, so when Saul graduated, Rothstein introduced himself. Although most Lubavitchers lived in the vicinity of the 71st precinct, after the riots Rothstein began coming around to the 77th, the precinct where Saul was stationed and that policed the predominately black area north of Eastern Parkway. He told Saul that he believed a presence there would be helpful in the ongoing quest to have the community's voice and situation understood by the outside world—especially since that outside world was just blocks away. The more police saw Jews as people worth protecting, the better, Rothstein reasoned. And in the past year, his face had become a familiar one around the precinct.

"Saul!" said Rothstein as the cab drove away.

Saul raised his hand in greeting and crushed the unsmoked half of his cigarette beneath his shoe. The men shook hands. Sweat dripped down Rothstein's brow, dampening his thin black beard. Saul ran his hand along his own face, thankful it was no longer covered in fur.

"You must be trying to lose weight standing here in the sun!" said Rothstein. "Don't tell me the air conditioning is out inside?"

"Just taking a break," said Saul. "You are well?"

Naftali sighed. "Zelda took the children to the country last weekend. I should have gone with her."

"Why didn't you?"

"I should have!"

Rothstein had a habit of not quite answering questions posed to him.

"Please," said Rothstein, shading his eyes from the sun. "Talk inside?"

Saul did not mind Rothstein—he found the hyper little man's attempts to ingratiate himself with officers and commanders irritating at times, but appreciated his desire to educate himself about the challenges of policing Crown Heights. What he did not like, however, was being called "rabbi," and it seemed to Saul that each time he was seen with Rothstein the nickname spread further, dug deeper.

Saul followed Rothstein through the front doors of the precinct and up the stairs into the waiting room. Rothstein took off his wide-brimmed hat and fanned his face, pulled a bit at the chest of his white oxford shirt.

"Terrible thing about that family on Troy Avenue. Some days I think perhaps the neighborhood is turning around. And then something like that happens. A little girl!" He shakes his head. "There has been an arrest?"

Saul nodded again. He could hear Olivetti laughing from behind the swinging door that led to the detectives' desks.

"Something to do with gangs? Drugs?"

"Looks like a family problem. We brought the teenage son in. A witness picked him out of a lineup. And we got a confession."

Saying the words made the whole scenario seem more plausible. Most homicide victims were killed by someone they knew. Stash houses were dangerous to bust in on because the people inside tended to be armed, but domestics could be just as risky. Angry husbands and girlfriends and even children went at officers and each other with kitchen knives and baseball bats and all manner of household objects, propelled by years of dysfunction or shame so overwhelming they could barely control themselves. Was it really so far-fetched to think a kid like DeShawn could kill his foster family? They weren't even his blood.

Rothstein made a clucking nose and shook his head. "Every little bit you do, Saul. Every little bit. It makes a difference."

Saul didn't respond, and once Rothstein stopped sweating, he bid his fellow yid farewell, and wandered into the back of the precinct to find the shift commander.

Sandra Michaels was greeted by whistles in the squad room.

Like any sane person, she'd taken her jacket off, exposing a high-collared but sleeveless blouse. Olivetti made a big show of pulling out a chair for her, and while she dug into her briefcase, he coughed, prompting snickers from everyone else in the room. She blushed, then looked at her armpits.

"It's fucking brutal out there," she said.

Of course, the men weren't snickering at the wet half-moons beneath her arms, they were looking at her nipples.

"*Brutal*," said Olivetti.

Sandra fanned herself with her hand and pointed her face up toward the vent.

"Thank God for AC," she said.

"Thank *God*," said Olivetti.

Sandra wasn't stupid. She knew she was being laughed at—she just didn't know why. Saul watched her eyes scan the room, looking for a clue, then hardening. Back to business.

"What do you have for me?" she asked.

Olivetti set a thin file in front of her and explained that it contained DeShawn's confession, as well as statements from Henrietta Eubanks, Dorothy Norris, and the Davises' neighbor.

"Should be a slam-dunk," he said.

Sandra glanced through the documents. "Was an adult present while he was being questioned?"

"You mean other than me?" asked Olivetti.

"You know what I mean, Detective."

"Well, Ms. Michaels, he *murdered* his foster parents. So, no, they weren't available to hold his hand while he cried about it."

"Could be a problem at the trial," she said.

"If anyone can convict him, Sandra, it's you."

The men in the squad room snickered again and Sandra Michaels stood up.

"I'll be in touch," she said, and walked what must have felt like many, many steps to the door.

Not fifteen minutes after that, the desk sergeant hollered for Olivetti.

"You back on rotation?"

"Yup."

"Congratulations," said the sergeant. He handed over a piece of paper with an address on it. "Stabbing on Park Place. One dead, one likely."

And they were off. Malcolm, Sabrina, and little Kenya now yesterday's victims. Their deaths just three more in the city's annual homicide count. DeShawn just another collar.

CHAPTER SEVENTEEN

Night
July 7, 1992
Bushwick, Brooklyn

He came through with the money: one thousand, cash. As usual, he arrived on foot. Hunny watched him walk up the block from the subway at the corner of Gates Avenue. Or at least that's where she figured he was coming from. She had no idea where he lived, if he owned a car, had a family. For all she knew he sunk into the center of the earth when he left and popped back up on their nights together.

He set the money on the sofa and told her to watch as he undressed, then instructed her, as usual, to fold his clothing and set the pile on the coffee table. They did it there in the living room, she bent forward over the sofa and him behind, barely making a sound. The bedsheet curtains she'd nailed above the windows billowed in the hot air. After he finished she went to the bathroom to clean herself, and when she opened the door he was standing, still naked, with a handgun pointed at her face.

"I should kill you now," he said. He pushed the barrel against her forehead, then drew it down, over her nose, and pushed it into her mouth. She tasted blood. Was there blood on the gun? Or was it her own? The barrel felt bigger than it looked. Her jaw locked around it. She'd lost two teeth that year and remembered hoping, ridiculously, that the hard steel wouldn't knock loose any more. It was difficult to see his face with her mouth spread wide, head tilted back, her eyes beginning to water. She felt a little bit of urine run hot down the inside of her leg.

They stood there, both naked and sweating, for what seemed to Hunny like a very long time. She thought about Gina finding her with her head blown open in the bathroom. She wondered if he'd leave the money and, if so, whether Gina would use any of it to bury her. Her jaw began to tremble. Could it actually come unhinged? Saliva built up in her mouth and her tongue tried to swallow, closing off the back of her throat. She gagged, pulling air in through her nostrils, feeling the wet snot and tears begin to leak out and slide down her face.

"I should kill you," he said again. He pulled the gun from her mouth. She coughed and wiped her face with her forearm, her eyes wide, searching his face for a sign of what to do next. Beg? Run? But he was no longer looking at her. She stood as still as she could manage while he dressed, and when he was finished he came to her again, putting the gun beneath her chin this time. He dropped down the safety with his thumb.

"I won't be far," he said.

He let himself out, and she ran to the window, watching as he walked back toward Gates.

For years after, she saw him in the profiles of men on the street, on the subway. She'd catch a glimpse and taste the metal in her mouth. It was never him. Or, if it was, he passed without a word or a glance. But the sightings took their toll. In the more than twenty years between the summer day he walked out of her door to the summer day he walked back in, she never once felt safe.

CHAPTER EIGHTEEN

On Monday morning, while waiting for my assignment, I call Amanda and fill her in on what I learned from the people at Glorious Gospel.

"Have you talked to DeShawn yet?" she asks.

"Over the phone."

"Do you think he's full of shit?"

"No," I say. "But I guess I don't know if I'd know, you know?"

"So, what's your next move?"

"I need to try to find the witness. It's a long shot, but maybe if she's less sure now that could be something. The issue is that she hasn't lived at the address I got from the *Trib* library for years."

"Did they run a national search?"

"I don't know. I guess I assumed so."

"It's not much more effort, but you have to click a couple more boxes to get non–New York info. Ask them to run it again. If they can't find it let me know, I've got some database access through the

Center. You gotta find that witness. If she tells a different story now, that's a game changer."

After we hang up I e-mail the library and have them run a national search on Henrietta Eubanks. Fifteen minutes later they send me a phone number and address in Atlantic City, New Jersey. I tell Iris and she decides it's the perfect excuse for a weekend road trip.

"I'm not officially on assignment," I say. "We'll have to pay."

Iris opens her laptop. "I just saw a Groupon for Atlantic City. They're practically giving rooms away." *Click-click-click* and she finds it. "One hundred fifty bucks for two nights at a hotel called The Coastal. We'll get a Zipcar and I can just wait outside while you interview her. I'll be, like, security."

I can't be sure Henrietta is still at the address from the library, but I have better luck getting people to talk to me when I show up in person than when I'm just a voice on the telephone. Plus, Atlantic City could be fun.

"You could invite your mom," Iris says when I hand her my credit card to enter into Groupon.

"My mom?"

"It might be fun. When was the last time you saw her?"

It's been a while. Months, I think. We had brunch in Park Slope one Sunday back in . . . April? May? When we finally met last year, I initially felt relief. It was like I'd been squinting at her all my life, and now she was in focus and I couldn't stop staring. Everything I learned about her was thrilling, and I was ready to forgive. She's endured a lot—being homeless in Maryland, friendless in Israel, shunned by her Brooklyn family, caring for her troubled brother—but instead of these experiences turning her into a gutsy free spirit, Aviva is conservative in middle age, even a little cowed. She leads a quiet life and seems almost allergic to attention. I know she was invited to join the interfaith nonprofit some of the people in and around Roseville established after the shooting. The goal was to create a foundation for understanding between the haredi and their upstate neighbors, and they reached out to a lot of people like Aviva who had left the ultra-Orthodox world. But she never went to a meeting. When I asked her about it, she wrinkled her nose. *They have lots of important people. They do not need me.* I tried to convince her that her experience in both worlds could be valuable, but I got the sense that she didn't think she deserved to have her voice heard. I felt bad for her until I realized that she was judging me for thinking that I do. At that last brunch I told her about a story I was reporting on a West Village landlord who planned to tear down a hundred-and-fifty-year-old tavern to build luxury condos.

"She's totally dodging my calls," I'd said, finishing my mimosa. "And she won't even admit she owns the building. It's all hidden behind an LLC."

"If she does not want to talk to you, why do you keep calling her?"

"What do you mean?"

"If she owns the building she can do whatever she wants."

"She *can*. But it's fucked up. F. Scott Fitzgerald used to drink at this place. And Dorothy Parker. It's history. The neighbors want to preserve it. And the last thing we need is more condos for rich people."

Aviva raised her eyebrows.

"What?"

"Nothing. It would make me very uncomfortable is all."

"What would make you uncomfortable?"

"Bothering people."

"I'm not *bothering* her. I'm trying to get her to admit the truth.

That's the whole point of my job. If nobody asks people doing shady stuff to explain . . ." I stopped myself. Aviva was no longer listening; she signaled for the check.

"We've only got one hotel room," I tell Iris. "Three people is too much. And I seriously doubt she's into gambling."

Iris does not say that neither of us are into gambling, either, which is true. She's made her point, and she knows when to stop pushing.

I pick up the Zipcar—a sapphire blue Kia Rio—after my shift on Friday and meet Iris on Canal, a couple blocks from the clogged entrance to the Holland Tunnel. Traffic leaving the city is monstrous, but a few miles out we're doing sixty. After about two hours, the highway becomes a boulevard lined by crab shacks and board rentals and fishing charters. The air is cooler and the breeze smells of seagulls and sand.

"There it is!" says Iris, pointing to the glass towers rising in front of us. Atlantic City looks a lot more impressive from afar than up close. Half the storefronts along the first street we turn down are boarded up, and more people on the sidewalks are pushing shopping carts than pulling luggage.

The plan is to door-knock at Henrietta's in the morning, so we drive straight to the hotel. The pink neon sign outside and lobby décor (zebra-striped pillows on white leather settees) attempt to convey a kind of art-deco look, but the effort is half-assed. The king-sized bed in our room has an enormous pink pleather headboard that rises halfway to the ceiling. Our window looks out over the parking garage.

Iris pops the bottle of prosecco I picked up at the wine store down the block from us in Gowanus, and I take a glass into the shower with me. We blow-dry and I borrow a Rag & Bone dress Iris got at a sample sale, then we stroll the boardwalk, lose a few dollars at the slot machines, and spend two hours at a "lounge" sipping cocktails, munching on coconut shrimp and fried calamari, people-watching, and occasionally getting up to dance. Just after midnight, I yawn and Iris laughs.

"We're so old!"

"Sorry," I say.

"Honestly, I'm ready to go, too."

The next morning, we turn the Rio into the parking lot outside a two-story apartment building about a mile off the main drag. Half a dozen children run around, spraying each other with water guns, squealing and shouting. Two women sit on the curb, drinking from giant 7-Eleven mugs, watching the children and chatting. Spanish music pumps into the air from the open window behind them.

"The library printout said it was apartment eight," I say as I turn off the engine.

"I might fall asleep," she says. "But I'll turn my ringer up loud. Call if you need anything. Or scream."

"I'll be fine."

I climb the concrete exterior staircase and knock on door eight. I see movement at the peephole, and then a woman's voice.

"Who is it?"

I hate introducing myself from behind a door. "Hi," I say. "My name is Rebekah Roberts. I'm sorry to bother you. Do you have a minute?"

"I don't need any subscriptions."

"No," I say. "I'm not . . . I'm a reporter. I'm looking for a woman named Henrietta Eubanks."

A pause, and then I hear the dead bolt turn. The woman who opens the door is wearing black pants and a black polo shirt with TRUMP TAJ MAHAL embroidered on the breast pocket.

"Hi," I say. "Are you Henrietta Eubanks?"

"How'd you get this address?"

"I . . . just looked it up. It's pretty easy nowadays."

"What you want?"

She's not angry, which is nice. Just suspicious.

"Sorry, are you Henrietta Eubanks?"

"I was. I go by Day now. Henrietta Day."

"Oh. Okay. But you used to live in Brooklyn?"

"What's this about?"

"I'm looking into an old case, from 1992, in New York."

"A case?"

"A homicide. Three people shot in their home in Crown Heights. You testified that you saw their son leave the house that night."

Henrietta's mouth falls open slightly, and she flinches, almost as if I've come at her physically.

"I was wondering if I could ask you a few questions."

For a moment, Henrietta just stares at me. It's hard to tell how old she is. Fifty, maybe? She has a long face, so oval it's practically rectangular, and a mole above her left eyebrow. I sense she's about to slam the door, and am ready to blurt out *Are you sure it was DeShawn you saw that night?* but instead she steps back, inviting me inside.

The tiny apartment looks more like a motel suite than a home. The sofa, eating table, bed, and kitchen—a sink and a mini-fridge with a hot plate atop it—all share the same space. The only interior door is for the bathroom. Henrietta takes a pack of Merit cigarettes from the kitchen table and lights one, then stands silent, arms crossed below her heavy breasts, looking at her bare feet.

"So," I say, "I've been working on a story about the murder of Malcolm and Sabrina Davis, and a little girl, in Crown Heights back in 1992. I guess you were a witness?"

Henrietta brings her cigarette to her lips, and I can see that she is trembling. She takes a shallow pull, then sits down at the little table. I sit, too.

"That was a long time ago," she says, the words coming through her teeth.

"I know," I say. "And I'm really sorry to bug you. I got a letter from DeShawn Perkins. He's the boy—well, man, now—that got convicted." I pause to see if she recognizes his name. Her lips pull back slightly. It's not a grimace so much as a brace. Like: what next? Hit me. Make it quick. "He insists he didn't kill his family. I know lots of people in prison say they didn't do it, but he didn't have any history of violence. I talked to one of his lawyers who said she thought the evidence against him was weak. And his girlfriend swears he was with her all night. She says the cops got her confused and the prosecutors didn't believe her."

Henrietta's face seems as though it is actually losing surface area. It's almost like she is shrinking as I speak. Her cigarette burns between her fingers, her eyes are unfocused.

"But obviously, your ID was pretty convincing," I say, slowly, not wanting to sound accusatory. "I guess I just wanted to know if you ever had any second thoughts about whether it was him you saw."

Henrietta puts her barely smoked cigarette out into a Taj Mahal ashtray, crushing it over and over, continuing to press it into the hard plastic long after the ember is extinguished. Smashing it for so long the white wrapping paper tears and what's left of the threads of tobacco inside spill out.

"Who you work for?" she asks.

"I'm freelance."

"What you mean?"

"I write for a few different places. The *New York Tribune*. A magazine called *American Voice* . . ."

"The *Trib*?" She almost smiles. "I miss that shit. But I definitely don't want to be in the *Trib*."

"Okay," I say. "We can talk off the record."

She furrows her brow, considering something.

"You recording this?"

"No," I say. "Totally off the record right now."

She nods, stares at the ruined cigarette. Finally, she says, "I didn't see nothing."

"What?"

"I didn't see nothing."

"I don't understand. You picked DeShawn out of a lineup, right?"

She nods.

"But you *didn't* see him coming out of the house that night?"

She shakes her head. "I didn't see nothing."

"I'm sorry, I don't mean to keep repeating, but, like, how did you pick him out then? Your statement said . . ."

"I lied."

"You lied? About seeing him?"

"I wasn't even in Crown Heights that night. I was up in Williamsburg with my roommate."

I stare at her a moment, my mouth open, my heart beating in my ears.

"Did. . . ? But . . . you testified . . ."

"I lied, okay."

"Can I ask you why?"

"None of this is going in your paper."

"Right," I say, thinking: how can I get this in the paper? "We're off the record."

"I had a trick," she says. "He paid me a lot of money to say I saw somebody running out of the house."

"He told you to pick DeShawn?"

"No," she says. "He just said to say I was there and saw a black guy running out."

"Why did you choose DeShawn in the lineup?"

She shrugs. "I was waiting in the precinct and they brought him in in handcuffs. I figured, you know, he'd done something."

I pause, not wanting to seem too enthusiastic.

"I know you don't want this in the paper," I say. "But, what about going to the DA? DeShawn retracted his confession. I think the only real evidence they had against him was your ID. He's been in prison for more than twenty years. You could get him out."

Henrietta pulls another cigarette from her pack. She looks at it between her fingers, twists it, brings it to her lips, lowers it.

"I'm sorry about that boy," she says. "It may not look like much in here, but this place, this job I got, this is more than I ever thought I'd have, okay? I been clean almost eight years. I got a church. I got a man, even."

The air-conditioning unit below the front window clicks on, blowing the thick curtains above it. I look at her and she looks at her cigarette. I suppose she doesn't have to explain. Even if they can't—or won't—prosecute her for making false statements, De-Shawn could sue her and take everything she has. I decide that, for now at least, it's not my place, nor would it be effective, to try to convince her to "do the right thing"—because there are probably a lot of ways that it's not the right thing for her. I try another tactic.

"This trick," I say, "do you think he was involved in the murders?"

"I mean, I never *asked*, but yeah, obviously. That's what I thought."

"Are you still in touch with him?"

"Fuck no."

"Is he why you changed your name?"

"Partly. I had a felony record. Couldn't get no straight work.

Not even cleaning rooms. So I can't be in the paper. I'll lose my job.
Probably go back to prison on some paperwork shit."

"Do you know if he's still in Brooklyn?"

"I don't think so. He used to send me postcards. Before I moved."

"Where were the postcards from?"

"A bunch of different places. Florida. Chicago. Boston."

"Is there anything you remember about him that you could
tell me?"

"He was Jewish."

"Jewish?"

"You know, one of those guys with the black hats."

PART 2

CHAPTER NINETEEN

1982–1991
Southern California

The first uniform he wore was for football. His mother signed him up for Pop Warner when they were still living in Fullerton. He put on the big plastic shoulder pads, and the jersey with the number, and the shoes with the blunt spikes, and he thought: this is who I am now. I am a Wildcat. He liked the fangs on the red and orange mascot and he wore the jersey to bed and to school so that the other kids would see and know. In school, everyone had their "thing." Some of the girls carried baby dolls and pretended to be moms. Boys aligned themselves with professional sports teams or players that they imagined matched their personality: the more aggressive liked the Detroit Pistons; the preppies liked the Chicago Bulls. Even the teachers had costumes. Mrs. Ellis wore silver rings on all her fingers. Mr. Williams had a thick mustache he dyed orange for Halloween and pink for Easter. Mrs. Ito exposed her toes in Birkenstocks no matter the season. His father's Ford Mustang, his mother's diamond earrings, his sister Jessica's stupid blue eyeliner—they were advertisements, he understood. They signaled membership in a group of like people.

The boys in the Wildcats weren't really like him, but they had a common goal and a common language, and that was enough for a while. He ran fast and hit hard, and his teammates and coaches cheered him on, patted him on the back, said "atta boy." He liked that. If he knew what people expected, he performed well.

The anger was always there, though, and there wasn't always someplace to put it. He was nine when he clamped his hand around Jessica's throat after dinner, pressing her into the wall of the bathroom they shared and squeezing, telling her in a steady voice that if she told anyone that he was still wetting the bed he could put a pillow over her head in the middle of the night and she would never wake up. He'd come up with the idea for the pillow when he pressed his own into his face the night before, nearly suffocating himself to silence the screams. If he hadn't screamed he knew he would explode. But if everyone heard the screams he would have to explain. *What's wrong?* It was not always a question he had an answer to.

His displays of aggression were never public. Other boys got into playground fights, sloppily swinging at one another, sweating and shouting, red faced, clothing askew. He cringed when he saw those fights, embarrassed for the boys who rendered themselves so clumsy and out of control. Did they think they were scaring anyone? Did they think their careless display did anything but reveal their weakness?

His father got the job at USC in July and their move to Los Angeles was rushed. He missed football tryouts and had to start seventh grade in a new school knowing no one. On the first day, he sat down alone near the back corner in science class, and a boy wearing a yarmulke took the seat next to him.

"I'm Ethan," said the boy.

"I'm Joe," he said. "I'm Jewish, too."

Ethan smiled.

"What shul do you belong to?"

"Shul?"

"Synagogue."

"You mean temple? I don't know. We just moved here." Joe's family went to temple once a year, on Yom Kippur. His sister complained that it was boring, but Joe didn't mind. He liked the way the Hebrew sounded, and he liked that he got to wear the little satin hat and she didn't. He'd never seen anyone wear one outside of temple, though.

"You should come to our shul," said Ethan. "It's cool."

When he got home, he told his parents he knew what temple they should join.

"I don't think so," said his mother when he said the name.

"Why not?"

"That's an Orthodox temple," she said. They were eating dinner at the dining room table, boxes piled around them. Dinner was important in the Weiss family. His mother, Nora, read books about raising children and believed that eating dinner together helped create a strong family and healthy children. The meals weren't fancy, or particularly tasty—macaroni and cheese, fish sticks, tacos, spaghetti—but she made an effort seven nights a week.

"My friend Ethan goes there. He said it was cool."

"Temple is not cool," said Jessica. She was so predictable.

"They're really strict, bud," said his father.

His parents hadn't been getting along since the move. His mother complained that his father worked too much and neglected to help her establish themselves in their new home. She wanted shelves and paintings hung, and she wanted her husband to hang them. Joe offered to help but she told him that it was his father's responsibility. Joe loved the new house. He got his own bedroom, which he was very thankful for. His mind was always going and he needed a private place to sit quietly and listen. Plus, there was a pool.

"What do you mean, strict?" Joe asked.

"I mean there are a lot of rules they think God wants you to follow every day."

"Like what?"

"Well," said his father, searching, "there are a lot of rules about food."

Andrew Weiss was raised in San Francisco by what Nora joked were "commie pinko Jews." His parents were professors—him of European history, her of American literature—who fled New York City, the story went, after a political meeting they attended was raided by police wielding batons. Joe's grandma and grandpa were atheists, and so was his father, but his mother believed in God. Before they got married, his father agreed to "raise the kids Jewish." Most of it was harmless, he figured. All the "King of the Universe" stuff rubbed him the wrong way, but he kept his feelings to himself.

"And you'd have to wear a yarmulke all the time," said his mother.

Joe shrugged. "That wouldn't be so bad."

"Are you kidding?" said Jessica, disfiguring her face the way only a teenage girl can. "Literally *no one* would be friends with you. You know that, right?"

"That's stupid," he said. "My friend Ethan wears one."

"Your friend? You just met him. Let me guess, he was the only one who would talk to you?"

"Shut up," said Joe.

"Stop it, you two," said his mother.

"He's the one that said shut up! What did I do?"

"Yom Kippur is soon, right?" asked Joe. "Couldn't we just go once?"

Joe looked to his father. He wanted him to make the decision. But his father looked to his mother.

The family "tried" Ethan's temple the next week, and everyone except Joe was in agreement afterward: this was not the temple for them. The service was too long, and there was too much Hebrew and not enough music. His sister pronounced all the kids "dorks," and his mother kept harping on the fact that she was the only woman wearing pants.

"It doesn't make sense to belong to a temple where we're so different from everybody else," she explained.

"I don't think I'm so different. I liked it."

"What did you like about it, bud?" asked his father.

"I thought it was cool how everybody was all into it. Did you see how they rocked back and forth sometimes?"

"Totally *freakish*," said Jessica. "It's like they're in a cult."

Joe wanted one of his parents to correct her. Sure, the rocking was a little weird, but if they were actually Jewish, why did it embarrass them? If they were gonna be Jewish, *be Jewish*. The way they tiptoed around their supposed identity was annoying. It made him think they were weak.

The decision was made. The Weisses "didn't feel comfortable there," but if Joe wanted to go with his friend, that was fine. So the next weekend, Joe spent the night at Ethan's house—which was much nicer than his—and in the morning they went to Hebrew school together. Ethan introduced Joe, telling the rest of the class that he had just moved from Fullerton. Joe appreciated that Ethan didn't mention that his parents had tried, and rejected, their temple. The Hebrew school teacher asked Joe if he was bar mitzvahed.

"No," said Joe. "Isn't that when you're thirteen? I'm twelve."

"You have to study a lot first," said Ethan.

"I don't mind that."

After class, the teacher introduced Joe to the rabbi, who said that he was welcome to join the class, but that he'd have to come for extra tutoring sessions to catch up. When he announced his intentions at home, the reactions were frustrating. His father said he wished he'd pick something more physically active as an after-school activity; his mother told him not to expect "one of those big crazy bar mitzvah parties;" and Jessica predicted he'd drop out within a month.

But he didn't drop out. He had always been good in Spanish class and the Hebrew came easily. His mother took credit for his apparent knack for languages. She studied abroad in Florence and took great pride in "keeping up her Italian." More than once he heard her tell someone "he gets his ear from me." Joe liked that she was proud. Feedback was important to him. It was hard to know how to feel without cribbing off other people's faces.

As part of the bar mitzvah curriculum, the rabbi took the class to visit different shuls—that was the proper word, Joe learned, not temple—around Los Angeles. In May of 1985, they visited the Chabad House. A bright-eyed young man with a wispy beard and a neat, black-brimmed hat gave them a tour. Joe thought the man, whose name was Shimon, was very impressive. His hat made him look important, and his wife, who gave the girls a tour, was pretty. He liked that they separated the girls and the boys when they went inside the shul for a prayer service. But in the backseat of the van on the way home, Ethan said he thought the Chabad people "went a little overboard."

"What do you mean?"

"All the men wear exactly the same thing," he said.

"So?" said Joe.

"They don't go to regular college, either."

"I don't care about regular college."

"You don't? I'm going to Yale, like my dad. Or maybe Dartmouth."

Joe shrugged. He didn't spend much time thinking about the future.

After his bar mitzvah, Joe started wearing a yarmulke every day. He told his parents he was joining the language club after school, but instead took the city bus to the Chabad House three afternoons a week. Most of the people riding with him were black, and he liked that his yarmulke marked him. He wasn't just a white kid. He was a Jew. He was proud and learned and powerful.

He planned his first attack for more than a month. He'd just begun his freshman year and the boys who teased him and Ethan in junior high were newly bold. One in particular, a blond kid named Matt who was popular because he made the varsity baseball team as a freshman, seemed to take particular pleasure in tormenting them. He made a game of trying to knock their yarmulkes off, sneaking up on one of them and whacking them across the top of the head in the parking lot, by the lockers, on the brown-grassed quad. He got Ethan's far more often than Joe's, but when Joe asked Ethan if he wanted to help him hurt Matt, Ethan said no.

"What do you mean, hurt him?"

"I mean punish him. Make sure he stops doing it."

"I told you I don't want to tell," said Ethan. Matt's bullying embarrassed Ethan; it embolded Joe.

"I'm not talking about telling, I'm talking about doing."

"I don't want to get in trouble."

Joe didn't push. He didn't need Ethan.

The idea for the padlock came from his father. About a week after Joe decided he was going after Matt, someone broke into two garages on the street where the Weisses lived. His father came home with a bag from the hardware store that included a lock for the broken side door.

"This'll do until I get someone out here."

Joe's mother had been complaining about the door for months. She muttered sometimes that she wished she'd married a man who could fix things. After the handyman came, Joe took the lock from the junk drawer in the kitchen and put it inside a sock. He trailed Matt for two weeks and discovered that the time he was most likely to be alone was after baseball practice. Matt might play varsity, but he was only fourteen, so he couldn't drive. Occasionally, he caught a ride home with an older player, but at least a couple times a week, big, bad, blond Matt Simmons could be found sitting on the curb outside the Language Arts building staring at the entrance to the south parking lot, waiting for his mom to pick him up. Joe simply stepped up behind him and swung. Matt must have turned slightly because the lock hit him in the eye. He grabbed his face and screamed, falling forward onto the blacktop. There was blood immediately, and Joe stood for a moment, watching the red pour through Matt's fingers. His screams were high-pitched. He sounded like a bird— *caw caw caw!*—and his feet kicked and kicked.

Matt was out of school for a month. When he returned he wore a black patch over the space where his eye had been. He was no longer on the varsity baseball team. Matt was never able to tell the police anything about whoever attacked him, but the story going around was that it was part of a gang initiation. The news was full of stories about the Bloods and Crips, and later that year the school amended the dress code to prohibit anyone wearing all red or all blue.

Maiming Matt satisfied something inside Joe. He felt calmer, more confident, and he dove into his studies at the Chabad House, telling his parents that he was joining the debate team in addition to the language club. Shimon wanted to meet his family, but Joe made excuses. He said his parents were atheists and had threatened to disown him if he continued to "waste his time" with religion. He wanted to try on Chabad without having to explain it to anyone, especially his father, who was always so reasonable, so sincere and inquisitive, so genuinely interested in Joe, and so desperate to connect. But Joe did not want to connect. He told Shimon that his father had a temper and that his mother was vain and materialistic.

The next Passover he told his mother that he was no longer going to eat "traif."

"Where did you learn that word?" asked his father.

"It's Yiddish. It means food that's not kosher."

"I know what it means. Did your friend Ethan teach you that?"

"No," he said. "God gets insulted when you don't keep kosher." Joe didn't care whether God—if he existed—felt insulted. He figured that if there was some sort of omniscient, omnipotent entity in the sky he wouldn't find silly humans like Jessica and his parents important enough to be insulted by. But Joe liked to stand out. He was different, and although he couldn't advertise his real difference, he wanted his family to see him that way.

"Who told you that?" asked his mother.

"Shimon."

"Shimon?"

"From the Chabad House." He prounced Chabad with a guttural flair.

"The *Chabad* House? How do you know someone at the Chabad House?"

"What's the Chabad House?" asked Jessica.

"I don't like living in a home where God is always being insulted."

His parents looked at each other.

"What's the Chabad House!"

"It's for Hasidic Jews," said his father.

"Hasidic?"

"You're so fucking stupid, Jessica. How can you know *nothing*
about your heritage?"

"My *heritage*?"

"Do not call your sister stupid, Joe. And don't swear."

"She's ignorant. That's the same as stupid."

"Jessica is not ignorant," said his father.

"Obviously she is." He knew he would get nowhere with his
family, so he dropped the subject. But he stopped hiding his trips to
the Chabad House and he began preparing his own meals. By the
end of his junior year he rarely ate at home. Shimon and his wife,
Sarah, had him for Shabbos dinner most weeks, and after the couple's
two small children were in bed, Shimon and Joe would talk late into
the night. It was Shimon who suggested Joe apply to the yeshiva
at the Chabad World Headquarters in Brooklyn.

CHAPTER TWENTY

Henrietta tells me that she knew the man who paid her to lie as "Joe."

"Sometimes a week goes by and I don't think about him," she says. "Then I'll see something—every once in a while those Jews come into the casino—and I get all jumpy. I still don't know why he didn't kill me. I don't know what stopped him. Maybe he just liked knowing he *could*, you know?"

"Do you think he was the one who killed the Davises?"

Henrietta shrugs. "Maybe. Or maybe he was working for somebody who did."

"Do you remember where he worked?"

"I never knew."

"How old was he?"

"Not old," she says. "Twenty, maybe, back then."

We both fall silent. I have to get her on the record.

"I don't want to, like, pressure you," I say. "But, this kid, De-Shawn. He's been in prison for twenty years. All you have to do is tell police what you told me, and you could set him free."

Henrietta shakes her head. "And I'd go to prison."

"Not necessarily . . ."

"I'm gonna tell the NYPD I lied? I watch *Law & Order*. You can go to jail for perjury."

"I think maybe there's a statute of limitations on that," I say.

"Did you not hear me when I told you he put a gun in my mouth? He was watching me. Those postcards. Sometimes they came every couple days. Half the reason I moved and changed my name was 'cause of him. Last thing I want is Joe—or anybody from back then—knowing where I am. I don't mean nothing to him. If he can shoot a little baby girl, what he gonna do to me?"

I decide to leave it there. I know DeShawn didn't do it. And I have a lead on the man who might have. I write my phone number down for Henrietta, and she reluctantly agrees to give me hers.

Iris is asleep in the driver's seat when I open the door.

"How'd it go?" she asks, rubbing her face. "Are you ready to head back to the hotel? I think I'm hungry."

"Drive," I say, pulling my notebook out of my purse. "She basically told me she completely lied to the cops."

"Holy shit!" she says. "So, you've got your story!"

"Not really," I say, scribbling. "She won't let me use her name or anything she said. And she says she won't go to the cops. But it gets better. Or worse, actually. She said a guy—a Jew, like, a black hat—who used to be one of her johns, paid her to lie. I gotta get all this down before I forget."

"Wait, like, one of your mom's Jews?"

"That's what she said."

"Jesus, you can't get away from this shit, can you?"

Right?

"Just drive," I say.

By the time we get back to the hotel I've got four pages of notes, everything I can remember about our conversation: what she said about Joe's schedule, his approximate age, why she picked De-Shawn in the lineup, and where she said she was the night of the murders.

Iris heads to the boardwalk for food and a little beach time. I tell her I'll join her in an hour or two. I want to call Amanda and figure out what to do next.

Amanda picks up after three rings. Children are crying in the background.

"Hold on . . . Jonathan—can you deal with them? I gotta talk to Rebekah." Footsteps, and a door closing. "Okay. I'm safe in the bathroom. Tell me everything."

I do.

"Two things strike me. First, most of the time people get killed by somebody they know. And with this case it definitely seems personal. Nothing was stolen, and he shot them in their *bed*, for fuck's sake. So my question is, how did the Davises know a Hasid?"

"The people at Glorious Gospel mentioned something about, like, an interfaith dialogue thing with the Jews in the neighborhood after the riots."

"Go back to them. You can't use what Henrietta said in print yet, but you *can* tell people what she said. It's gonna be really hard for anybody who actually knew them to ignore all this now. They know DeShawn has always said his confession was coerced, they just didn't believe him. Add this, and unless they're total assholes, they're gonna want to get involved and help make it right."

"Totally," I say. I scribble: *call pastor green, dorothy morris* into my notebook. "What was the other thing?"

"The other thing?"

"You said two things struck you."

"Oh! Yeah. Shit. I forget! Oh my God, my brain on pregnancy . . ."

I laugh. "It's cool."

"I'll remember and call you back, I promise."

"I really appreciate your help," I say.

"I can't believe you got that woman to admit she lied. That's pretty awesome."

"I'm not sure how much good it'll do," I say.

"I bet she comes around. Seriously. You've planted the seed. In my experience, people can't live forever with lies."

We hang up, and just as I'm stuffing a hotel towel into a beach bag, she calls back.

"I remembered the other thing! Did she tell you the guy's name? The one who paid her?"

"Yeah," I say. "Joe. But who knows if that's even his name."

"Well, it might be his name. What kind of paperwork do you have on the case?"

"So far just what DeShawn sent you, which isn't much. He said he's sending me more, though. And Judge Sanchez was going to help me get the appeal file."

"Good. There might be something in there—maybe they interviewed someone named Joe, or he was a neighbor or something. And keep in touch with this woman, the witness. If you go interview her again, bring donuts or something. Call her every few days to check in. She may not agree to talk to the police, but I guarantee she'll be thinking about it. And the more comfortable she feels with you, the more likely she is to go on the record."

I find Iris lying on her stomach, bikini straps undone, reading a *W* magazine. I set my towel down beside her and sit, pulling my knees to my chest like it's cold.

"Anxious?" she asks.

I nod.

"What does Saul say?"

"Saul?"

"This was his case, right?"

"Right. But I haven't actually told him I'm looking at it."

"What? Why?" She turns over and props herself up on her elbows, holding her top with one forearm.

"I was waiting until I knew more. I didn't want to make a big deal out of nothing."

"Don't you think he deserves to know? I mean, it affects him, clearly."

"Yeah."

"I don't get it. I thought the whole point was that this was something he could help you with. You said the blog girl gave you files from a bunch of different people. Were they, like, less interesting?"

She does get to the heart of it, doesn't she?

"No," I say.

For a few moments neither of us says anything. I look out at the ocean and watch a woman with a parrot tattoo that covers her entire calf stand still, letting the water carve out sinkholes for her feet. I remember that it seemed like a big secret when my dad showed me how the tide could make your toes disappear. I never stood still long enough to get buried to my ankles like he and my brother did, though. The wet sand felt constrictive, and I always hopped out of the slippery pockets with a feeling like something was chasing me.

"This is about your mom, isn't it?" says Iris. She sits up, fastening her top with one hand. "You're not calling because you don't want to talk to her."

"I don't know," I say. "I feel like . . . I don't think she likes me very much."

Iris sighs, pulling her sunglasses down over her eyes and turning her face away from me. "It doesn't fucking matter if she likes you. Or if you like her. She is yours. You are hers. Like what you can, focus on that. Focus on the fact that you found her. She's *alive*."

Iris's mother died of breast cancer when we were in college. Back then it would have been inconceivable that one of us would reject a mother should she somehow appear. But that's exactly what I'm doing. And I haven't given a thought to what it must feel like to Iris.

"I'm sorry," I say, putting my hand on her leg.

"You don't have to be best friends," she says. "But you can't avoid her so hard it, like, *negatively* impacts your life. This is your work. Your fucking career. You could be missing something major by not talking to Saul. If it wasn't for your mom you would have called him, right?"

Right.

CHAPTER TWENTY-ONE

Instead of telling Saul about Henrietta over the phone, I text and ask him if I can come by Sunday night after Iris and I get home. He texts back that I'm welcome for dinner, and that my mom is going to be there, too.

She's looking forward to seeing you.

I get off the Q train at Brighton Beach at a little before seven. It's probably at least five degrees cooler out here by the ocean. At the entrance to Saul's high-rise, a half-dozen wispy-haired women in visors sit on low beach chairs fanning themselves with magazines.

"Is that Rebekah or Aviva?" says the woman in the open-toe terry cloth slippers.

"It's Rebekah, Evie! Jesus!" says the woman with the root-beer-colored hair.

"What, what? They look so much alike!"

Does it make me a bad person that I have no desire to learn the names of these women?

"Rebekah," I say, pushing out a smile.

"That's what I said!"

"I heard you!"

"Enjoying the sunshine?" I ask, because, polite.

"Oh, we are!" says cloth slippers. "Tell your handsome man to come visit with us sometime. We never see him!"

"He's not her handsome man! She could be his daughter!"

"She knows what I mean! You know what I mean!"

"I do," I say. "I'll let him know."

Saul calls the ladies "the force." There is a security desk in the lobby, but I've never seen anyone behind it. Saul says the ladies are better guards than a bored former transit cop any day.

I can smell the meal the minute I get off the elevator. Aviva cooked for me a couple times at her house in New Paltz, and she really gets into it. My mother is kind of an all-or-nothing person. She either brings home fast food for dinner or spends all day in the kitchen fixing half a dozen elaborate dishes that she'll freeze or give away.

It's been almost three months since I've seen either of them, and I hesitate before knocking on Saul's door. Part of the reason I didn't call when I read his name in DeShawn's file was because I liked the feeling of knowing something he didn't. Saul and Aviva have always been a couple steps ahead of me. He knew my mother was alive and in New York weeks before he told me. And for two decades she had the power to appear in my life anytime she wanted. It wasn't until Iris reacted with such surprise to the fact that I hadn't been communicating with Saul about the case all along that I realized I'd probably made the wrong decision by avoiding him—not to mention, for the wrong reason. It's time to come clean.

Saul answers the door to 16H wearing a mildly ridiculous pair of mirrored aviator sunglasses.

"Nice glasses," I say.

"Your mother got them for me," he says. Saul has lost weight since he and Aviva fell in love. I don't think she specifically encouraged it, but I get the sense that he feels lucky to have a girlfriend who is ten years younger than he is, and he wants to keep himself fit for her. It's kind of cute.

I relay the ladies' message, and Saul escorts me into the kitchen where Aviva, barefoot and dressed in denim shorts and a Coney Island Mermaid Parade T-shirt, is stirring a pitcher of iced tea. She smiles when she sees me, but waits for me to come and hug her. I do.

"Smells amazing," I say.

"You'll have to take some home. I made too much. Tea?"

"Sure," I say.

"There is wine, too."

"Tea's good for now," I say.

"Everything's all ready if you and Saul want to go sit down. I'll bring the borscht."

"Can I help?"

"No, no," she says. "Just make yourself at home. I'll bring the borscht right out. Do you like borscht?"

"That's soup, right?"

"Cold soup. There is sour cream or horseradish to put on top."

"Sounds good," I say.

Saul picks up the pitcher of tea, and I follow him to the table on the balcony. He goes back into the kitchen and I sit, looking through the metal bars at the ocean. Someone I can't see is flying a kite—a big orange and red bird with long streamers flapping behind it. Tomorrow is a workday, but there are hundreds of people still on the beach; blankets and umbrellas and little nylon tents stretch into the distance in both directions. I can see the Ferris wheel and the parachute jump, and hear the rumble of the Cyclone and the screams of the passengers as a train of cars rushes down the old roller coaster's rickety track.

Saul returns, and while we wait for Aviva to bring dinner, we chitchat about my job and his. He's still doing freelance private investigation work. He talks more than I do; it's probably apparent I'm a little nervous.

"Save room," says Aviva, carrying bowls of pink soup onto the balcony. "I've got brisket and asparagus, and sweet kugel for dessert."

"You hit the jackpot didn't you, Saul," I say.

"I'm a lucky man." He looks at Aviva and smiles. She waves him off. Aside from the time I saw them embracing on the grounds of the school where Connie Hall shot seven people in Roseville last year, I've never seen Saul touch my mother. Nor, for that matter, have I seen her touch him.

After we eat the brisket, I decide it's time to bring up Henrietta.

"So," I say to Saul, "I actually wanted to talk to you about a possible story." I tell him about the Center's cocktail party, and meeting Amanda. "I've been looking for something interesting—a feature, you know, something more than the day-stories at the *Trib*. Anyway, I've been reading a lot about wrongful convictions. People getting exonerated now that we have DNA evidence and stuff. So this girl, Amanda, we were talking and she gave me some letters she's gotten from people who say they're innocent." I lean over and pull DeShawn's envelope out of my bag. "She gave me this."

"You'd like an ex-cop's eye?"

"Well, yeah. But . . . it's a case you worked on."

"Ah." He bends forward and pulls the papers out of the envelope. "Just a minute," he says. "I need my reading glasses." He gets up and while he's gone Aviva takes our plates to the kitchen.

"Let's see," he says, sitting back down, putting on his glasses.

"I hope you're not . . ."

"It's all right, Rebekah," he says, not looking up. "I'm not offended."

Aviva returns with three small plates of kugel. I pick at mine while Saul reads DeShawn's letter, then glances at the reports.

"I remember this case. The day after the Fourth of July. Horrible, *horrible* scene. It was the first murdered child I'd ever seen."

"So what do you think?"

"What do I think about the letter? I think this is a man with nothing but time on his hands. There was an eyewitness in this case. That's hard to argue with."

"What if I told you the witness lied."

"Lied?"

"I tracked her down. She's in Atlantic City now. She said somebody paid her to lie."

"And you believe her?"

"I think so," I say. "I'm not sure why she'd lie now."

"She lied then," says Aviva.

I look at her. "She says the man who paid her threatened her. She said he put a gun in her mouth. She also said he was Hasidic."

Aviva rolls her eyes. "Of course she said that."

"What do you mean, of course?"

"I mean the blacks hate us."

"'The blacks?'"

"Oh, please, Rebekah. Don't you see she's just trying to stir up trouble? It is trendy to make the police look bad now. And anti-Semitism is a very big problem. Have you been reading about what is happening in France? The Jews are all having to leave! Just like before the Holocaust."

My mother has gone from Henrietta to Hitler in two sentences. I look at Saul. "Is that what you think, too?"

"I have no way of knowing." He looks at the file again. "The boy confessed."

"Right," I say. "But he says the detective—this Olivetti guy—coerced him. That's what happened with the Central Park Five kids, right? And you know there's been a lot of research about how common false confessions are, especially with teenagers. DeShawn was only sixteen. I can't tell if he had a lawyer present, but—"

"I don't know about any research," says Saul, interrupting me. He closes the file and takes off his glasses. "How much money are those Central Park boys getting? Millions, right? I'm sure there are a lot of people in prison who see that and think, maybe I can get some, too."

"You don't think they deserve some compensation for spending ten years in prison for something they didn't do?"

"They may not have done the rape, but those kids were up to no good in the park. We know that."

"Up to no good? What does that mean?"

"I mean that the officers didn't just pluck them out of thin air. They were running around the park, assaulting bicyclists, terrorizing people."

"But . . ."

"I know, Rebekah," he says. He takes a deep breath. "I'm sorry. I don't like what happened to those boys any more than you do. But things were very, very different in New York twenty-five years ago. I don't think it's even possible for you to imagine what it was like. Every single day there were at least five murders. Five! Now we go days, sometimes a week, without even one. And murder was just part of it. Stabbings and shootings and rape and robbery and assaults. Constantly. *Constantly*. People could barely keep a business open in parts of Brooklyn for all the smash-and-grabs and the fires and the drugs. We were working fourteen-, sixteen-hour days. It was a tidal wave. Nonstop."

I wait for him to continue, but he doesn't. I suppose I shouldn't be surprised that he is reacting defensively to my looking into an old case, but I can't help being a little disappointed. When I met Saul last year all he seemed to care about was justice: a woman had been murdered and he believed that her insular religious community would cover it up. He wanted to get to the truth, no matter the cost. Is it possible he doesn't think the Davis family deserves the same thing? What kind of person does that make him?

"Okay," I say. "I hear that. I just . . . what does that have to do with whether this guy—or anybody—is innocent or not? I mean, it makes sense that with so much coming at you things would get . . . mistakes might get made. Right? I mean . . ." I trail off, hoping he'll agree, but he doesn't. "I talked to DeShawn a few days ago and he said their family was getting threatening letters. And there'd been some vandalism at their house. That's another lead. Do you remember that?"

Saul sniffs, wipes his mouth with a paper napkin, and sets it down. For a moment I think he's about to leave the table.

"Everything pointed to this boy," he says, and begins ticking points off on his fingers. "He was a messed-up kid. He had a history of arrests. He ran from us when we tried to interview him. I don't think he had an alibi. . . ."

"I actually talked to a woman who says she was his girlfriend," I say. "She says she was with him all night but that the police didn't believe her."

"I don't recall a girlfriend. But how do you explain that this witness picked him out of the lineup?"

"She told me she saw him in handcuffs and figured he must have done something wrong."

Saul is trying to appear unmoved—his back is straight, stiff, as if to project confidence—but he's not looking at me. There is doubt somewhere.

"She's not taking the easy way out saying all this now," I continue. "She basically admitted to lying to police, and lying to the court and sending a kid to prison for the rest of his life. She could face a lot of shit for what she did."

"People say a lot of things," says Saul. "Maybe she is looking for attention. She was a drug addict, am I right?"

"So what? She's clean now. She's got a job and an apartment, and she's just living her life like the rest of us. And she's fucking *scared*, Saul. There's some crazy Hasidic murderer . . ."

"Rebekah!" says my mom.

"What? Oh, now you're all protective? This is exactly the kind of shit I thought you guys hated. You don't think it's *possible* she's telling the truth? Why? Because she's black?"

Saul sighs and looks at the sky. "Rebekah . . ."

"Don't patronize me, Saul. I don't deserve it. I may not be a cop but I'm not an idiot. If DeShawn didn't kill his family someone else did. Someone else walked into that home and shot three people—a little girl—in bed. That is a person that needs to be locked up. That is a person who has probably killed again. Right?"

Saul doesn't say anything. Part of me wants to storm off. But storming off is juvenile. Storming off won't make anything better. And I could really use Saul's help.

"People make mistakes, Saul," I say. "It doesn't mean you were a bad cop."

"Of course he wasn't a bad cop," says Aviva.

I ignore her, look at Saul. "You know what I'm saying."

"Yes, Rebekah."

"What if she's telling the truth? Without her ID the case would have been a lot weaker, right? I mean, maybe that confession would still have convinced a jury and the appeals judge, but maybe not. And just the idea that a Hasidic man paid her to lie—that's a real lead. I mean, was there any indication the Davises even knew people from the community?"

"Not that I recall."

"That opens up a whole line of investigation. If she'd told you this back then you would have at least tried to find out who this guy was, right?"

"Yes."

I can tell by the way he says yes that I've made my point.

CHAPTER TWENTY-TWO

August 1991
Crown Heights, Brooklyn

Joe arrived in Crown Heights one week after the riots. His mother watched the coverage on the evening news and read the articles in the newspaper out loud to him.

"They are *literally* killing Jews there," she said. "Why would you want to walk into that?"

Joe didn't tell her that he was excited to be walking into what the paper called a "war zone." In their Shabbos talks, Shimon told Joe that Rebbe Menachem Schneerson, the revered leader of the Lubavitch-Chabad movement, said a Jew must be a master of his emotions, that the mind can channel and control the passions of the heart. *Emotions are like oxen,* Shimon explained. *They are unruly and destructive when left alone. But yoke them and they can plow a field.* Joe knew his emotions were unruly and destructive. He tried to yoke them with his mind, but his mind was just as disorderly. Perhaps what he needed was a place to channel them. He was ready to get out of his quiet California neighborhood and into the fires of Crown Heights.

But once he got to Brooklyn, Joe was stuck in a classtoom. The yeshiva kept the boys busy. He spent his days improving his Hebrew and learning to read Aramaic—endeavors that quickly became tedious. Shimon had advertised the yeshiva as the place where the brightest young Jewish minds went to discuss big ideas. But Joe was stuck doing grammar exercises. The first time he was able to go even five blocks from the Eastern Parkway headquarters was when Daniel Grunwald, the neighborhood mentor he'd been matched with, invited him to Shabbos dinner with his family. At that dinner, Joe met Daniel's uncle, Isaiah. Isaiah Grunwald, Joe learned from his new friend, had been born in Israel and fought in the Six Day War. This impressed Joe. When they discussed politics or even the Holocaust, Shimon always reminded him that the Rebbe taught his followers to use their voices, not their hands, to respond to violence. Joe found this edict frustrating: would the six million have perished if they had taken up arms? Shimon never had an answer that satisfied him.

After dinner, Daniel and Joe and Isaiah lingered at the Shabbos table.

"How are you getting along with your studies?" Isaiah asked.

"He is bored," Daniel answered.

"I was speaking to Joseph, Daniel."

"It's true," said Joe. "I thought I would be *doing* something."

"Would you like a job?" asked Isaiah.

"What kind of job?"

Isaiah explained that he owned about a dozen buildings in Brooklyn and that Daniel sometimes helped him evaluate complaints and do light maintenance work.

"The yeshiva won't like it," said Daniel. "You are not supposed to be doing anything except studying, especially your first year."

Joe shrugged. "I don't have to tell anyone."

"It is dirty work," warned Isaiah. "Many of my tenants live like animals. Do you understand what I mean?"

"I think so."

In Los Angeles, Joe saw crime on the news, but in Brooklyn it was up close; the smells and sediment of it inescapable. Police vehicles rolled down the streets, but the officers stayed in their cars, ignoring the men openly imbibing liquor and smoking marijuana, the prostitutes propositioning every passing pedestrian, the boys spraying their gang names on buildings and tossing glass bottles into the street, the drunks urinating into gutters, onto buildings, behind Dumpsters. It was the dirtiest place he'd ever seen. It was lawless.

Isaiah started Joe in the office. The landlord had a file on each tenant and kept them in two drawers: one for addresses south of Eastern Parkway, where Jews lived, and one for his other properties, which were, he told Joe, mostly populated by blacks. Joe's first job was to go through the latter pile and use red flags to mark the files of tenants who were behind on their rent or had paid late more than once. When people in this pile called to report problems—clogged toilets, mold, broken radiators, vermin—Isaiah would know that fixing the issues was not a priority. Those tenants, Isaiah said, were taking advantage of his generosity. Isaiah understood that sometimes money was tight, but his Jewish tenants at least respected his property. In Isaiah's opinion, if you could not pay your rent *and* you treated the home your landlord was providing you as a dump, you were not entitled to have the owner of your building—the owner who you might as well have been stealing money from—attend to all the problems you caused.

And there were, Joe learned quickly, lots of problems with Isaiah's buildings. Every day there were calls. Rats were the biggest complaint, but nonfunctional toilets and sinks, as well as crumbling ceilings and walls were common. Raisa, the woman who answered the phones, spoke with the tenants and passed their messages to Joe. Joe identified the tenant by his or her file and informed Isaiah of the day's complaints. Isaiah had a small group of handymen—a mix of *goyim* and Jews, including Daniel—who worked for him, and several mornings a week the men came to the office to receive a list of repairs they were to accomplish. Isaiah tended to prioritize issues that, if left untouched, could further degrade the value of the buildings. Roaches and rats he shrugged off as either encouraged by the tenants' poor sanitation habits or an inevitable part of urban living. Burst pipes always got attention, as did crumbling façade— anything that could fall and harm a passerby and spark a lawsuit or a visit from one of the city's agencies.

About two months after he began working, Isaiah suggested that Joe accompany Daniel to a building where the tenants were complaining of a leak in the ceiling. The building was in Bushwick, a barren, industrial wasteland where Isaiah owned two four-story buildings across the street from a Department of Sanitation garage. They parked in front of a fire hydrant and Daniel told Joe to take work gloves and a paper mask from the box behind the driver's seat. A line of garbage trucks, apparently awaiting repair, stretched down the block, fetid juice dripping from their exposed bellies. The door to the apartment building was propped open with a shoe, and inside the hallway Joe smelled cooking grease and feces. He covered his nose and mouth.

"What did I tell you?" said Daniel. He knocked at apartment 1F, and a dark-skinned woman wearing a dress three sizes too small answered.

"It's about time," she said. There was a gap between her two front teeth and a gold cross pendant inside her massive cleavage. Joe felt a surge of blood to his groin. None of the girls in his high school were interested in him after he began wearing his yarmulke, and the girls he met at the Chabad House were saving themselves for their husbands. For a while, he convinced himself that sexual discipline was an important part of his new identity. If he was to belong—and he wanted to belong—he had to live by the rules, even if they meant nothing to him. He didn't crave intimacy, so porn magazines sufficed. But standing in the doorway that afternoon, inches from this woman whose clothing said, clearly, *come and get me*, he decided that he would no longer force himself to suppress his desire to do just that.

The woman let them into the apartment and pointed them to the bathroom, which was the first door past the living room off a narrow hallway. The carpet was soaked halfway back toward the bedrooms, and an inch of filthy water pooled around the base of the toilet and sink. Someone had used towels to try to keep the damage contained to the bathroom, but they lay, soaked through and useless, on the floor. Part of the ceiling was open—melted, apparently, by a cascade of water from upstairs. A cascade now turned to a trickle, browning the wall behind the toilet.

"You know I've been calling about this leak for a month, right? If y'all had come the first time—"

"We're here now," said Daniel, cutting her off.

The woman put one hand on her hip and one hand in the air. "Don't you *even* get mouthy with me," she said. "I pay my rent. I got rights. I should be calling the city to report your asses."

Daniel told the woman they would be back, and when they left her apartment he whispered to Joe that she was a prostitute and wouldn't be calling any authorities.

A mentally retarded man answered the door at the apartment upstairs. His head lolled sideways and his tongue hung between his lips. There was food on his chin and the zipper of his pants was open.

On the sofa behind him was a middle-aged woman attached to an oxygen tank. The galley kitchen was swarming with flies; food containers and dishes were piled on every surface, and bags of trash covered the floor, rendering the room unusable. Applause and laughter and ringing bells screamed from a game show on the television. The volume was turned up far too loud.

"Turn that down," Joe said to the woman.

"Uh-uh," said a voice from down the hall. "You don't get no say in how Mom watches her TV."

A shirtless man appeared from inside one of the bedrooms. He had, judging by the creases on the side of his face, just woken up. He buttoned his jeans and ran his hand through his hair. His chest and arms were muscular and there was a tattooed image of a praying woman on his left bicep and a Puerto Rican flag across his pectoral muscle. Joe could smell marijuana coming from either the man's breath, or the bedroom.

Daniel did not argue with the man; instead, he turned his attention to the bathroom, which was worse than the kitchen. The toilet was full of paper and feces; days' worth without a proper flush. Someone had actually defecated on top of the clogged pile. The tile that had presumably once lay between the base of the toilet and the tub was gone and the floor beneath rotted away. Joe knew from his time spent with the files in Isaiah's office that his boss had only owned these two Bushwick buildings for three months. How long had these people been living like this? It was a disgrace. Renting an apartment owned by someone else was a privilege. These people were guests. The woman should be in a hospital, the retarded man should be in a home, and the drug-smoking shirtless man should be in jail. And yet here they were, standing around useless as Isaiah paid Daniel and Joe to fix their mess.

"We been calling," said the shirtless man. Daniel ignored him and kneeled to examine the hole in the floor. "This isn't something we can fix today."

"When you gonna fix it then? Shit!"

Daniel stood up and began to leave the bathroom. The man stepped closer to him, got in his face.

"I want this shit fixed *today*."

The man didn't expect Joe to push him, and just a shove sent him tumbling, his bare feet useless on the slick floor. He fell spectacularly, stumbling first into the tiny vanity, his tailbone landing audibly on the tile, his arm splashing against the mountain of shit in the toilet.

They were all silent for a moment. The man was stunned, shaking his head. Before he could get up, Joe and Daniel left. Neither spoke for the first half of the ride back to Crown Heights. When they crossed Eastern Parkway, Daniel asked, "Do you think he's hurt badly?"

"No," said Joe. "He just slipped."

CHAPTER TWENTY-THREE

I call Judge Sanchez first thing Monday morning to tell her about Henrietta.

"I can't believe it," she says. "I mean, I *can* believe it. I do believe it. That poor boy. I tried to argue that she wasn't reliable because of her drug habit, but . . . I should have sent someone to scour her neighborhood. She wasn't even in Crown Heights! We might have found that roommate if we'd tried. *Fuck*."

I almost say, it's not your fault. But I don't.

"But she won't go to the cops?"

"No, at least not yet."

"If you could get her to write down what she's saying and sign it . . . it might not be admissible. But it might be enough for the DA to at least take a second look at the case. They're starting to do that—reexamine old cases."

"I can try," I say. "I was going to call her again today or tomorrow. I don't want to be too pushy, you know. She's scared of this guy, Joe."

"Joe. Could you get a more common name? And it's probably not even his name. She thinks he's Hasidic?"

"Yeah," I say. "Well, at least that's how she said he dressed. Black hat and the whole thing."

"Unreal. Do you have any idea why the Hasids might have been interested in the Davises?"

"No," I say. "But I'm going to call their friends at the church and ask."

"Good," she says. "Keep me in the loop."

When I call in for my assignment, the *Trib* receptionist transfers me to Mike, who tells me there is mail waiting for me in the newsroom.

"It's from the Coxsackie Correctional Institution," he says. "This for a story?"

"Maybe," I say. I didn't want to give a convicted felon my home address, so I had DeShawn send everything to the *Trib*. This, I realize now, was stupid. I haven't mentioned the story to anyone at the office because I've been working on it in the hopes that the Center might give me a grant. But I can't tell Mike that. "It's sort of preliminary. A possible wrongful conviction on a triple murder in Crown Heights back in 1992."

"Oh, yeah? Morgan's been asking about investigative stuff. He wants us all to bring ideas to a meeting on Friday. Can you have something for me by then?"

"Um, maybe?"

"Give me the gist."

"The guy who the packet is from was only sixteen when he got convicted. He says the detective on the case manipulated him into confessing—you know, like the Central Park Five?"

"That's it? Everybody says that."

And then my ego gets the better of me.

"I actually tracked down the key witness who flat-out told me someone paid her to lie to the cops."

"That's on the record?"

"No," I say. "Not yet. She's scared of him. She changed her name and moved, but she's worried she'll get in trouble for lying if she comes forward now."

I can hear Mike typing.

"Mike. It's not on the record."

"What?"

"You're typing."

"I'm taking notes, Rebekah." More typing. "Okay. Things are a little slow. Come to the office and see what he sent. I might have to send you out, but you can work on this in the meantime."

I hang up the phone and head to the bathroom. The conversation has alighted my anxiety and when it hits these days, it always hits in my guts—literally. Iris knocks on the door.

"Should I do my makeup in the living room?" she asks.

"Yeah," I call out. "Sorry. I might be a minute."

"Everything okay?"

"I told Mike about Henrietta, and now he wants to pitch the DeShawn story to Morgan on Friday. I don't trust him not to, like, exaggerate what I've actually got. Which is nothing—at least not on the record."

I finish in the bathroom, light a match, and get dressed. Iris and I ride the F train into the city together and just as I'm about to push through one of the four revolving glass doors into the midtown high-rise where the *Trib*'s newsroom is, Aviva calls.

"Hi," I say, plugging my ears against an ambulance screaming up Sixth Avenue.

"Rebekah? Can you hear me?"

"Yeah. Sorry. I'm in midtown. Are you still in the city?"

"Yes. I am driving back to New Paltz today. I would like to talk to you. Can we meet?"

"I'm working all day," I say. "What's up?"

"I would like to see you in person."

"Is something wrong?"

"I would rather discuss it in person."

What doesn't she get about *I'm working*?

"I can probably take lunch," I say. "But if something comes up and they send me out, I have to go."

"I understand."

We agree to meet at a deli around the corner from the *Trib* building at twelve thirty. As I ride the elevator upstairs to the newsroom, I dig through my bag for my bottle of anti-anxiety pills. For twenty-three years my missing mother existed exclusively inside me. She was a feeling: a fist around my heart, quicksand in my stomach; real, but not real. And she had tremendous power. I always figured that if I met her I could take that power back. That it was the mystery of who she was and why she left that debilitated me. But now, as I pop a pill to dull the dread of seeing her in a few hours, I have to confront the idea that having her in my life creates as much hurt as it heals. And all that hurt, the new and the old, it isn't like some tumor I can just excise. The fact that it didn't just drop out of me when I learned the secret of where she'd been and who she was means it's wormed its way into all my corners and pockets. It's in my body like a virus.

The packet DeShawn mailed to the *Trib* is thin. I pull out the paperwork and the handwritten note attached:

Dear Ms. Roberts,
Here is everything I have on my case. I got it all from the

office of the woman who did my appeal, Theresa Sanchez. I had a friend in here who found information in the prosecutor's file that wasn't given to his defense attorney, so in 2009 I filed a Freedom of Information Act request to get my file from the Kings County DA. I waited and waited and when they wrote me back they said my file was burned up in a warehouse fire in 2001.

Thank you very much for taking an interest in my case. I am innocent of this crime. Somebody else shot my family. Someday, I hope I find out who.

Sincerely,
DeShawn Perkins

Aside from the confession and Henrietta's statement, which DeShawn already sent to Amanda, the packet contains mostly copies of motions filed by his attorneys, including a request for a delay after his first attorney died (denied by the judge), and a motion requesting that DeShawn's confession be thrown out (denied by the judge). There is a short summary of an interview with someone named Virginia Treble, who apparently lived above the Davises; boilerplate motions about DeShawn's appeal and the judge's ruling (the original verdict stands); the Kings County DA's response to DeShawn's FOIA. No crime-scene photos or sketches, no ballistics reports, no autopsy reports, no more interviews.

I call Judge Sanchez and give her the inventory. "DeShawn says he FOIA'd the DA for their copy, but they told him it was destroyed in a warehouse fire."

"Huh," she says. "I guess that's possible. There's definitely more than what he sent. He said he got it from my office?"

"Yeah."

"They're supposed to send everything, but honestly, back then the office was ridiculously understaffed. It still is, but now there aren't quite as many cases. Whoever filled his request was probably rushing and figured they'd cut some corners at the photocopy machine. I'll tell you what. Let's go to the courthouse. I can't do it tomorrow. Can you meet me first thing Wednesday?"

"I think so," I say. I'm scheduled to work a shift, but I'll figure something out.

"I'll call and ask them to get the file up from storage if they have it. Meet me in records—it's on the fourth floor."

"Thanks," I say.

"Thank *you*, Rebekah. Most people don't give a shit about guys like DeShawn. We chew them up and spit them out every day. I've lost sleep thinking about what kind of defense the people I represented could have gotten if they'd been able to pay for it. And once you're convicted that's pretty much it. Reporters are the ones who've done the work getting people out. Well, reporters and lawyers. But honestly, I like reporters better." She laughs. "Not much of a compliment. I like you better than a lawyer."

"I'll take it," I say.

I spot Aviva from across the street. She is standing outside the deli on Forty-Sixth Street wearing the same shorts and T-shirt as she was at Saul's, plus dirty white running shoes and socks with little green balls at the heel. Her red hair, brighter now that she started using drugstore color to cover the gray, is drawn back in a rubber band. As I wait for the light to change, I watch a woman wearing filthy clothing far too heavy for the weather approach her. The woman speaks and Aviva listens, then she reaches into her purse and hands the woman a dollar.

"Hi," I say. Neither of us moves to hug the other.

"Saul was very upset after your visit."

"Okay."

"I do not know if you know this, but Saul was going through a divorce when this case you are talking about happened. It was the worst time of his life. His wife was very angry and spiteful and she used his son against him. Those memories are very, very painful now that his son is dead. Saul feels he did not do enough. He feels responsible for his son's death because he chose to leave the community."

"I know."

"I understand that you are doing your job," she continues, "but perhaps you can find a different story?"

I lift my hand to shade my eyes from the sun. I want to say, I don't have time for this, but instead I sigh. "Can we go inside, please? It's too hot."

"All right."

We enter the deli and I walk straight back past the hot-and-cold lunch bar, stuffed with fifteen long feet of salad toppings and rubbery pasta and steaming fruit cobblers, to the first metal table I see. It was stupid of me to suggest we meet somewhere with food; seeing my mom makes me queasy enough.

"I'm sorry this is tough for Saul," I say when we sit. "Really. But, honestly, it's a lot tougher for this man who's been sitting in prison for twenty years for something he didn't do. He's been locked up more than half his life, and I'm the only person who's taken the time to actually do anything."

"I just don't see why it's your responsibility."

"It's not my *responsibility*," I say. "Did Saul ask you to come talk to me?"

"No. I am looking out for him. You have not had the kind of hardship in your life that he has, and I think it is important that you understand how terrible this time was for him."

This is the second time my mother has asked me to lay off

reporting on someone she loves. Last year, she didn't want me to tell my editor that her brother might have been involved in a shooting. She pleaded that he endured miseries I couldn't possibly understand because I grew up in such a loving, stable family. Since then, I've had imaginary conversations with her in which, instead of silently acquiescing, I say that while it might make her feel better to focus on my father's strengths and the family he built in her wake, I grew up battling some pretty significant psychological and emotional trauma, too. Trauma she caused when she decided to slip out the back door while we slept.

"Like I said, I'm really sorry this happened when things were bad for Saul. But he had a job to do. Being a policeman is a powerful position. It's a responsibility. You can really screw with people's lives if you don't do it right. I'm not saying he did anything wrong on purpose. But if he has to endure a little bit of discomfort in order to help get an innocent person out of prison, I think that's an okay trade-off."

"I think you are being very selfish, Rebekah."

Oh, you have *got* to be kidding me.

"Look, if you knew me at all—which you don't because you bailed on me before I could speak—you would know that there is literally no fucking way that I am going to not report a story because you think it's going to hurt your boyfriend's feelings."

"Rebekah . . ."

"This is what I do. Okay? This is who I am. I am a reporter. And guess what? I'm good at it. It's a hard job—it's an *important* job—and I'm good at it. Most moms would be proud of their children for doing the kind of work I do."

"I'm not . . ."

"Right, I know. You're not really a mom."

I stand up and walk out, though I can barely feel my legs.

When I get outside I start walking north toward Central Park. I need shade. I need a bench. I need a place to cry.

I spend the rest of my shift doing rewrite, and just as I am about to head into the subway to go home, my phone rings.

"Hi, this is Rebekah," I say.

"Rebekah, this is Bob Haverford. You called me last week about someone I represented back in the nineties. DeShawn Perkins."

"Yeah," I say, "thanks for getting back to me."

"I'm sorry about . . . how I reacted before. Listen, I'm in the city. Do you have time to meet right now?"

An hour later, I meet Bob Haverford at a café in the West Village. He is there before me, sitting at a tiny bistro table on the sidewalk. I recognize him from his photo on the Haverford & Haverford Web site: ashy blond hair with a boyish but sun-worn face. He is wearing a striped oxford shirt, dark blue jeans, and expensive-looking European-style loafers. A nearly empty martini glass sweats on the tabletop.

"Bob?" I say.

"Rebekah, how are you?"

"Good," I say, dropping my purse under the table and sitting, carefully, on the chair beside him. Our entire setup is atop the metal door into the basement. I've been avoiding even walking over these things since we did a story in June about a woman who died after an improperly latched one on Second Avenue gave way beneath her; she broke her neck falling down the concrete stairs below. Hopefully that won't happen this afternoon.

The waiter comes and asks what I'd like. "The coldest beer you have," I say.

Bob makes a noise like a chuckle, but can't muster a smile.

"I basically haven't slept since you called." He presses his thumb and forefingers into closed eyelids, wincing. "I want to help you but. . . . Can we talk off the record?"

Ugh. "Okay." Build trust, I think. Build trust and the quotes will come.

"That case, DeShawn—it was the low point of my life. My wife was leaving me. She was the whole reason I'd started at Legal Aid to begin with. We were dating and I did it to impress her. Make myself look like I was some do-gooder. Which I'm not. I mean, I'm not a bad guy. But you have to be a saint to do the shit I was doing. We had, like, thirty cases at a time. And it wasn't as if we had money to hire investigators or spend any time actually researching anything or tracking people down for interviews. Most of the time we just pled shit down as best we could.

"Anyway, we'd only been married two years, and she basically came home one day and was, like, I'm not sure if I was ever in love with you."

"Ouch," I say, but I doubt I sound terribly sympathetic. Aviva is trying to get me to excuse anything Saul might have done wrong because it was a tough time in his life, and now this guy. Tell it to DeShawn, I think. Tell it to his dead family.

"It was all I could do to get out of bed."

The waiter brings my beer, and as he sets out a napkin, Bob finishes his martini.

"I'll take another," he says.

I sip my beer and Bob blows an exhale like he's trying to expel something ugly, and rubs his hand over his mouth.

"I should never have been assigned the case to begin with. They always give homicides like that to people with a lot of experience. But the original attorney had a heart attack about a month before trial and they had to divvy up all his cases really fast. I tried to get the trial postponed but the judge wasn't having it. The whole system was backed up. I mean, every day we each got another five or six clients. Seriously. And this was a tough case to begin with, okay? The kid had a record, and the cops had an eyewitness and a confession. That's basically insurmountable. Or it was back then. They didn't have much in the way of physical evidence. They never found the gun. But, honestly, DeShawn wasn't a lot of help. He kept getting into fights at Rikers. Twice I went to see him and they turned me away because he was in segregation for some infraction."

"What about the girlfriend?" I ask. "She said she was with him the night they died."

"I think she flip-flopped. Told the cops she wasn't with him, then said she was. She wasn't reliable. Putting her on the stand wouldn't have helped DeShawn."

"The jury believed the witness," I say, "and she was a crack addict."

"Yeah, but at least she told the same story the whole time."

I nod. "Did you check it at all?"

"Her story? Not really."

"I just visited her in Atlantic City a few days ago. She told me she lied. She wasn't even in the neighborhood that night."

Bob's eyes go wide, his mouth slack. He takes a deep breath and rests his head in fingers.

"I brought up the fact that the woman had a record. But like you said, the jury believed her. I guess, to tell you the truth, I believed her, too."

CHAPTER TWENTY-FOUR

September 1992
Crown Heights, Brooklyn

When his wife and children were not at home, Naftali Rothstein often ate Shabbos dinner with the yeshiva students in the basement cafeteria of one of the dorms just south of Eastern Parkway. He was inspired by their youthful energy and enjoyed engaging in the impassioned discussions about Talmudic law. When his father died suddenly of a stroke, the then twenty-year-old Rothstein had cut his formal studies short to begin earning money to help support his four brothers and sisters who were still living at home. He couldn't bring himself to completely leave yeshiva life, however, and found work first as a secretary to the man who coordinated visas and housing for students coming to Crown Heights from across the United States and abroad. Rothstein quickly established himself as an enthusiastic advocate for the community. He was a natural multitasker, and if the phone cord was long enough, he could photocopy, file, and type up meeting minutes while reminding a skeptical mother that, yes, the area surrounding the yeshiva was dangerous, but sending her son into the fray—as it were—was a mitzvah. But in 1986, when a student from London was robbed and beaten so badly he spent three weeks in a coma—a story that made international news in part because the young man's father was a cousin-in-law of Shimon Peres—Rothstein began to wonder if the future of Chabad was actually imperiled by the "bad" neighborhood in which Rebbe Schneerson had planted his flag.

And so, Rothstein went to his superiors at the Crown Heights Jewish Council with a proposal: allow him to create a public relations and development office. It took some convincing, but after a few weeks of meetings, he was granted permission to call himself the Council's Community Relations Manager and to spend some of his time forming relationships with reporters and civic leaders in New York City in order to advance the interests of the movement and better protect the population.

But he could only spin the situation in Crown Heights so far. The police needed constant reminding that the taxpaying, law-abiding citizens of the neighborhood were watching when they rolled past corner drug deals and let thefts and assaults and vandalism go virtually uninvestigated. It took two months for the commander of the 77th precinct to agree to meet with him. The relationship was not a warm one, especially now, a year after the riots, when the neighborhood had become an international symbol of ineffective civil authority and citizen unrest. It didn't seem to matter to Commander Greg Harbrook that it was the blacks—not the Jews—who destroyed entire blocks with fire and baseball bats. Let it burn, seemed to be the precinct motto. Harbrook actually said as much in an emergency meeting with Rothstein and senior Chabad leadership the day after Yankel Rosenbaum was murdered in the street.

"We don't have enough manpower to control every angry nigger in Brooklyn. And now with Sharpton bringing his people in . . ." He shook his head. "Let them get it out of their system. It'll die down eventually."

Rothstein did what he could to use the riots to build support for community. And in some ways, the experience created a kind of lore around the Lubavitchers of Crown Heights. The Jews on the Upper West Side had fled to Westchester in the sixties, and as the blacks moved into Brownsville and East New York, those Jews moved to Long Island. But *not even a virtual civil war* could uproot the men and women of the Chabad movement. Donations began to pour in from as far away as Russia and as close as Prospect Park West.

Isaiah Grunwald was one of those donors. Rothstein knew many of the men who owned buildings in the neighborhood, but Isaiah was not particularly active in the community, so when the stocky Israeli appeared in Rothstein's office in the fall of 1991, Rothstein didn't recognize him. Isaiah handed him an envelope and said that he could count on the same donation each quarter. Naftali opened the envelope and saw a check for five thousand dollars.

"You know that my wife and I have not been blessed with children," said Isaiah.

Naftali nodded. It was a great sorrow for a Lubavitcher couple to be childless, but some were, of course. Naftali did not know Isaiah's wife, and he wondered if she, like other chassidish women who were barren, felt out of place in the community. It occurred to him that it would be a mitzvah to use some of Isaiah's donation to create a group for those couples. A monthly meeting space, perhaps, to share and comfort. He made a mental note to ask his superiors about the idea.

"We cannot raise Jewish children of our own," continued Isaiah. "We would like to help the community educate and care for the students who come here to learn."

Isaiah did not stay long. Unlike many donors giving far less than he was, Isaiah did not appear to want Rothstein to flatter him, or to arrange a special seat in shul or a one-on-one meeting with the elderly Rebbe. In fact, while the checks came each quarter, Naftali did not see Isaiah until nearly a year later, a few weeks after the Davis murders. Rothstein was in his office working on his monthly newsletter when Isaiah appeared in the doorway.

"Good Shabbos," said Rothstein, inviting the man inside.

"Good Shabbos," said Isaiah.

The two men asked after each other's families and made small talk of the upcoming trial of Yankel Rosenbaum's murderer, the Rebbe's health, the weather. There was nodding, and then Isaiah lay an envelope on Rothstein's desk.

"Hashem has blessed me with a particularly profitable year. This gift is in addition to my quarterly contribution." He gestured to the envelope, encouraging Rothstein to open it. Inside was a check for ten thousand dollars.

"This is very generous," said Rothstein, clearing his throat in a bumbling attempt to mask a wide grin. Rothstein had recently approached the Council's leadership for a raise. His wife was pregnant with their sixth child, and in May his father-in-law lost his entire retirement in a bad land investment in New Jersey, forcing Rothstein to step in to make mortgage payments so his wife's parents didn't lose their home. Leadership promised to take his request into consideration at the monthly financial meeting, scheduled for next Tuesday. A surprise ten-thousand-dollar addition to the quarterly balance sheet, thought Rothstein, might just make the difference.

"I wonder if you might be able to assist me with something," said Isaiah.

"Anything."

"One of my tenants has come to me for assistance. His brother was murdered in July. Shot to death in his home on Troy Avenue, along with his wife and daughter."

"Yes!" exclaimed Rothstein. "I remember the case. A horrible, horrible tragedy."

"Unthinkable. My tenant's only consolation has been that the murderer—the man's own son, if you can believe it—confessed."

Rothstein nodded.

"But now, it seems, the murderer has changed his mind. He is pleading not guilty."

"No!"

"Yes. And my tenant is concerned that the prosecutor might be lenient because he is still a teenager. They are not wealthy people, but they have scraped together enough money to hire a private attorney to ensure that the family's interests are represented.

"I know that you have developed a relationship with police, and I am hoping that perhaps you might be able to help the family obtain the documents the police have on the case. I believe there was an eyewitness, for example."

Rothstein nodded his head. "It is very generous of you to help this family," he said. "As it turns out, I am friendly with one of the officers involved. Let me see what I can do."

Isaiah stood up. "I knew I had come to the right man." He reached forward and squeezed Rothstein's hand. Rothstein saw that Isaiah was missing the tip of his right index finger. He had heard that Isaiah fought in the Six Day War, and although he was certainly not one to fetishize violence, at that moment he felt a surge of respect for his donor. There were many in the community who disliked Isaiah Grunwald. They felt he was insufficiently pious, and there was talk about his business practices. The Rebbe instructed his followers who were able to help establish housing for Jewish families: apartments with more than three bedrooms, two sinks for kosher cooking; buildings with outdoor space suitable for building a sukkah. Isaiah Grunwald had done this, and then, people said, he got greedy, and bought crumbling buildings in other areas, looking for a quick profit. But who was Rothstein to say? And while some would have seen Isaiah extending himself for a black family as suspect behavior, Rothstein, who believed that peace with their goyish neighbors was in the best interest of the community, admired it.

"I will look forward to hearing from you," said Isaiah.

Rothstein wasted no time. Shabbos did not begin for another two hours, so he donned his hat and jacket, set the newsletter aside for Monday, placed Isaiah's check into his locked desk drawer, and set out for the 77th precinct. September was a beautiful time of year in Brooklyn, and Rothstein, feeling particularly optimistic, decided to take a chance and walk up Utica instead of hailing a taxi. The yeshiva students were all outside, too, holding their binders and books, laughing, smoking cigarettes on the benches along Eastern Parkway. Rothstein envied the young men, and some days the envy soured him. But today, with ten thousand dollars in his desk drawer and a mission to assist a grieving family, he felt as if the work he was doing was helping to strengthen this place he loved. Perhaps, he thought, people like Isaiah and himself, people some might call too modern, too involved with those outside the community, perhaps they were playing an essential role in protecting the Jewish community, in allowing it to thrive in this hostile place. Perhaps the fact that he cut his studies short was a blessing for the community, even if it felt like a burden to him. He would do well to adjust his attitude toward that part of his past, he thought. He looked forward to expressing this new idea to his wife at dinner.

He smiled and nearly skipped across Albany, noticing but not despairing in the overturned garbage can and broken beer bottles at the corner. The black people on the street watched him, but he did not feel afraid. If someone threatened him, he imagined himself saying, *I am on an errand to help your brother! We are neighbors, all of us!* In the imaginary encounter the imaginary black man shook his hand and patted him on the back, sending him on his way.

He arrived at the precinct at shift change. Uniformed officers, some with handcuffed men in tow, filled the two front rooms. Rothstein caught the desk sergeant's eye and the cop waved him past. What a fortunate man he was, to be known and respected here. He found Saul Katz at a corner desk, poking at a typewriter with two fingers. He looked weary, his shoulders hunched over, and Rothstein noticed that Saul's head was bare, his *kippah* laying atop a stack of folders.

"Good Shabbos," said Rothstein.

Saul looked up and returned the greeting, then turned his attention to his typewriter.

"You will have to excuse me," he said. "My shift commander wants this report . . ."

"Absolutely!" said Rothstein. "I see it is a bad time. I have a question but it can wait." He patted his breast pocket where he kept his copy of the Tehillim, the Book of Psalms. "I will busy myself until you are available."

"It shouldn't be long," said Saul. "Thirty minutes."

"We have plenty of time before sundown," said Rothstein. And then: "Saul! Do you have plans for Shabbos dinner?"

"Naftali . . ."

"Yes, yes, I know, you are busy. But please, would you join us? It would be an honor."

"Fine," said Saul. "Now . . ."

"Say no more!" Rothstein made a gesture like he was zipping his lips. He wrote his address on a slip of paper. "Can you make it by nine thirty? I will meet you after shul."

Naftali's wife had prepared a roast chicken for dinner and was delighted when Saul appeared in her dining room.

"Wonderful!" she exclaimed. "Someone to appreciate my cooking!"

"Your husband is not enough?" gasped Naftali playfully.

Zelda waved him off. "My husband will eat anything," she said, beaming at Saul. "He is not at all discerning. I could serve boiled fish every night and he would be pleased. It is no fun to cook for him."

"It smells delicious," said Saul.

Zelda ushered the men into the tiny dining area, where the table was set neatly with tall white candles burning in silver candlesticks, paper plates, paper napkins, and plastic utensils. When their fifth child was born, Zelda announced that she was finished washing three meals worth of dishes for seven people. Cookware and serving plates and the baby's bottles were enough. Naftali knew enough not to argue—even if, as the Rebbe instructed, he occasionally rolled up his sleeves to help her at the sink. The dining chairs were upholstered in pink and yellow fabric, and covered in plastic; the table was overlaid with a mauve oilcloth. Like many chassidish families in Crown Heights, the Rothsteins were poor. Furniture and clothing was second- or third-hand, meals were simple, utilities carefully conserved, brand names unheard of. But, as Naftali motioned for his guest to sit next to him, Saul could see that their poverty was material, not spiritual. The apartment was cluttered, but there were tracks in the carpet from a recent vacuuming. Zelda yelled for the children, and all five came running: three boys and two girls, ages three to fourteen. One of the girls brought the challah to the table, then returned to the kitchen to bring a plate of salmon and crackers. Another brought a bowl with salad, and finally Zelda appeared with the chicken. Over dinner, Zelda quizzed the children about what they had learned in school. It was the second week back, and there were many stories about new teachers and new rules and new students. Saul filled his plate twice—he could scarcely remember the last time he ate a homemade meal—and marveled at the lively discussion. When Zelda told the children their guest was a police officer, the kids went wild, asking if he got to arrest people, asking if they made him shave off his beard, asking if they could see his gun.

"Why aren't you with your family for Shabbos?" asked the eldest boy.

"Mendel!" shushed Zelda.

"It's fine," said Saul, smiling at Zelda. "I was working late. Your tatty came to see me and told me how wonderful your mommy's cooking was. I simply had to eat some myself!"

The boy furrowed his brow. He was not satisfied by Saul's response, but did not press him further. Saul took a sip of wine and saw Naftali and Zelda exchange a smile. How he envied them. Why had he been cursed with such doubts? Such discontent? Such blasted contrariness? Look, he said to himself, look what you could have had. And yet he knew he and Fraidy would never have been like Zelda and Naftali. When she gave birth to Binyamin, Fraidy had nearly died, and the doctors had to do an emergency surgery to remove her uterus. The shock of it stunned them both, and neither had the emotional tools to comfort the other. They sought help from their rabbi, who suggested prayer, of course, but they simply could not come together. And so each sought solace separately. Fraidy turned to her sisters, bringing Binyamin to meals and playtime with his cousins, sometimes staying for days in New Jersey, obsessed with the idea that he should become as close to them as he would to the brothers and sisters he would never have. Saul, working then at her father's hardware store in Borough Park, turned to his radio, finding meaning and moments of joy in the music, but also the voices of the men and women who read the advertisements. Their excited sales pitches occasionally carried him off into another world. A world where a new mattress or a trip to Atlantic City could change every-thing. He tried to tell Fraidy the way the radio made him feel. How the news reminded him that they were not alone in their suffering, and how the music reminded him that there was still beauty in Hashem's world. But she would not listen. The radio was forbidden. That—not her husband's misery, his loneliness, his bumbling at-tempts to soothe himself—was what she cared about. She was a small-minded woman. And he began to hate her.

After dinner, Zelda and the girls cleared the table and cleaned the kitchen while the boys disappeared into a bedroom. Saul asked Naftali what he had wanted to speak about when he came to the precinct that evening.

"I was hoping you might be able to help me obtain what I believe are public documents," he said. "Do you remember the family that was murdered on Troy Avenue in July? Mother, father, and a little girl."

"Yes," said Saul. Truthfully, he hadn't thought about the Davis case in a while. After working with Olivetti, he was moved to the newly created sex crimes unit. Homicide had been difficult, but he would have gladly returned to it after just a week on this new rotation. The depravity he encountered each day seemed to know no bounds.

He had seen children—*babies*—literally torn apart, ripped open by ravenous monsters masquerading as human beings. Dead bodies could not recount the moment their killer pulled the knife or the gun, could not describe the fear, or the feeling of the hammer on their skull, the bullet in their gut. But these living victims, with their still-bleeding wounds and their shame, they burdened his soul and tested his sanity in ways he could never have anticipated. Each day seemed to bring an attack more vicious than the last, a victim more stunned and debilitated. Saul knew, looking at the women lying in their hospital beds, that the justice he was there to help mete out was not likely to comfort them. Many refused to co-operate with the official investigation. Their attackers were often friends or family members, and even if a jury convicted—which was rare—they would never, truly, be free of them. By the time he appeared at their bedside, or in their home, the victims were so fundamentally altered by what had happened to them that Saul felt he was no better than a newspaper reporter, picking at their pain in the name of "the job."

"The son confessed," said Saul, "if I remember correctly."

"Yes," said Naftali. "But he has decided to plead not guilty and take the case to trial. One of my most generous donors is a landlord, and apparently one of his tenants was related to the victims. The family, as you can imagine, is distraught. They have hired an attorney to represent their interests but have been unable to arrange a meeting with the prosecutor. They are concerned the murderer may be treated lightly because of his young age." Naftali made up the part about not being able to meet with the prosecutor. He was on a roll. "They are hoping to get a copy of the case file to make sure that everything is being done properly—all the *i*'s dotted and *t*'s crossed."

It seemed like a reasonable request, and as Zelda brought slices of homemade cinnamon babka to the table, Saul said he'd be happy to make a photocopy of the file.

"Why don't you come by Monday," he said to Naftali.

The next Monday afternoon, Naftali collected the file from Saul, and that evening Isaiah Grunwald collected it from Naftali.

CHAPTER TWENTY-FIVE

Wednesday morning Judge Sanchez is at the records office before me, arguing with the clerk, a young Latino man with a sliver of a beard shaved across his jaw.

"Let me talk to your boss," she says.

"She's not going to tell you anything different," says the man. "Everything before 1995 was in storage in Red Hook and got destroyed in Sandy."

"Well, that's remarkable, since we've already been told this particular file was destroyed in a fire in 2001."

"I don't know what to tell you," he says.

"Just get me your boss, please. Tell her Judge Theresa Sanchez is here."

The clerk disappears and Judge Sanchez turns to me.

"The incompetence is un-fucking-believable. Please tell me you brought DeShawn's file."

"I did," I say, digging into my bag. I open the manila envelope and pull out a letter explaining that the prosecutor's file on DeShawn's case was not available because it was in storage in a warehouse that caught fire in 2001. The letter is signed by the Kings County Clerk, Chris Hancock, and dated April 2010.

"I can't wait to see how they explain this."

"Me, too," I say, thinking, if nothing else, this might be a story in itself. How many other people are being told their files were destroyed?

After another minute, the clerk returns with a woman who looks about eleven months pregnant. Her arms and legs are tiny, but her belly is shocking—it's hard to figure how she's upright.

"How can I help you?" she asks.

"My name is Judge Theresa Sanchez, I run the Brooklyn Community Court. This is Rebekah Roberts with the *New York Tribune*. We'd like to take a look at a case file from 1992."

She sits down at the computer. "Do you have a case number?"

Judge Sanchez turns to me. I read the case number off the letter DeShawn sent me and she types it in. *Click click click.*

"Your assistant here said that everything pre-1995 was destroyed in Sandy," says Judge Sanchez.

"Much of it was."

"But what's odd," I say, "is that the man whose file we're looking for was told back in 2010 that his paperwork was destroyed in 2001 in a warehouse fire."

"Obviously it's not possible for both things to have happened," says Judge Sanchez.

"Obviously," says the clerk, not the least bit rattled by Judge Sanchez's indignation.

"The clerk who signed this letter was named Chris Hancock," I say. "Is he still here?"

The clerk shakes her head. She's still looking at the computer, scrolling with a mouse. Finally, she speaks. "It's possible that this file is in our basement storage."

"Unbelievable," says the judge.

"I said it's possible," says the woman, looking up. "We *have* had files destroyed in both fires and flooding. And prior to 1997, very little was computerized. This may never have been properly entered into our database, which may explain why it has been difficult to track down."

Judge Sanchez isn't having it.

"What a reasonable excuse," she says. "I'm sure the people sitting in prison being told their files are gone will be pleased to know how difficult your job is."

"Would you like Andre to show you to the storage room?"

"That would be wonderful," says Judge Sanchez. "And can we get your name?"

"My name is Anna Brannon."

I write that down.

"Did you replace Chris Hancock?" I ask.

"Yes."

Andre walks us to the elevator bank and escorts us to the basement of the courthouse. We follow him down a long hallway and through an unmarked door.

The cardboard file box with DeShawn's case number scrawled in Sharpie on the side is smashed beneath a much heavier box. I pull it down and Judge Sanchez and I walk toward the front of the storage room to a desk that looks like it hasn't been occupied in a decade. The files inside don't even fill half the box. It's kind of unreal to think that this measly pile of paper is everything the state had on DeShawn—and it was enough to take his life away.

We start pulling files and comparing them to the paperwork

DeShawn sent me. I open one unmarked manila envelope and find two things inside: a police report and a Ziploc bag. According to the typed summary on the police report, Malcolm Davis came into the 77th precinct on June 2, 1992:

> *Complainant alleges that his family is the victim of vandalism, specifically the word "SNITCH" spray-painted on his front door.*

"Check this out," I say, handing Judge Sanchez the report. As she reads, I open the Ziploc bag: inside are three envelopes. One, postmarked June 14, 1992 in Brooklyn, is addressed to Malcolm Davis at the apartment on Troy; there is no return address. The other two were not mailed, apparently. I open the postmarked envelope and unfold the piece of paper inside. Just as DeShawn described, the text is made up of letters cut out from magazines: YOUR FAMILY WILL SUFFER.

"Look at this."

The judge looks up from the police report.

"What the fuck?" She reaches for the paper, then stops. "Put that down."

I do.

"We didn't have *any* of this."

"When we talked on the phone, DeShawn said somebody was threatening his parents. He said they were getting hang-up phone calls and letters like this. But he said his original defense attorney told him the cops never found any."

"Well, clearly *that's* not true. Jesus. *Jesus!* They just didn't turn this shit over. We need to get these letters tested for fingerprints, first of all. And DNA. They might be able to find something from whoever licked the envelopes."

"What about the police report? You didn't have that?"

"Definitely not."

"Sandra Michaels prosecuted this case," I say, my voice low.

"Yes, she did. Un-fucking-believable. Honestly, I wouldn't have expected this from her. I thought she was a straight shooter."

"Do you think it's enough to get the case reopened?"

"It might be," she says. "It should be."

I pull out my cell phone. "I'm gonna get pictures," I say. "Just in case."

"Oh, I am *not* letting this shit disappear," says Judge Sanchez, pulling out her own phone. "One of my best friends is still a prosecutor. She does sex crimes. I'll have her send someone down. We will not leave this box until it is safe in her office."

"You're sure you can trust her?"

"Absolutely. We grew up together. She's gonna hit the roof. Especially once she finds out I've got a *Trib* reporter with me."

I take photos of the first letter, the envelopes, and the police report, then follow Judge Sanchez and a clerk from her friend's office back upstairs. Her friend, ADA Felicia Castillo, is in court, but she's told her clerk to let us wait in her office.

"I wonder how many other cases Sandra Michaels withheld evidence on," I say.

Judge Sanchez shakes her head. "They're going to have to look back at everything. Two *decades* of convictions. What a shit show. This could end her career."

"Can I quote you on that?"

"No," she says. "Not that. But I'm on the record saying we didn't have any of what's in that file. The letters and the report, I mean."

Felicia Castillo returns to her office at a little past noon.

"Whose case was it?" she asks Judge Sanchez.

"Sandra's."

Felicia doesn't even attempt to hide how the news makes her feel. She drops into her seat.

"I don't know what's worse," says Judge Sanchez, "that she withheld all this from the defense, or that this office has been telling the defendant that the files we just found in about five minutes were destroyed more than a decade ago."

"None of it's good," says Felicia. She's staring at the box like she's never seen one before. For a moment, no one speaks, then Felicia comes out of her trance and looks at me.

"This meeting is off the record," she says to me. "I have to figure out what the fuck is going on."

"Okay," I say. "But I'm obviously going to want a comment from Sandra Michaels."

"Are you planning to run this tomorrow?"

"Maybe," I say. I need to talk to Mike, but my guess is he'll want copy immediately. This morning, DeShawn's story was just a possibly interesting feature idea that could pad Mike's pitch list at a meeting. Now, it's the center of a legit scoop on a powerful woman whom everybody in the city is already talking about. Was it just Sandra Michaels who withheld evidence? Or was that how the Kings County DA did business back then? How many DeShawns are there?

"I'm due back in court at one," says Felicia, looking at her watch. "I'll have someone call you."

Outside the courthouse, Judge Sanchez tells me to call her if I don't hear from the DA's office by tomorrow.

"Can you get in touch with DeShawn?" she asks.

"He has to call me, I think. But I'll try the prison and see what happens."

"He's, what, forty years old now?"

"Almost," I say.

"Un-fucking-believable," she says again, raising her hand to hail a cab. "I don't know how a guy like that doesn't go completely insane after all this time. Maybe that's why so many of them get religious. Let go and let God. Me? I'd wanna burn it all down."

Ninety minutes later, I'm with Mike, Gary, and Larry Dunn—the paper's longtime police reporter—in Albert Morgan's office on the eleventh floor of the *Trib* building. The *Trib*'s leadership structure is absurdly male. There are plenty of female reporters, but almost no one making editorial decisions has a vagina. I wonder, standing there, if it's because the boys like it that way, or if they've actually tried to get women on board but they're smart enough to know what this place will do to them long-term.

"I hear you have another scoop for us, Rebekah," says the managing editor from behind his enormous desk.

"I do," I say.

"And it doesn't even involve Jews," says Mike.

I decide it is not the time to mention that Henrietta told me the man who paid her to lie was Hasidic. For one, I don't think it's immediately relevant to the Sandra Michaels angle of the story. But even more, that particular piece of information feels dangerous. I've done a lot of reporting in the haredi world in the last two years and, frankly, I've never come across—or even heard about—anyone cold-blooded enough to behave the way Henrietta says this man did. Not that it's not possible. I just know how cavalier the *Trib* can be, and the last thing I want to do is start a rumor that incendiary based only on the word of an admitted liar who won't go on the record.

"Do we have a comment from Michaels on this?" asks Morgan, after I've briefed him on DeShawn's case and the evidence Judge Sanchez and I found.

"No," I say. "I literally just came from the courthouse. I'm waiting on a call."

"Gary, can you spare one of your reporters?"

"Sure."

"Get somebody calling defense attorneys. See if anyone else ever accused Michaels of anything like this."

Gary nods.

"Tell him about the eyewitness," says Mike.

"She told me—off the record—that she lied."

Morgan raises his eyebrows. "Good work, Rebekah. Are you still freelance?"

"Yeah," I say.

"Gary, aren't you hiring for your desk?"

Gary avoids looking at me. "We actually just brought Jack Owens on . . ."

"Who?"

"He, um, he's been here about six months. Columbia j-school."

"Hm," says Morgan. He moves on. "So, we've got two parallel stories. There's DeShawn's case with the lying witness, and there's the Sandra Michaels-withholding-evidence story. I want to focus on Michaels. It has implications for Kendra Yaris, and that's what's trending now. If she didn't turn over evidence in this case, how many other cases did she withhold on? Is she still doing it? What else is she doing? Does the NYPD know? Are they colluding?" I start scribbling, thinking, those are questions you could spend three years trying to answer. "Write up what you have and get it to Mike. I want our first story to run tomorrow. If we can get it online earlier, even better."

The last time I was in this room, I was terrified. I'd made a couple really big mistakes and was pretty certain I'd lose my job. Today, I feel differently.

"I can get some of those answers," I say, "but it'll take a couple days. There's not a huge rush. No one knows I was looking into this case. The missing evidence—that's totally exclusive. Plus, I can't call DeShawn. He has to call me. If we could just wait until tomorrow I might be able to—"

"No," interrupts Morgan. "Michaels could call somebody at the *Times* who's sympathetic and get her side of the story out first. This is too big to sit on. We can fill in the holes later. This story is going to get picked up, and I want every news outlet in the city to have to say, 'as first reported by the *New York Tribune*.'"

CHAPTER TWENTY-SIX

When I wake up the next morning, my article is online. It doesn't get top billing (that goes to the cover story on a round-up of arrests after a man dressed as Cookie Monster and another dressed as Elmo got into a brawl in Times Square), but it's number three on the site, with a red banner reading TRIBUNE EXCLUSIVE atop the headline:

SANDRA MICHAELS ACCUSED OF WITHHOLDING EVIDENCE IN TRIPLE MURDER
by Rebekah Roberts

The woman many expect to be the next Brooklyn DA is accused of withholding critical evidence in the triple murder trial of DeShawn Perkins, a teen convicted of killing his foster parents and sister in 1992.

"It's a disgrace," says Judge Theresa Sanchez, who was Perkins' appeals attorney.

Perkins was 16 years old when he was convicted of shooting Malcolm and Sabrina Davis, and 3-year-old Kenya Gregory, on July 4, 1992.

Sandra Michaels had been with the Kings County DA's office less than a year when she prosecuted Perkins. She won praise for putting the supposedly violent teen behind bars.

And she may have cheated.

Buried in a case file in the Kings County Courthouse basement, the *Trib* found bizarre letters sent to the victims in the months before their deaths, and evidence that family's home had been vandalized.

But none of this evidence was ever turned over to the teen's defense attorneys.

Perkins is now 38 years old, and has spent more than half his life in prison.

"I did not kill my family," Perkins told the *Trib*.

Perkins retracted his original confession, which he says was coerced and made without an adult present. But the jury believed the witness—an admitted crack user and prostitute—who said she saw him leave the scene of the crime.

Other than that, Sanchez says the case against him was "thin."

Perkins has been stalled in his quest to have his conviction overturned because the Brooklyn DA's office told him his case file was destroyed in a 2001 fire.

But when a *Trib* reporter requested the file on Wednesday, she was told it was destroyed when a Red Hook storage warehouse flooded during Super Storm Sandy in 2012.

Neither was true.

The file Perkins wanted was in the basement of the Kings County Courthouse—along with the missing evidence that might have freed him.

Richard Krakowski, the spokesman for the Brooklyn DA, says the office is investigating the situation.

Judge Sanchez, who now presides over the Brooklyn Community Court, has vowed to get the case reopened.

"What else are they hiding?" asks Sanchez. "How many people are sitting in prison because the prosecutors lied?"

With DA Stan Morrissey undergoing treatment for cancer, Sandra Michaels is now running the office. She is currently under pressure to indict NYPD Detective Jason Womack in the shooting death of Kendra Yaris.

The *Trib* was the first to report that Womack has a history of use-of-force allegations.

Attorney Andrew Perlstein, who represents Yaris' family, told the *Trib* that he isn't surprised the DA's office is accused of withholding evidence in a case against a young black man.

"Even in supposedly liberal New York City, black defendants and victims simply don't get real justice," he said.

"If Kendra Yaris had been white, her killers would have been indicted immediately, without a doubt."

Additional reporting by Jack Owens

No one ran the quote from the Yaris family attorney by me. Apparently Jack couldn't find anybody who had accused Sandra Michaels of tampering with evidence, so they just decided to throw in a link and a nod to the story that's currently getting the most clicks on the site. Just as bad, Mike added that the witness against DeShawn was a drug addict and prostitute, which wasn't necessary and will likely piss off Henrietta and make it harder to convince her to go on the record. It would be awesome to work for an editor I could trust.

My phone rings at 9:00 A.M.

"This is Rebakah," I say.

"Hold for Mike."

I hold.

Mike comes on. "Sandra Michaels is doing really well on the site. We need a follow for tomorrow. Have you heard from the kid?"

"DeShawn? No. Hopefully he's not pissed we ran the story without checking with him."

"Try to get in touch," says Mike, ignoring my concern. "Call the prison. And go down to the courthouse to see if you can corner

Michaels. We need a comment from her. Larry's gonna look into the precinct, see if there were shenanigans there around the same time. Call me back at noon so I can give an update at the meeting."

"You made some changes in the Michaels story," I say.

"What?"

"Henrietta isn't going to trust me if I called her a crackhead in the paper."

"You said she was a crackhead."

"I said it but I didn't write it. Can you ask me next time before you make changes like that? Please?"

"I can't run every edit by you, Rebekah."

"I'm not asking you to run every edit by me."

"Fine. Call me at noon."

I'm pretty sure I just made the situation worse. I call the DA's spokesperson and leave a message requesting an interview with Sandra Michaels. Just after I click off, my phone rings with a blocked number.

An automated voice says, "You have a call from the Coxsackie Correctional Facility. Will you accept the charges?"

"Yes," I say.

"Rebekah?"

"DeShawn?"

"I saw the article! You have to be kidding me!"

"I know," I say. "I'm sorry I couldn't run it all by you. I'm so glad you called."

"I can't believe they had those letters all this time! My lawyer said the cops never found nothing."

"Well, somebody lied."

"Ms. Sanchez is a judge now?"

"Yeah," I say. "I don't know if I would have found this stuff if it weren't for her. She's on the warpath." It's time to tell him about

Henrietta. "And there's something else. I tracked down the eyewitness. The woman who picked you out of a lineup. She's clean now, and she's moved to New Jersey and changed her name. She wouldn't let me quote her, but DeShawn, she says she lied. She says she wasn't even in Crown Heights that night. She said somebody paid her to make up a story, and she picked you because she just happened to see you in the precinct that night."

Silence at the other end of the line.

"DeShawn?"

"I'm here. I'm just . . . she really said she lied?"

"She did. But I don't have it on tape. And she says she won't go to the cops. She's afraid of this guy who paid her."

"Who is he?"

I could tell him what she told me, but what if Aviva is right? What if Henrietta just said the man who paid her was Jewish to settle some old score? Until I have more than her word, I decide to keep that part to myself.

"I don't know," I say. "She won't tell me. I'm going to keep trying, though. I'm gonna call her and tell her what we found and basically beg her to come forward."

"I don't even know what to say," says DeShawn.

"I'm working on another story for tomorrow. What would you say to them—to the DA—if you could?"

"I'd say they should all be ashamed of themselves. I was just a kid. I didn't know nothing. And they're gonna lie and cheat just to make some case? What the hell? They took my whole life, man. My whole damn life."

I scribble the words he says into my notebook, but I wish I could scribble the way he says them. At the beginning of the conversation DeShawn was energized. But after I told him about Henrietta, he deflated. I don't know what he is thinking, but I know what I'm thinking: the last twenty-two years of his life spent locked in a cage weren't just some random, awful twist of fate. They were the result of machinations by people for whom the truth of what happened the night someone slaughtered his family was less important than a win—or in Henrietta's case, some cash. Whatever faith in humanity DeShawn managed to hold on to these past two decades has probably been hard won. This shit—I imagine it's enough to undermine that entirely.

"Judge Sanchez thinks there's a good chance they'll reopen your case now," I say, trying to sound hopeful. "I mean, if it's not prosecutorial misconduct, it's definitely negligence." I don't really know what I'm talking about, and before I can make any more empty promises, a recorded voice breaks into our call and says we have ninety seconds remaining.

"DeShawn?"

"I'm here."

"I know this is a lot to lay on you."

"I been dreaming about something like this for so long. I just . . . I don't want to get my hopes up, you know?"

"Totally," I say. "But listen, you've got people behind you now. The DA's office knows they fucked up. And I won't let this drop. Neither will Judge Sanchez."

"Okay."

"Call me tomorrow? Same time?"

"Yeah," he says. "Thank you. No matter what happens now. Just this article . . . thank you."

And the line goes dead.

DeShawn isn't the first person to thank me for reporting a story—people who loved both Rivka Mendelssohn and Pessie Goldin told me they were grateful someone outside the insular haredi community was looking into their deaths. But Rivka and Pessie were dead. My efforts to bring them justice would never change the essential fact that their lives were over before I'd ever heard their names. DeShawn, on the other hand—if I do this right, he could walk out of prison and live for fifty years in a world he would never have seen had I not opened his letter to Amanda. That feels good.

I get dressed and brush my teeth, and at a little after ten, I call Saul. He doesn't pick up.

"Hey, Saul," I say to the voice mail. "I just wanted to see if you saw my story today. Give me a call when you can, 'kay?"

My next call is to Henrietta, but she doesn't pick up, either. I leave a message, and as I do another call comes in. I click over.

"Hi, it's Rebekah."

"Rebekah, this is Richard Krakowski at the Kings County DA. I can get you ten minutes with ADA Michaels this afternoon. Come to the third floor at one thirty."

CHAPTER TWENTY-SEVEN

Sandra Michaels looks like shit. She doesn't appear to have slept, and without the soft Plaza lighting and armor of an elegant suit and professional blow-out, what you notice about her are the prominent tendons in her skinny hands, the hurried eyebrow pencil, the sunspots.

For a few seconds she doesn't speak, she just looks at me.

"Do we know each other?" she asks finally.

"No," I say. "I mean . . . I was at the Plaza the other day."

"I know that. That's what I'm talking about. Did I *do* something to you?"

"I don't understand."

"You did that story about my ex, and now this shit from, what, 1992? Do you have something against me?"

I don't bother protesting that I didn't actually write the story about her ex. I'm the face she associates with it, and splitting that hair will probably aggravate her even more. I decide to focus on DeShawn. "A lot of people are looking into old cases. . . ."

"You think I don't know that!"

Her face contorts dramatically and without all the makeup she was wearing last week I can see that she's had work done. The way her face moves doesn't make sense. The skin beside her eyes scrunches up, but the skin below doesn't budge. Plastic surgery makes me sad, especially on accomplished women. What does it matter what a prosecutor looks like? Maybe I'll think differently when I'm thirty. Or fifty. "Just so I'm clear: this isn't personal? I didn't prosecute your boyfriend or something?"

I shake my head, waiting for more hostility, but she changes tack.

"You're going to have to give us some time on this," she says.

"What do you mean?"

"I mean we have to figure out what happened."

I sense weakness and decide to exploit it. "What happened with what? That the office has been saying the file was destroyed? Or that DeShawn's attorney says she never saw the evidence inside it?"

"She *says* she never saw it. Do you know definitively that it wasn't in the appeals file?"

No.

"Of course not," she continues.

"Are you saying you did turn it over?"

"I'm not saying anything. That's not true. This is what I'm saying: I have never knowingly withheld evidence in a case. That's on the record. You can print that. Everything else is off the record. As Richard explained." She pauses. "You realize this is going to effect the Kendra Yaris case, don't you?"

I decide I don't need to answer.

"That's all I've got for you," she says.

I am dismissed. Outside the courthouse I pull out my phone and am about to call Mike with Sandra Michaels' quote when I get an incoming call from a 718 number I don't recognize.

"This is Rebekah," I say.

"Rebekah, this is Dorothy Norris. We spoke last week at Glorious Gospel."

"Hi, how are you?"

"I saw your article this morning. I hadn't put it together before, but I remembered something that might be useful. Before they died, Malcolm started collecting signatures against a landlord. I don't remember his name, but he owned several buildings in the neighborhood that were in terrible condition. I think one of Malcolm's kids from the YMCA might have lived in one. I believe he complained to the landlord in person—on their behalf—but if I recall correctly, he'd been frustrated by the response. Or lack of response."

"Do you remember the landlord's name?"

"No," she says. "I'm sorry to say I don't. But he was Jewish. I remember that because Malcolm didn't want to tell Pastor Green about it. Like he told you, Red felt it was important for us to get along with our Jewish neighbors, especially after the riots. He was very embarrassed by the way the community behaved. Red does not have much patience for violence or law breaking. Not that I do, either, of course. And Malcolm certainly didn't. But I suppose we were a little more sympathetic to the frustration, especially among the young people then."

"Do you know if Malcolm ever talked to anyone at the city? Maybe made a formal complaint I could look up?"

"Well, Sabrina worked in the city's housing department."

"She did?"

"Yes. I don't know if she was involved, though."

"Okay."

"If DeShawn really is innocent, my husband and I want to do everything we possibly can do help him."

It's about time, I think.

I call Mike and fill him in on what DeShawn, Dorothy, and the DA had to say.

"The vic was collecting signatures against a Jewish landlord?" he asks.

"She thought so, but she didn't have a name."

"More fucking Jews. You're like a magnet."

"Thanks."

"You didn't find signatures in the box with the letters?"

"No," I say.

"Okay, ask the DA's office if they know anything about that. What about the witness?"

"I'll call her. She's in Atlantic City," I remind him, "so I can't just door-knock."

"Okay, Morgan's more interested in the Michaels angle anyway." I know. I was in the meeting, too. "Send me whatever you have by four."

I end the call and find a Starbucks to start plunking out a draft of what I have so far. I splurge on an enormous Frappuccino and text Saul:

> *Just got a tip that Malcolm Davis may have had some sort of conflict with a Jewish landlord before he died. Any thoughts?*

CHAPTER TWENTY-EIGHT

December 1991
Crown Heights, Brooklyn

Two months after the man with the tattoos fell into the toilet, Daniel invited Joe to a meeting on Albany Avenue.

"What sort of meeting?"

"Wait and see," said Daniel. "I think you will find it interesting."

The apartment was on the top floor of a two-story home. By the time Joe and Daniel arrived there were already four men there. Three were standing at a dining room table eating pastries out of plastic bags. One man sat on the floor, fiddling with a radio.

"Avi," said Daniel to the man on the floor, "this is Joe."

Avi rose. He was easily six foot three, with broad shoulders and red hair. He shook Joe's hand and invited him to sit, then called for the rest of the men to gather around the coffee table.

"Did Daniel explain our mission?"

Joe shook his head.

"We came together last year after Shmuli's sister was attacked." Avi looked to the dark-haired man sitting on the far end of the sofa.

Beneath his beard, Shmuli's face was red and mountainous with acne. He cast his eyes down when Avi mentioned his sister.

"I will not offend you with details, but she endured violence no woman should endure. Shmuli's family contacted the police, but as I am sure you can imagine, they were useless. Shmuli took matters into his own hands several weeks later. His sister was brave enough to return to the street where the incident occurred, and she identified the man. Shmuli followed him home, and the next day Eli and I accompanied him to the address, where we were able to detain the man when he came outside."

"Detain?"

Avi smiled. He leaned sideways and unhooked a pair of handcuffs from his belt. "We did not wait for the police to come get him. We brought him to the police. Not surprisingly, the man was on probation for another crime. He is now off the streets."

Avi explained that as students they were not allowed to join the neighborhood's official *shmira,* or patrol group. But even if they could, Avi said, the men in the room believed that the assiduously law-abiding shmira were ineffective. Reactive, not proactive; not willing to, as Avi said, "get their hands dirty."

"You are new to Crown Heights, yes?" Avi asked.

Joe nodded.

"When you read about the riots at home, what did the newspapers say?"

"What do you mean?"

"Did they say that blacks and Jews were fighting? Killing each other?"

"I think so. I don't remember exactly."

"The newspapers had it all wrong. Jews and blacks weren't fighting each other. Jews were being attacked. And we didn't raise a hand! But did that matter? No. The story was that everyone resorted to violence. We were all at fault. Al Sharpton and his people talking about how unfair life is for the blacks. How the police target them and treat the Jews so well. Ha! Who was burning the city? Not Jews! Who was stabbing and beating people in the street? Not Jews!"

Avi shook his head.

"No more. The Rebbe says not to raise hands in violence. But if the world already thinks that is what we are doing . . ." He paused. "You see what I am saying?"

Joe saw. He stayed at the apartment until very late that night, and volunteered to patrol with the group the next evening. It was December, and Joe's first experience with temperatures below freezing. The cold made him feel limber and clearheaded. The air was stimulating, like a shot of adrenaline. He met Daniel, Avi, and another man called Barry at the bakery across the street from Isaiah's office. Daniel handed him a foot-long metal pipe.

"Don't start trouble," Avi said. "But don't run from it, either."

The foursome split into twosomes; Joe and Daniel went west, Avi and Barry east. They would reconvene at midnight. The first hour was uneventful, but Joe felt powerful with the pipe in his jacket. At about seven thirty, they heard glass shatter near the corner of Albany Avenue and Union Street. Two black men ran past. Joe and Daniel started after them, but when the men darted into the traffic on Eastern Parkway, Daniel stopped.

"It's not worth the risk going north after dark," he said. "Even with two of us. They have guns and we don't."

"Why not?"

"Why don't we have guns?"

"Yeah."

Daniel, somehow, seemed to be considering this for the first time.

"I suppose they aren't very easy to get. And we're the good guys. Guns are for bad guys."

Joe found Daniel's response ridiculous, but did not say so. They walked back to the street where they had heard the glass break and found a woman standing beside a minivan with two of the windows smashed.

"Did you catch them?" she asked.

"No," said Daniel. "But we will make sure to add this street to our patrol."

The woman made a disgusted sound. She peered into the vehicle. "This is the third time since Sukkot these same men have broken into cars on this block. I told my husband not to buy another radio after the last time. It only encourages them!

"Do you know how many times I have called the police? They don't even bother to come unless they steal the entire car!"

The rest of the night was busy. They shouted at three men urinating in public, confronted the drivers of two cars obviously trolling for prostitutes, and, brandishing their pipes, broke up two clear drug deals. At just after 10:00 P.M., a young haredi woman, barely out of her teens by the look of it, came running up to them on President Street. Three men had just attacked her husband and he needed help. When they got to the man he was sitting on the curb, his lip split and his white shirt stained with blood. The woman explained that they had been walking home from her parents' apartment when the men came from behind and grabbed her purse.

"Ezra went running after them," she said, breathless. "I screamed for him to stop but . . ." She looked at her husband, who was rubbing his jaw. "One of the men punched him right in the face and then the other one began to kick him. I screamed and screamed and finally they ran off."

"They took our money," said the man. "And now, with her identification, they know where we live. When will they be back for more?"

Neither Joe nor Daniel had an answer for him.

They split up at midnight, and instead of returning home immediately, Joe walked north, toward Eastern Parkway. He hailed a
taxicab and told the driver to take him to Bushwick. He was wide
awake. Since seeing the prostitute in Isaiah's building, he had been
nearly unable to control his desire for a woman like her. A woman
with no dignity; a slab of meat to bite and lick and explode inside
of. In the taxi, he put his brimmed hat in his backpack and replaced
it with the Dodgers cap he'd brought from California. He directed
the driver to a corner a few blocks from the building with the leak
in the ceiling. As much as he wanted to knock on the big-breasted
woman's ground-floor door, he knew he had to find someone else,
someone who could not connect him to his life in Crown Heights.

With his backpack over one shoulder, he strolled, scanning the
street for women. He walked two blocks up one side of Wilson
Avenue, then crossed to the other side and walked the same two
blocks in the other direction. He approached a bodega in the middle
of the block, its piss-yellow awning torn, its windows fogged with
filth and dusty canned goods, a neon Budweiser sign blinking. Outside stood a woman in an oversized military-style coat, her legs bare,
feet stuffed into high heels. He slowed.

"You want a date?" she asked.

It was that easy.

Ten minutes later, around the corner and up the stairs into a
sparsely furnished apartment, Joe no longer needed to control himself. He pulled down her shirt and squeezed, then sucked, lost, as if
in a dream. It was finally real. He told her to take off her shorts, and
she did. He told her to get on her knees, and she did. He came in
her mouth. He roared, excited by the volume of his voice. Who
could hear him now? Who could stop him from doing exactly what
he wanted?

The prostitute took her clothes into the bathroom and he heard the water running. She was dressed when she came out.

"No," he said. "We're not done."

He told her to take off her clothes and sit on the sofa. He told her to open her legs so that he could see what was there. He looked, intrigued and appalled.

Afterward, he gave her twenty-five dollars, five more than she had told him it would cost.

"Next week at the same time."

The woman nodded. "I'm Hunny," she said.

"Joe."

A week later, he was back on the street with the patrol group, this time paired with a small, bespeckled man named Lazer, with whom he quickly became exasperated. Just fifteen minutes after beginning their patrol, the pair spotted two skinny, filthy men huddled in the doorway of an abandoned storefront on Brooklyn Avenue. They were smoking crack. Joe began to jog toward the men, but Lazer grabbed his sleeve.

"What are you doing?"

"I am going to tell them to move or we will call the police."

"They could be dangerous. Avi says, don't start trouble."

"I'm not starting the trouble. They're the ones doing drugs."

He shook Lazer off and pulled the metal pipe from his waist. The men in the doorway did not see him until he was standing just a few feet away, and when he kicked one in the stomach, the other was so startled he didn't even run. Joe kicked the man again, and then brought his pipe down on his ribs. The man vomited blood.

"Stop!" screamed the second crackhead, throwing himself toward Joe's feet. Joe stepped back calmly, disgusted at the display.

"This is my neighborhood," said Joe. "I will kill you if I see you again."

The men nodded frantically, like children. The friend took the injured man's hand and together they lumbered north. Joe watched the men go, their pants falling off their skinny hips, their sneakers scratching along the sidewalk. When they disappeared around the corner of Bergen, Joe turned and waved Lazer over.

"You have a kit?"

At first, Lazer appeared not to hear him. He looked to Joe like one of those tiny dogs the Puerto Ricans kept; twitchy and useless.

"Lazer!"

Lazer dug into the knapsack slung across his chest and handed him a pair of work gloves and a small broom and dustpan. Joe swept the glass from the broken pipe into the plastic dustpan. He handed the dustpan to Lazer, then, when his partner turned to dump the glass in a garbage can, Joe picked up a tiny plastic bag with what he assumed were two pieces of crack cocaine inside. Rocks, he had heard them called. He put the plastic bag in his pants pocket, and later that night, he gave the bag to Hunny and asked her to smoke one before they had sex.

He didn't have to ask her twice. She pulled a glass pipe from her purse—it was just a little tube, really—put the rock at the end, and flicked a lighter. The smell was chemical and sour, and Joe was impressed with the white cloud of smoke she blew after her inhale.

"How does it feel?" he asked her.

She leaned back on the sofa and spread her legs. "It feels like I wanna get to fucking."

The next day, Joe dozed off in his morning Hebrew class. The droning of the students' recitations entered the dream: he and Hunny were walking in Bushwick. It was summer and he was wearing shorts, a T-shirt, flip-flops: the clothing of his childhood. The men in black hats were all around them, crowding the sidewalk, their mouths moving, moving, moving. He had to push them aside like overgrowth in a forest. First with his hands, then he had a pipe. *Smack*. The instructor's hand on the desk where his head lay. Joe startled awake, felt the cold wet of drool on his chin. The instructor stared down at him, performing disgust for his obedient, obnoxious pupils. Joe didn't think, he just swung: fist to chin, and the man fell.

CHAPTER TWENTY-NINE

December 1991–February 1992
Crown Heights, Brooklyn

Daniel brought the news of Joe's expulsion to Isaiah. The second floor was busy that morning. A Lubavitcher couple and a black woman sat on folding chairs in reception, and the secretaries darted around, apparently unable to find whatever paperwork was necessary to attend to them. Isaiah yelled from behind his desk and when Daniel poked his head in, the landlord said he would have to wait. An hour later, Daniel closed the door behind him and relayed what the yeshiva's principal had described.

"Does he deny it?"

"No," said Daniel.

Isaiah raised his eyebrows.

"What do you think of him?" Isaiah asked.

"Think of him?" Daniel considered this. He was reluctant to say that he didn't really know Joe any better now than he did when they were introduced in August. His mentee was friendly and articulate. He was polite and he expressed reasonable opinions about the Talmud and the neighborhood and the collapse of communism across Eastern Europe, but every time they interacted, Daniel couldn't help feeling as if they had just met. They ate meals together, worked together, walked the streets of Crown Heights together, but there was no intimacy between them. Was that abnormal? Daniel didn't know. They were from very different backgrounds, after all.

"Were you surprised when you learned what he'd done?" Isaiah asked when Daniel did not seem to be able to come up with an answer.

"No," said Daniel. "I have seen him be aggressive. But against blacks."

Isaiah nodded. He explained that he was getting pressure from his partners in the UK to turn a bigger profit on his buildings and may have to start evictions in order to replace his current tenants with people who would pay more.

"I need someone to accompany me on what are occasionally unpleasant visits."

Daniel understood. "I think he would be good at that."

The next day, Isaiah summoned Joe to his office.

"Would you like to stay here in Crown Heights?"

"Yes," said Joe.

"Good. I have been looking for someone with a certain skill set. As you know, some of the people who live in my buildings are very different from you and I. They do not understand what it is like to have to make a living. They do not understand the responsibility of owning something." He paused. Joe sensed Isaiah needed a nod, so he nodded. "Of course, we always conduct ourselves as best we can. We try not to draw attention."

"Of course."

Isaiah paid Joe a month's wages upfront, in cash, so that he could rent a furnished apartment. With a job and a place to stay he did not have to go home. With a job and a place to stay he could deflect his parents' anxious inquiries. With a job and a place to stay he could live exactly as he pleased.

Typically, Isaiah was vague about what he wanted. He told Joe that the building on Bedford had only three apartments still occupied, and that without heat it would be very difficult for the remaining tenants to stay through the rest of the winter. So Joe went to the building and took a wrench to the boiler. When the tenants called to complain, the women at the office took a message. By spring, the building was empty.

And then Malcolm Davis came along.

At first it was just phone calls requesting a meeting.

"Is he a tenant?" Isaiah asked the receptionist one morning when she informed them that there was another message on the machine overnight.

"No," said Goldy. "He says he is calling on behalf of someone on St. John."

"On behalf?"

"Listen to the message, why don't you!"

"Press the button," said Joe.

This message is for Mr. Isaiah Grunwald. My name is Malcolm Davis and I have called several times on behalf of Roberta Wilcox. Ms. Wilcox has a ten-year-old son with asthma and the mold in the apartment is making him very sick. She is going to begin withholding her rent until the problem is fixed. She will be filing a complaint with the Department of Housing.

"Let her complain," said Isaiah. "If she does not pay her rent, we will evict her."

Two weeks later, Isaiah got a call from Gabriel Sachs, the son of a fellow former IDF solider. Gabe worked in planning at the city's housing department.

"There is a woman here who is trying to convince my superiors to open an investigation into your business," Gabe told Isaiah.

"A woman?"

"Her name is Sabrina Davis. She is a secretary. Apparently her husband works with children and some of their families have made complaints."

"Should I be worried?"

"Possibly. Most complaints never trigger an inquiry, but much of the time it is haphazard. You don't want someone bringing up your name constantly."

"And that is what she is doing?"

"Yes."

That afternoon, Isaiah informed Joe that the Davises seemed to have become fixated on him.

"We need to avoid an investigation."

CHAPTER THIRTY

The follow-up story on Sandra Michaels withholding evidence isn't much. Just a "no comment"/"we're looking into" placeholder. Jack Owens got a quote from a defense attorney whose client was exonerated in 2013 after serving twenty-eight years for a murder ("Some prosecutors will do anything to get a conviction") and on Monday morning the office issues a statement announcing that ADA Michaels has been taken off the Kendra Yaris case "pending investigation into allegations of past mishandling of evidence."

Mike calls and directs me to Crown Heights to get reaction from the Yaris family. But just after I get off the subway at Nostrand, Judge Sanchez calls.

"I'm at Felicia's office," she says. "They think someone slipped that evidence we found into the file recently."

"What makes them think that?"

"Apparently somebody came in asking about the same file a couple days before we did. And they have him on surveillance video."

Forty minutes later, I'm in ADA Felicia Castillo's office with Judge Sanchez and Richard Krakowski, the DA's spokesman.

"Before we go any further, we need to set some ground rules," says Krakowski. "Our official statement is that the prosecutor who tried this case *did not* have the evidence you uncovered—the letters and the police report—at the time of the trial. We are actively investigating whether what you found is authentically part of the case and, if so, how—and when—it was put into the case file."

I scribble what he's told me into my notebook.

"Now, we're going off the record," says Felicia. "I want you to know, I would never—*never*—give this kind of access to a reporter if Theresa were not involved."

"I told her I want someone outside this office—someone outside the court system—to see this," says Judge Sanchez. "If this video disappears . . ."

"It's not going to disappear," says Felicia.

"It better not."

The four of us gather around Felicia's desktop computer. Krakowski opens a plastic CD case and slips a disk into the drive. He clicks open the icon that appears and up pops a black-and-white image with a time and date stamp in the corner. The camera is mounted above the doorway leading into the storage room Judge Sanchez and I were in together.

"We don't get a lot of people asking for paperwork this old," explains Krakowski. "I talked to the clerk this morning, and it turns out she was sick early last week. She asked her people and was told that a man came in on Monday looking for the same file. Her replacement had an assistant escort him downstairs, and the assistant told me he brought the box down for the man, but left him alone after he showed an ID from the PBA."

"The police union?" I ask.

Krakowski nods, then clicks the video image, and after a few seconds we watch two men walk into the room. Because of the angle of the camera, we can't see their faces.

"That's the assistant," says Krakowski, pointing at the first man.

The two disappear out of the camera's range. About a minute later, the assistant appears again—he's facing the camera, so we see his face—and walks out the door. Another minute passes, and the second man walks back into the frame.

"That's him," says Krakowski, pausing the video. "In the sunglasses."

Mirrored aviator sunglasses. It's Saul.

"Do we think he's a cop?" asks Felicia.

"If he's not a cop he was pretending to be one," says Richard.

"If he's a cop, though, why show a PBA card? Why not his shield?"

Because they took his shield away, I think.

"What does the assistant say?" asks Judge Sanchez. "It looks like he wasn't alone long."

"Long enough to slip something into the box," says Krakowski.

"How many people have seen this?" I ask, trying to keep my voice steady.

"The clerk and the assistant. And ADA Michaels."

"And nobody recognizes him?"

"The sunglasses make it hard, but we'll print up a still image and start asking around. I've got a call in to the original detective on the case."

For a moment, everyone is silent, staring at Saul's frozen image.

"This doesn't show anybody actually slipping anything into the file," I say.

"No," says Krakowski. "But obviously, we need to talk to this man."

Yeah, I think. So do I.

Outside the courthouse in the blazing sun, I stare at my phone. Who do I call first? Mike, to tell him we have an exclusive on the fact that the DA suspects someone—someone only I know was one of the officers who arrested DeShawn—slipped crucial evidence into the Davis file two decades after the case was closed? Or Saul, to give him a chance to explain? But what possible explanation could he have for being in that storage room the day after I came to visit *other* than to fuck with the file? And if he did fuck with the file, that's a crime. It might be a bunch of different crimes. Even if Henrietta never comes forward, what Saul did might be enough to get DeShawn's conviction overturned. If that happens, the DA is going to shout Saul's name from the rooftops. DeShawn and some lawyer will sue the shit out of him. He might even go to prison.

And maybe he should.

CHAPTER THIRTY-ONE

Saul was taking his daily walk along the boardwalk when he received Rebekah's text about the landlord: *Just got a tip that Malcolm Davis may have had some sort of conflict with a Jewish landlord before he died. Do you remember anything about that?*

He put his hand on the railing and found a bench. How could he have been so stupid? He closed his eyes and saw Fraidy's spiteful face; he heard Binyamin's voice saying "I don't want to see you anymore;" he smelled the mildew in the lonely room in Coney Island. He had come so far from the misery of that time. But what he had done—and what he had not done—lived on. Rothstein wanted that file for a landlord. And he gave it to him. No questions asked.

Until he received the text, Saul had forgotten about the favor entirely. What sent him to his basement storage locker was what Rebekah said about the eyewitness. Her identification made it easy to do what he had done.

The Ziploc bag was inside a cardboard box of mementos from his life on the force. A certificate from the academy; a photograph of Saul shaking hands with the commissioner at graduation; a ribbon for placing in the NYPD 5K; his white dress gloves; a letter from a rape victim whose attacker he'd helped convict. He brought the box upstairs. Aviva was back in New Paltz and he had the apartment to himself. What would she think of what he'd done? Probably she would understand. Her daughter, on the other hand, would not. Aviva's moral code was less rigid that Rebekah's. Perhaps it was a function of her age. Saul once thought he had a rigid moral code. It was that code, ironically, that told him putting the letters and the police report in the Ziploc bag was the right thing to do.

It was a week after they handed the Davis case to the ADA. Saul was sitting at a desk in the precinct, going over his statement about why and how he had shot and killed a twenty-seven-year-old named Eric Overland the day before. Overland was the suspect in the double stabbing that he and Olivetti had been called to on Park Place. The scene was more gruesome, even, than the Davises'. The mother, forty-five-year-old Pauline Rodriquez, died in the apartment. Her daughter, Lisa—who had been dating Overland—was nineteen, and died at the hospital. Both had been tied up, sexually assaulted, and stabbed and slashed so badly that pieces of their bodies were severed. They found Pauline without nipples. Lisa arrived at Kings County Hospital unconscious, the four-month-old fetus inside her exposed by the gaping wound in her abdomen. Olivetti and Saul tracked Overland to his cousin's house on Staten Island three days later.

"Keep your hand on your weapon," Olivetti had told him before they stepped out of the car. "This guy is a sneaky motherfucker."

What they'd learned about Overland was that four years earlier he'd been acquitted in the choking death of his seventeen-year-old girlfriend. When Saul talked to the ADA who prosecuted the case, he said the defense created reasonable doubt by introducing love letters from one of the girl's classmates. Overland's attorney speculated that it could have been this lovesick high school boy—not the girl's older boyfriend—who'd murdered her out of jealousy. If not for those stupid, harmless letters, Overland would have been in prison, and Pauline and Lisa Rodriguez would be alive.

Before they even knocked on the cousin's door, Saul sensed this arrest was going to go badly. The front window was open and he heard shouting, then a crash, like a piece of furniture being knocked over. Olivetti drew his weapon; Saul did the same.

The detective banged his fist on the front door.

"NYPD!"

Heavy footsteps, and then the door swung open. A man held his hands up and said, "He's upstairs."

Olivetti pulled the man onto the home's little front porch.

"Cuff him," said Olivetti. Saul obeyed.

"Is he armed?" Olivetti asked the man.

"He's got a knife. And my sister's in there."

"Why didn't she come out?"

"She's trying to talk to him. He showed up last night. Drunk as shit. I fucking *told* him to leave."

"But you didn't call the cops."

"Come on, man, that's my cousin."

"Your cousin stabbed a pregnant woman and her mother to death."

"He said it wasn't him."

"And you believed him?"

The man didn't answer.

"Put him in the car," said Olivetti. "Hurry up. And radio for backup."

"What'd I do?" asked the man.

"You harbored a felon, for starters."

Saul sat the man in the backseat of the cruiser. He got on the radio and gave their address, said they were preparing to apprehend an armed murder suspect.

Back on the porch, Olivetti was itching to get inside the house.

"If there's a woman in there she's in danger."

As if on cue, they heard a scream inside.

Olivetti kicked open the screen door, his gun pointed in front of him. Saul followed.

"Eric!" shouted Olivetti.

Another scream, and Eric Overland appeared at the top of the staircase just inside the home. He held a young woman in front of him, a knife to her throat.

"Drop the knife, Eric," said Olivetti. Olivetti seemed calm, but Saul's hands were shaking. When they crossed into the house, Olivetti stepped right and Saul left, which put him at the foot of the stairs. His vision narrowed; everything surrounding the man and the woman above him became blurry.

"Stay the fuck down there!" shouted Eric.

Saul heard the words, but they sounded as if they were coming from far away, inside a tin can. Both he and Olivetti had their weapons pointed up, but there was no way they could shoot and not risk hitting the woman. She was silent now; a knife at her neck and two guns pointed at her.

"Let your cousin go," said Olivetti.

"Shut up!"

"Your family's been good to you, Eric," he said. "You're gonna need them. Let her go, drop the knife, and we'll talk. Just talk."

"Fuck you! I ain't stupid."

"Let her go, Eric. We can help you if you let her go. If you don't let her go, things are going to get really bad really fast."

In the distance, sirens.

"Let her go, man," said Olivetti. "Those sirens are for you. When those sirens get here all hell is gonna break loose. You're gonna die and your cousin's gonna die. Let her go and we can still talk."

The cousin started wimpering. Eric pushed her sideways and started down the stairs, the knife held strong out in front of him, pointed at Saul.

Saul pulled the trigger. Later, they told him he fired five shots. Four of the bullets hit Eric Overland.

No one thought he'd done anything wrong. The suspect was coming at him with an edged weapon. But in one instant, Saul became a man who had killed another man. Even in those first hours afterward he knew that fact would change him in ways he could only begin to imagine. He hated Eric Overland for that. He hated the cousin who didn't call the cops. And he hated the twelve members of the jury who had let Overland off four years earlier.

So when the woman from the evidence collection team found him in the precinct that mid-July afternoon and handed over the "possibly relevant" items they had taken from the Davis home, Saul made a decision. He was not going to be responsible for letting another murderer go free over some bullshit reasonable doubt. They had the confession. They had the witness. They had the perp.

If Saul is honest, and when Rebekah texts him twenty-some years later he has lost whatever ability he once had to be dishonest with himself, he has to admit that he hadn't thought once since about the papers he tucked into a drawer in his room at Coney Island, and then carried around from apartment to apartment in a box, until her visit. When he finally did think about it, he knew he'd done wrong. But, he thought, maybe I can make it right. Let Rebekah look into the case. Let her find the evidence—meaningless or meaningful. Let the truth come out, whatever it is.

PART 3

CHAPTER THIRTY-TWO

Spring–Summer 1992
Crown Heights, Brooklyn

Once Joe had their phone number, finding the Davises' address was simple. He started with spray paint, something dramatic: big red letters across the front door. He hand-delivered the first letter, hopping quickly onto the porch after watching the family leave in the morning, then mailed the next two, thinking better of being seen on their street.

The letters were vague: *YOUR FAMILY IS IN DANGER* and *YOU ARE BEING WATCHED.* No details that could be traced to Isaiah.

He made the first phone call at dinnertime and a woman answered. Children's voices in the background; pots and pans.

"Hello?"

He was silent.

"Hello? Who is this?"

He called again a few days later and a boy answered.

"Davis residence, this is Ontario speaking."

In the background a woman asked: "Who is it, Ontario?"

"Who is it?"

The woman—Sabrina, he assumed, the wife who was complaining to her bosses at the housing department—came to the phone.

"Hello?"

He hung up.

He called every other day, at different hours, from different pay phones. If Malcolm answered, he hung up. If it was Sabrina or one of the children, he remained on the line, listening as their confusion turned to frustration and then to fear.

"Stop calling here!" begged Sabrina one evening.

"You are being watched," he said.

"What is this about?"

He decided he could tip his hand on the phone. No hard evidence, just a voice saying words no one else would ever hear.

"Stop bothering Isaiah Grunwald."

"Who? Isaiah . . . you mean . . . Oh my God. Malcolm!"

He hung up.

If they had just done as he asked, it would have ended there. But Malcolm Davis got self-righteous. One of Isaiah's handymen stopped by the office about a week later and informed them that a black man named Malcolm was knocking on doors at one of the buildings in Bushwick, asking people to sign a petition.

"What kind of petition?"

"I didn't get a look at it, but something about failure to maintain the building."

"Who does this man think he is?" shouted Isaiah. "What is this obsession with me? What have I done to him?" He turned to Joe. "I thought you were taking care of this?"

"I am," said Joe. "I will."

"This family needs to know that nothing good will come from challenging me like this."

Joe began to watch the Davises, to learn the patterns of their life. They attended church on Wednesday evening and Sunday morning, and went grocery shopping at the Associated market on Utica on Saturday. On Sundays after church they went to Prospect Park, sometimes with a larger group, sometimes alone. Sometimes they stopped at a restaurant and bought food for a picnic, sometimes they brought Tupperware from home. Mommy and Daddy and a little girl and boy. Sometimes a teenager was with them. Malcolm and the boy played catch, and Sabrina sat with the little girl, reading to her on a blanket, or watching as she climbed on the playground equipment.

He got the gun from a man who worked at the bodega on Hunny's block. All he had to do was ask, and hand over the cash.

"Have you shot one before?"

Joe said he hadn't, and the man suggested he take the gun on the Metro-North to a range outside Peekskill. They won't ask you for paperwork, he said. You should be fine.

Joe took the train from Grand Central Station and spent the day shooting at paper targets in a field. His aim was good for a beginner. And the small pointers the instructor gave—pull the trigger on the exhale, be prepared for the kick—helped. But he was astute enough to realize that it would take time to become truly proficient with the weapon. And he did not have time.

On the ride home, he noticed his ears were still ringing. The noise and his inexperience with the weapon were liabilities. He needed to attack while the family was as helpless as possible—and as isolated. On the street, they could run or fight back. On the street someone could intervene. Ideally, he would shoot the couple in their home. Ideally, he would be hiding somewhere and wait until they were asleep. But gunshots in the middle of the night would alert neighbors quickly. The train stopped to pick up more passengers and that was when he saw the red, white, and blue bunting.

TARRYTOWN ANNUAL FOURTH OF JULY PARADE!

Gunshots could be mistaken for firecrackers.

It was June thirtieth. He had five days to prepare.

When he got back to Brooklyn that night, he walked from the subway to the Davises' address. They lived in a small house that was separated into two apartments; ground floor and above. Several things about the home worked to his advantage: it was the last house on the block, and there was a small alleyway behind it, meaning there were multiple ways in and out. The most promising entrance appeared to be a window he could reach with just a little boost. He found a paint bucket a few houses down and used it to peek inside: bunk beds and strewn clothing and posters on the walls. The window was open for the breeze, he guessed. But what kind of parents did not have bars on the window in their child's bedroom? More proof, Joe thought, that they deserved what was coming to them.

The paint bucket gave him the idea to disguise himself as a handyman, just in case anyone asked him what he was doing in the almost entirely black neighborhood. On July second, he tested the costume: work boots, paint-dusted pants, a roller, and a small tarp, all taken from one of Isaiah's vans. He watched as the family left their home in the morning, then laid the tarp under the window—cracked open again—climbed onto the bucket, and let himself in. No one said a word. He took his shoes off once inside. The house hummed softly; a refrigerator, or maybe an air-conditioning unit on the floor above. He walked down the hallway to what was obviously the master bedroom. A pile of laundry sat unfolded in a basket on the bed. There were framed photographs on the bureau: a wedding day, a visit to a tropical location, school portraits. A jewelry box. A mirror with a corsage of dried flowers hanging from one corner. Matching bedside tables with matching lamps. On the woman's side was lotion, a datebook, Kleenex. On the man's side there was a clipboard with a piece of paper on it, and on the piece of paper, signatures. He snatched the clipboard. They would think they had misplaced it, and in two days they would be dead.

There was a clothes closet in the bedroom, but it was small, with two sliding doors—not a good hiding place. The hall closet was also unsuitable, filled with built-in shelves that held linens and cleaning supplies. He could curl beneath the lowest shelf, but if someone opened the door, he would be cornered. Nothing presented itself in the second child's bedroom, either. He had two choices: a small space between the wall and the living room sofa, or beneath the master bed. Both were risky, but the living room seemed more so. If the family came home and sat down to watch television, the kids might run around and find him. The bedroom, he decided, was less likely to be a center of activity. Yes, someone might look under the bed for something, but a decision had to be made. He would enter the house while the Davises were at the Independence Day festivities—he made the assumption that they were the kind of family that would take the children to some sort of celebration— and shoot the parents in their bed once the family was asleep. From inside, he could unlatch and lift the window in their room, hop into the alleyway, and walk home.

He visited Hunny the next night and gave her a hundred dollars cash, and the addresses of the Davises' home and the precinct on Utica Avenue.

"Say you were in the neighborhood after the fireworks and saw a black man running out of this house. Say you saw him carrying a gun."

"I don't talk to cops," she said. She had smoked her drugs before he arrived; he could tell because of the way she kept licking her lips, and she couldn't stop moving.

"Sit down," he said.

She sat, knees bouncing, eyes moving around the room like she was following a fly. When she was like this she would fuck him more than once for the same price. But she wasn't as attractive to him as she had been when they first met. She'd lost weight, and didn't bother fixing herself anymore. Her apartment smelled like garbage, and she had turned lazy. At the beginning, she took charge of their nights, giving him new experiences and allowing him to relax and enjoy. But now he had to ask her to do every little thing. When this was over, he would stop seeing her.

"I don't talk to cops," she repeated.

"Five hundred dollars," he said. "And you aren't helping the police. You're lying to them."

He wasn't sure if she heard him. Or if she heard him, he wasn't sure she understood. If he had thought it might help, he would have hit her. But he did not want to risk her becoming angry and stubborn. Hunny did what she did for money, pure and simple. Enough money and she'd do anything.

"One thousand dollars," he said. "All you have to do is go to the precinct and say what I told you."

"A thousand?"

He nodded.

She picked up the twenties from the table between them, flipped through them like she was counting, but her eyes were unfocused.

"You trying to jam somebody up?" she asked.

He didn't answer. He didn't need to. She didn't really want to know. He stood up and began to unbutton his shirt, thinking, as he did, that the next time he was in this ugly little room he would be a killer.

The Fourth of July fell on a Saturday. He couldn't have planned it better. The streets near the Davises' house were swarming with people running amok, throwing bottles and blasting music, shouting and laughing. He kept his head down and his hands in his pockets as he walked up Utica from Eastern Parkway. No one noticed him. He had hidden the paint bucket in the alleyway, and he was ready with a response should someone question him as he popped the screen on the window and slipped inside. *I work for the landlord. They're having a problem with the latches.* But there were no questions. Before he slid under the bed to begin waiting, Joe used the toilet in the hall bathroom. He peed and flushed and put the seat down, using his knuckles so as not to leave fingerprints. There were three toothbrushes in a plastic cup on the sink and a sticker on the mirror, an *S*—the symbol for Superman. He smiled as he looked at himself beside the emblem. He pulled his handgun from his waistband and posed, pointing it at the mirror, moving his wrist around and watching the way he looked with the weapon in his hand. In the planning, he had not allowed himself to indulge in excitement. What he was doing was not about him, or what he wanted; it was about his commitment to Isaiah. But, he decided there in the Superman mirror, there was nothing wrong with taking pleasure in his work.

From beneath the bed, Joe felt the floor shudder when the Davises came in. Children running. A woman's voice.

"Ontario, will you help Kenya with her shoes please?"

"Kenya! No shoes on the carpet!" said a little boy.

"Gentle," said Sabrina.

Adult footsteps came into the bedroom. Joe saw gym socks. Malcolm Davis switched on a lamp.

"Do you want me to run a bath?" he called.

Sabrina came in. Bare feet, toenails painted pink.

"I think we can skip it tonight. It's late. If you do teeth and pajamas, I'll get them down."

"I thought maybe he'd be home," said Malcolm.

"I know," said Sabrina.

"I don't know what to do anymore. Does he even want to be here?"

"I think he does. I think he's just . . . having a hard time."

"I'm worried about how all this is affecting Ontario. It's exactly the wrong thing for him to see right now."

"I know."

Malcolm sat down on the bed.

"Red thinks he has a girlfriend. He told me she's nice. A track star. Why wouldn't he want to share that with us?"

"Maybe he will."

"He can't stay out all night. We can't just let this go."

"It's only eleven. He might still come home."

"And if he doesn't?"

"I don't know, Malcolm. If he doesn't we . . . talk to him."

"It's not enough. It's not *working*."

"What else can we do? I'm not giving up on him."

"I'm not saying we should give up."

"I know what you're thinking."

"We have to consider all the options. We have to consider Ontario, and Kenya."

"Giving up our son is not an option," said Sabrina. "I don't want to talk about this anymore tonight. There is nothing we can do.

Stay here. I'll get them ready. Try to relax. Try to see the big picture. He's sixteen. He hasn't hurt anybody. . . ."

"He's hurting me! He's hurting you. He's hurting this family."

"Shh!"

From down the hall the little boy shouted, "Kenya needs help on the potty!"

"It's going to be okay, Malcolm," said Sabrina. "If we keep loving him, it's going to be okay."

Sabrina left the room, and Malcolm sat on the bed. It was very hot. Joe's armpits and forehead itched. He heard the children talking, water running. Outside, the celebrations were ongoing. Shouting and pops; sirens, car horns. Malcolm switched on an electric fan and went into the bathroom. He brushed his teeth and changed his clothes, then got into bed. Soon, Sabrina came in and did the same.

"We should think about an AC unit for the boys' room," she said. "He doesn't complain, but even with the fan, it's uncomfortable in there. He's been opening the window, which makes me nervous. Should be sales coming up soon. I wouldn't mind one in here, either."

"Sounds reasonable."

"What are you reading?" asked Sabrina.

"Abel recommended it."

Bodies adjusted on the bed.

"You want a little lovin'?" asked Sabrina.

"Not really," said Malcolm. "I'm just . . ."

"It's fine."

"I love you."

"I know you do."

"I can't stop worrying about him."

"I think he's going to be okay," said Sabrina.

"The way he's been speaking to you . . ."

"He's testing us, Malcolm."

Malcolm sighed. More adjustments on the bed. Quiet. After about ten minutes, the bedside lights switched off.

"I love you," said Malcolm again.

"I love you."

He needed to wait until they were asleep, so he lay there in the dark, listening to them breathe. He would shoot Malcolm first, then Sabrina. When he heard the snoring, his stomach clenched. It was time. And then there was a scream. It came from down the hall.

"I'll go," said Sabrina.

"Just bring her in," said Malcolm.

Sabrina climbed out of the bed and Joe realized he would have to kill the girl, too. She was young, yes, but it was possible she could tell the police something. Even that he was white would be enough to contradict the story Hunny would tell. And what kind of life would she have anyway, with both parents dead? She would probably never recover. It was, he decided, the right thing to do, under the circumstances.

The little girl and the woman came back. Soon, he heard the snoring again, and decided it was time. He crawled along the carpet slowly, staying low as he emerged from beneath the bed on Malcolm's side. He came to all fours, and then stood, taking relief in the breeze blown by the fan, the cool against his sweat-soaked T-shirt. He aimed the weapon inches from Malcolm's head, face turned toward his wife, mouth slightly open. The bullet entered just in front of his ear, blowing his head apart. Sabrina sat up, sucking air. She turned his way, eyes wide. He aimed at her chest. Two shots and she fell back, slumped over. The little girl dove toward the end of the bed. There was less of her to aim at. Joe jumped to meet her before she could climb down. She stopped and stared up at him. There was a blond princess on her sleeping shirt.

"This is just a dream," he said. "Go back to sleep."

He pointed the weapon at her face, closed his eyes, and pulled the trigger.

CHAPTER THIRTY-THREE

July–September 1992
Crown Heights, Brooklyn; Fort Jackson, South Carolina

The Davis murders did not make the front pages. The morning after the bodies would have been discovered, Joe bought a copy of the *Trib* at a bodega down the street from his apartment and found the article on page four: "Three Dead in Savage Crown Heights Home Invasion."

The article said that police were interviewing a "person of interest." The next day, the paper reported that the Davises' teenage son was in custody. A day after that, the paper said the boy confessed, and that police had a witness who saw him leaving the scene. Each of these days, Joe went to the Kingston Avenue office ready for Isaiah to congratulate him. He did not expect a celebration, of course, but a nod. An acknowledgment. He had done his job. Yet Isaiah said nothing. Joe knew the landlord read the newspaper, and a triple murder in the neighborhood—even if it was on a black block—should have caught his attention, especially once he read the victims' names.

Finally, on the day the newspaper covered the funerals, Joe brought a copy to the office and laid it on Isaiah's desk.

"You have been reading the articles?" he asked.

Isaiah was silent.

"Everything is taken care of," said Joe. He opened the newspaper to the page where he'd slid the signatures from Malcolm's bedside table.

Isaiah looked up, and their eyes met. Joe saw immediately that the landlord was not pleased.

"There is no need to worry," said Joe. "The son confessed."

"Never come to this office again," said Isaiah. "If I were you, I would leave New York."

Joe withdrew what was left in his bank account that afternoon and took a taxi to Bushwick to get drunk and look for Hunny. He told the bartender he'd just been fired, and she poured them both a shot of whiskey.

"To new opportunities," she said.

"Yeah," said Joe. "New opportunities."

By nightfall, he'd forgotten about Hunny. He hailed a cab back to Crown Heights and walked through the streets for the last time, alternately mumbling and shouting about Chabad being full of phonies and cowards and idiots. How he got back to his apartment, he didn't remember, but the next morning he packed a bag and got a hotel room near Port Authority. He slept all day, then followed the crowds toward Times Square at night. And right there, in the center of it all, was the military recruiting station.

The whole process took less than an hour. Two days later, he took the ASVAB. When his score came back the Army recruiter told him that if he passed a background check he could start basic training in South Carolina in two weeks.

"Anything going to come up on the check?" asked the recruiter.

"I was expelled from school for fighting," he said.

"That shouldn't be a problem."

Basic training was more difficult than he expected. What bothered him was not the physical exertion—he had no problem stretching his body's limits—but the demands from his trainers. A year earlier—six months, even—he would not have felt the need to challenge the men barking orders at him. A year earlier, he would have accepted, even respected, the chain of command. He would have found pleasure in keeping his clothing and his bunk tidy, in pleasing his superiors, in conquering obstacles. But what he'd done in the Davises' bedroom changed him. He was more than just a rule follower. More than just a deviant looking for a place to park his problems. He was a man of action. He didn't want to be told what to do anymore. He could survive on his own.

Six weeks into training his marksmanship instructor criticized his shot grouping.

"Where's your control, Weiss?"

Joe turned and looked the man in the eye, then raised his rifle and fired it inches from the instructor's head.

"I'm better up close."

In the brig, he met Lawrence Franklin. Lawrence had gotten court marshaled for driving drunk on post and taking a swing at the officer who cuffed him.

"Fuck this shit," Lawrence said during one of their first nights sharing a cell. "We got skills. Come with me back to Chicago and we can make some real money."

CHAPTER THIRTY-FOUR

"You can't print that picture without warning him," says Iris.

We're on our third round at the cocktail bar down the block. The bartender (excuse me, mixologist), a lanky white boy from California with a man bun and Gothic script tattooed across his collarbone, wants to fuck Iris, so he's making us elaborate drinks, one after the other. Iris is sipping at a stemless champagne flute with pomegranate seeds floating in it; mine is pisco-something. Dinner is the free popcorn.

"I could," I say. "I almost did. If I hadn't recognized him I would have brought the printout to the office three hours ago and it would be online right now."

"But you did recognize him. You have more information, so you have a different responsibility."

"My responsibility is to the truth," I kick back. "Saul broke into that file. At the very least he tampered with evidence."

"You don't know that for sure. You don't have any photos of that."

I would respond, but instead I launch into a coughing fit. The popcorn is peppered almost maliciously. Mixologist brings a glass of water as I right myself, wipe my eyes.

"I'm kind of surprised you're so ready to turn on him," says Iris.

"I'm not turning on him. He lied to me. Again. He was like, I barely remember this case. And he made me feel like shit for questioning him. But DeShawn didn't kill his family. Henrietta proves that."

"You're sure you believe her?"

"Why is it so hard to believe that I believe her?"

"It's just such a crazy story. And she's obviously good at lying. She convinced a jury and Sandra Michaels and everybody."

"I don't get the sense they took much convincing, you know? There were a couple murders every single day just in Brooklyn back then. Now there's one in the whole city, if that. I bet they were like, cool, we got a witness, we got a confession, onto the next."

"I don't see how you confess if you didn't do it," she says, then puts her hand up. "I know, I know. The Central Park Whatever, but seriously. Would you ever say you murdered three people if you didn't? I mean, that's insane."

"The fact that your privileged ass can't imagine doing it doesn't mean someone else wouldn't."

Iris rolls her eyes. "Fine. Fine. Even if Saul lied, even if he somehow fucked with the case, shouldn't you give him a chance to explain before you put him on blast to the whole city? Journalism 101. Get both sides of the story."

"Running the photo doesn't necessarily ID him," I say.

"You're saying you're going to give the *Trib* the photo and not tell them you know who it is?"

"I don't know! I mean, I guess I have to tell them, right?"

"Probably. But talk to Saul first. Just get it over with. Call him now."

She picks up my phone, plugs in my passcode.

"Stop," I say, snatching it back. "I will."

"Your mom will understand."

"I don't think she will," I say, my voice quieter. "I'm trying, I really am. But she thinks I'm spoiled. And selfish."

"Well," says Iris, "she doesn't really know you. And if you keep avoiding her she never will."

I don't respond.

"You need to try to look at it from her point of view. She's gotta be dealing with a shitload of guilt every time she sees you. I'm not saying she doesn't deserve it. It's just . . ."

"We don't have to talk about it," I say. What I mean is, I don't want to talk about it.

"You need to call him."

I suck the last of my cocktail through the little black straw.

Mixologist appears immediately. "Call who?"

"Tell her to call him," says Iris.

"Call him," he says.

"Tell her you won't make her another drink until she calls him."

"I won't make you another drink until you call him."

Does he think this makes him attractive?

"I don't need another drink," I say.

"Just do it," says Iris. She actually pokes me with her finger.

"Do it," says the mixologist.

"Fucking Christ," I say. "Fine."

The story Saul tells is reasonable. Wrong and fucked up, but reasonable. When he is finished talking, his face is red. He hasn't looked me in the eye since I walked into his apartment, where he summoned me promising to reimburse the late-night livery cab fare.

"Why didn't you just give the evidence to me?" I ask.

"Because I was trying to stay out of it."

"That doesn't make any sense! You can't really have thought you could sneak that stuff into the file and no one would notice. And what about Sandra Michaels? You're cool with her just getting blamed?"

"She'll be fine," says Saul. "She is very powerful now. She has lots of friends. And it is just one case. There are many possible explanations for something like this."

I am, for the first time I can remember, stunned to silence. He was just going to let her take the fall.

"You don't have to use my name to tell your story," says Saul.

"Saul, you *are* my story. An innocent man has been in prison more than half his life because the cop working his case buried evidence in a fucking *box* in his apartment!"

"That is not the only reason he is in prison."

"Saul . . ."

He stands up abruptly, knocking a mug of coffee onto the carpet. We both stare at the floor, watching the brown stain spread.

"I am not proud of what I did, Rebekah. I am asking you . . . They will reopen every case I ever worked on."

"Maybe they should! How many other times did you do this?"

Saul raises his eyes to me. "None. I give you my word. The day that woman from evidence gave me those letters was the most terrible day of my life, Rebekah. I had just killed a man. My relationship with my son was over." He pauses. "He was afraid of me. Can you imagine? No, you do not have children, so you cannot. But please try. He did not want to see me because he had been convinced that I was a threat to him. Me—his father. I would have died for him, suffered for him. And when he learned what I had done. That I had taken a life . . . I knew Fraidy would never let him see me after that. It was the perfect excuse. *Your tatty is a killer. Forget him.*"

Saul waves his hands in front of him like he is trying to flick something off them. It's a gesture I know well: trying to fling the pain inside out.

"I have to run the photo," I say. "It's not just about you."

Saul does not respond.

"Someone will probably recognize you."

"Perhaps."

"It's only a matter of time, Saul. I can't believe you thought you'd get away with it."

"I took a chance," he said. "In my experience, security cameras in public buildings in this borough are nonfunctioning at least half the time."

I almost laugh. Almost.

"Before you make your decision I want you to come with me somewhere," he says.

"Where?"

"Crown Heights."

Saul and I step off the elevator on the third floor of the Crown Heights Jewish Council just after noon the next day. A receptionist shows us into Naftali Rothstein's office, where two men are waiting.

"I was hoping we could meet alone," says Saul.

"You and Daniel are here to discuss the same problem," says Naftali. He looks at me. "This is Daniel Grunwald. He runs the Crown Heights Shmira."

"Shmira?" I ask.

"It is like the shomrim," says Saul. "A different word for the patrol group."

"We are off the record, Miss Roberts," says Naftali.

Figures.

"Fine," I say, thinking, as always, build trust now, get quotes later.

"Do you remember a man named Joseph Weiss?" asks Naftali. Saul shakes his head.

"There is no reason you should," says Daniel. "He was only in the community about a year."

"Joseph?" I ask. Then look at Saul. "Joe."

"What?" asks Naftali.

"Last weekend I went to Atlantic City and talked to the only witness in the Davis murders. She told me that a Jewish man named Joe paid her a thousand dollars to lie and say she saw a black kid running out of their house that night. Could it be the same person?"

Daniel breathes in deeply through his nose. "Yes," he says.

For the next twenty minutes, Daniel tells us about "Joe from California" who worked for his uncle Isaiah, a landlord, from September 1991 to July 1992.

I hear the word *landlord* and look at Saul. If this Isaiah instructed Joe to kill the Davises to stop their investigation into his business, the story I write is going to confirm every ugly stereotype about Jews imaginable. This is exactly the kind of shit that got nine utterly innocent Jewish students and teachers slaughtered in Roseville last year. What if Ontario, or DeShawn, or even Toya—people whose lives are divided entirely by what happened before the Davis murders and what happened after—get it in their head to get some revenge? It's easy to get a gun in Brooklyn. It's easy to find a Jew on the street.

When Daniel finishes speaking, Naftali looks at Saul, whose face has gone white.

"I know what you are thinking. Yes, Isaiah Grunwald was the

man who asked for the Davis file. He lied to me, apparently, about his relationship with the family. Obviously, if I had known he might be involved in some way . . . if I had even *suspected* . . ."

Saul lets him trail off. "I should not have handed it over in the first place."

"What are you talking about?" I ask.

"There is nothing we can do about that now," said Naftali. "I've asked the yeshiva to look for any paperwork they have on Joseph. Daniel wants to go to the police. I would like to speak with Isaiah first."

"Why?" I ask. "He's the one who benefited from their deaths, right?"

Naftali and Daniel look at me.

"What do you mean, benefited?" asks Naftali.

"A friend of the Davises told me that before they died Malcolm and Sabrina were trying to get the housing department to investigate a landlord."

Naftali looks at Daniel. "Did you know about this?"

Daniel nods.

"And yet you said nothing," says Saul.

"Do you remember what it was like here in 1992?" says Daniel, raising his voice. "Can you *imagine* what would have happened if a chassidish man was accused of slaughtering a black family? Jewish blood would have run in the streets!"

I raise my eyebrows, which upsets Daniel.

"You think you are so smart. You have *no idea* what we were dealing with then. Now it is fashionable to live here. When this happened you could not *give away* a home in Crown Heights. My uncle . . ."

"Daniel," says Naftali.

"No. No. My uncle invested in this neighborhood. He may have made some mistakes but . . ." Daniel stops himself. "When this happened, I was not certain that Joe—or my uncle—was involved."

"And now?" asks Saul.

"Now," he pauses, "now I wish I had not been so careless. Or so blind."

Naftali clears his throat. "We are not certain this man committed these murders. And we are definitely not certain Isaiah was involved. If this is just a coincidence, I do not want to bring unnecessary scrutiny to the community. Joseph is a very common name."

"Do you have a picture of him?" I ask.

"The yeshiva should have a class photograph," says Naftali.

"Good," I say. "I know a woman who can tell us for sure."

CHAPTER THIRTY-FIVE

September 1992
Crown Heights, Brooklyn

Isaiah kept the signatures in a safe deposit box along with his birth certificate, his citizenship papers, and $750,000 in gold bars. The bars he had been amassing since the late 1970s. They were the only insurance policy a Jew in this world could rely on. With gold bars, a man need not stay longer than is safe in a country whose leadership has suddenly changed. Gold could get Isaiah and his wife plane tickets and new identities in Mexico, or Indonesia, or South Africa. His mother's entire family perished together in 1941, lined up and shot by Nazis along with 35,000 other Jews at the lip of a mass grave outside Minsk. Somehow, the spray of bullets only grazed eighteen-year-old Sonia Baran. For hours she lay still beneath a thin layer of sand, bodies below and beside and atop her, many still writhing and moaning. At nightfall, she climbed out and ran through the forest. She made it to a suburb where no one on the streets wore a yellow star. What she needed were papers that did not identify her as Jewish. With those, she could escape to Israel or America. For two days, she hid in a storage shed behind a bakery.

The smell of the bread coming from the ovens nearly felled her—
Isaiah remembers her telling him that she hadn't eaten bread that
didn't chip her teeth in a year—but she remained out of sight, watching the proprietor and his family through a crack in the door. The
baker and his wife appeared to have only one child, a daughter about
her age. On the third night, after two days eating the flour and sugar
dust off the floor of the shed, she broke the window of the bakery,
stuffed yesterday's bread down her shirt and, while the family was
downstairs assessing the damage, snuck into the apartment above.
She found the daughter's identification documents folded neatly in
a leather envelope on the bureau in her bedroom. For six months,
until she got to Israel, Sonia Baran, born in 1923, became Dasha
Garmash, born in 1925.

Isaiah was born in Tel Aviv in 1944. Many of his peers' parents
had stories like his mother's, and each took something different as a
moral. The Rebbe taught that, more important than searching for
lessons from the Holocaust, one should guard against despair. If
the Jews who survived sunk into despair, they became victims of
the Nazis, too. Jews should live with joy; serve God with joy. Isaiah
agreed with the Rebbe, of course, but he also believed that after
Hitler, a Jew who did not plan for a quick escape was a fool. And
Isaiah Grunwald was no fool.

So when Joe Weiss came to work grinning in the days after the
Davis murders appeared in the newspaper, Isaiah experienced not
just the shock of what had been done in his name, and the fear of
the consequences for himself and his fellow Lubavitchers, but the
unmooring knowledge that he so badly misjudged this man. How
could he have failed to see what he had let into his life? For two
days he did not eat; he lay in bed and could not sleep. He had taken
a step—many steps—in the wrong direction. He had crossed lines.
He had sinned. The sins had seemed minor; the victims removed

from his daily life, the actions not technically his. But there could be no doubt that he set into motion the series of events that led to the slaughter of three innocent people. It mattered little that he had not intended for Joe to commit murder. What had he intended when he instructed him to make the problem go away? A threat. What kind of threat? If he wanted someone to reason with the Davises, he could have tasked Daniel. But he chose Joe. Would he have approved of a black eye? A broken leg? A menacing note handed to a child? Where did what was moral turn into what was immoral? He turned these questions over in his mind until he realized that the answers made no difference. He had not intended the specific outcome, but should have foreseen it. He had encouraged— or at least allowed—Joe and the others who worked for him to think of the people in his buildings as unworthy of the help they would give fellow Jews. If they were lesser human beings, it was just another few steps to barely human at all.

He avoided Joe for three days. The California boy with the handsome face was a monster, and now Isaiah had a decision to make.

When Joe came to his office with the newspaper and the signatures he had taken from the Davis home, Isaiah did not give the speech he had been constructing in his mind. He did not yell or even question. Standing on the other side of his desk, Joe felt to him like a bomb about to explode. The longer Joe remained in Crown Heights, the more likely what he had done would be discovered. And if it were discovered, Isaiah feared that what had happened the summer before—the fires and the stabbings and the mayhem; the hate writ large on every face—would be repeated, magnified. With the match lit by a Jew, he knew that whatever sympathy the police and the goyim of the city had for his community would be obliterated. The death of that poor little boy on Utica Avenue had been an accident. This was murder. And he and his fellow Jews would be made to pay for it.

So Isaiah told Joe to go. Go and never come back.

"You have done the wrong thing," he said as the young man turned to leave his office. If Joe heard his boss, he did not respond. Isaiah remembered that Joe had the newspaper tucked beneath his arm, folded open to the page with the photograph of the mourners. As if he was proud.

When enough time passed that it didn't look suspicious, Isaiah asked Naftali Rothstein for the file on the murdered family and learned that the police did not appear to have anything that could connect him—or Joe—to the crime. After that, he did what he could do, what was all too easy for him: he wrote three checks. One was made out to Glorious Gospel, with the words "In memory of Malcolm and Sabrina Davis, and Kenya Gregory" written on the note line. The second, mailed in the same envelope as the first, was made out to Ontario Amos, "For the care and education of the child." The final check he took to an attorney outside the community. He instructed the man to create a trust for DeShawn Perkins. Invest it, he said, and send a little to his prison account each month. Isaiah knew DeShawn had been sentenced to life, but perhaps someday he would get out. If he did, he would need money.

The checks came from a bank account for "The Canada Fund, LLC," but all a curious soul would find if he went searching for the entity was a PO box on the Lower East Side. A PO box that Isaiah closed once the checks were cashed. He named the fund for Ontario, the little boy left behind. Maybe, he reasoned, the boy's mother had a connection there. Maybe she named him for a good memory.

Over the next few years, he sold his interest in most of the apartment buildings Joe and Daniel had visited. Let his former partners manage the tenants. Let them make those daily decisions that had led to this. By the summer of 2014, when the article about DeShawn appeared in the *Tribune*, Isaiah Grunwald owned only the four-story building on Kingston Avenue that housed his office on the second floor and his home on Crown Street. The rent from the storefront and two apartments at the Kingston address was enough to live on. He was getting old, and the gold bars meant he didn't need more for his family's security. Certainly, he did not deserve more.

CHAPTER THIRTY-SIX

I am sitting in a café on the ground floor of the Jewish Children's Museum on Eastern Parkway when Henrietta calls.

"That's him," she says. "How'd you find him?"

"It's a long story. You're sure that's who paid you to lie to the police?"

"Positive. I almost forgot how young he was. But he scared me good. Little shit." She pauses. I can hear slot machines ringing in the background. "I gotta get off before my shift manager sees me talking."

Henrietta hangs up before I can ask if she'll go on the record. I call back, but she sends me to voice mail.

I look at the photo of this man who I now know likely murdered three people and got away with it. He is, I have to admit, attractive. Large hazel eyes and a heart-shaped face. A man you would feel safe opening the door for. He is smiling at the camera in the portrait. Chin up, like he is proud; preening almost. Naftali and Daniel and the other Lubavitch men milling around me wear a black-brimmed hat that is slightly different from the ones the men in Borough Park and Roseville wear—it is angled down at the front, more like a fedora than a top hat. It occurs to me that that hat, which always seemed so stodgy and old-fashioned, is also, on Joe at least, almost rakish.

Mike calls at noon, and he isn't happy.

"The *Ledger* just went live with a story about some guy planting evidence in your cold case," he says. "They've got a surveillance photo and a comment from Michaels' office. Why don't we have this?"

"I . . . um . . . I actually had it, but I wanted to confirm . . ."

"You had it? What the fuck! We need to get this up *now*. And we need to advance."

I make the decision quickly. The photo is out there; if someone sees past the sunglasses and identifies Saul, I'm screwed. It'll look like I withheld the information because of my relationship with him. Which, of course, I did.

"I know who it is."

"What? Who? Is it on the record?"

"It's Saul Katz."

"Saul Katz. Why do I know that name?"

"Because he was my source on the Rivka Mendelssohn murder."

"Who?"

"Crane lady."

"Crane . . . oh, Jesus! You're kidding me. The disgraced cop?"

I figure I might as well go all in. "He's dating my mother."

"Fucking fuck, Rebekah. I . . . I'll call you back. Do not call the DA's office. You are off this story."

He hangs up and I sit, listening to the roar in my ears. My face is hot; it feels like needles are poking into and out of my skin.

My hands are shaking as I call Saul's cell.

"Where are you?" I ask. We left Naftali's office only an hour ago.

"I am home."

"You're going to get a call from the *Trib*."

"I see."

"I'm sorry. The *Ledger* has the photo online. Someone in the DA's office must have given it to them. It was only a matter of time before someone recognized you."

"Perhaps."

"Henrietta just called and she ID'd Joseph from the photo Naftali gave us. That's the man who paid her to lie to you. If he didn't kill the Davises, he knows who did."

I expect Saul to respond, but he doesn't.

"Saul?"

"I'm going to have to call you back, Rebekah. I need to make some arrangements."

And he's gone.

I e-mail the *Trib*'s library and ask them to run a backgrounder on Joseph Weiss, originally from California (*He'd be 40-something now. Lived in Brooklyn in 1991–1992ish*), and then pack up and head to Isaiah Grunwald's office. It's a little bit cooler out than the last few days, and the yeshiva students—all male, of course—are lingering on the sidewalks, chatting, sipping sodas, typing on smartphones. Two women, each pushing a double stroller, walk past with purpose.

The door to 318 Kingston is slightly ajar, so I push in. A bulletin board just inside lists Grunwald Management as being on the second floor. Halfway up the stairs, I hear a woman screaming.

"I don't know!" She says something else but I can't make out the words above the howls of another female voice. "Please! Come now! Help!"

I step inside the door marked Grunwald Management and find a woman in the reception area kneeling over a man who is splayed on the carpet, convulsing. Her arms to her elbows are blood smeared, and I can see her underwear beneath her flesh-colored pantyhose.

She appears to have pulled off her skirt in order to press it against the man's chest. The man, I realize as I step closer, is Naftali.

"Give me your shirt!" screams the woman when she sees me. I pull my flimsy H&M blouse over my head and hand it to her. She presses it against Naftali and it is soaked through in seconds. She tries to pull her own shirt off, but her hands are shaking so violently she cannot control her fingers to grasp the blood-slick buttons.

"Did you call 911?" I ask.

"Yes! Yes!" The woman turns to her colleague, a much younger woman—probably a teenager—who has her back pressed against the wall. Her eyes are wide and she is huffing a half-scream half-grunt with each breath. I watch as her face turns from white to purple.

"Hella!" shouts the woman on the floor. "Give me your skirt!"

But Hella can only gasp for air.

I look around for something else to press against Naftali's chest. Through a doorway about ten feet away I see the tail of a black coat. I crawl toward it and realize it is attached to a man. A dead man. Daniel. And he is not the only dead man in the office. An older man is bent backward over the arm of a leather desk chair, his eyes frozen open, a pink ring across his forehead where his hat pressed into his skin.

"What happened?" I whisper, almost to myself.

"He just started shooting!"

"Who?"

"I don't know! I don't know! Hella! Give me your skirt!"

But Hella's skirt won't help. Naftali is gone.

When help arrives, the only person they are able to assist is Hella, who gets oxygen, a stretcher down the stairs, and whisked away in one of the waiting Hatzolah ambulances. Someone brings the other woman, Goldy, a blanket to cover herself. I sit, shivering in my bra until an EMT hands me an FDNY T-shirt that is four sizes too big. The blood is everywhere. I won't be able to get it out of my cuticles for days.

Goldy tells the detectives that Naftali and Daniel came to the office unannounced—probably immediately after meeting with me and Saul—and that the three of them had been behind closed doors when the man with the gun arrived.

"Do you have any idea who he was?" asks the detective, Anne Richter.

"He was frum, but I never saw him before."

I pull out my phone and scroll to the photo of Joseph Weiss.

"Was this him?"

She looks hard for several seconds. "Maybe," she says. "Hella was the one who greeted him. I was at the photocopier."

Detective Richter turns to me. "Who is this?"

I explain, and when they are finished questioning me I call Henrietta, but she doesn't pick up. I leave a rambling message, then boil it down in a text:

Joe might have just shot 3 people in Brooklyn. Be careful.

On my way home in a livery cab, I text Amanda:

I've got some info on a shooting in Crown Heights

CHAPTER THIRTY-SEVEN

Spring 1993–August 2014

He'd been lucky, and smart, and he'd stayed out of prison. He didn't have to do jobs more than three or four times a year to live the way he wanted—which was alone. After Chicago, he rented a house on Martha's Vineyard during the off-season and returned most winters. He walked on the beach for miles and didn't see a soul. The people he met in bars, the girls who came over to fuck—paid and unpaid, though there was overlap—didn't ask a lot of questions.

But in Brooklyn, they had his real name, and they might even have his DNA. He avoided the borough entirely for twenty years; in 2002 he actually turned down fifty grand for an easy job in Bay Ridge because he knew that his first kills had been careless. He kept up on the news, however, and when he saw the article that said they'd found the letters he sent the Davises, he knew he needed to take care of it. Immediately.

He ordered the black pants and jacket and hat online, and two days later, at just after noon, he parked his car—a silver Hyundai; forgettable, dependable, with all the interior bells and whistles, and

the registration and insurance up to date—along the eastern edge
of Prospect Park. He walked toward Kingston Avenue with his gun
in his pocket.

Isaiah and Daniel did not have time to recognize him. The
third man, well, that was his bad luck. The woman who asked him
to wait at reception must have hidden herself when she heard the
shots, and he decided it was not worth hunting her down. The sooner
he was out of Brooklyn, the better.

His buddy with the tech job at the FBI had gotten him Hunny's new address. He figured he had less than twelve hours to exe-
cute before she got word there'd been a shooting in Crown Heights
and got on her guard.

There was a gas station across the street from her apartment
complex, and he stopped there to watch. At sunset, she drove into
the parking lot and took the stairs to the second floor. She'd gained
weight, but not as much as some women. Maybe, he thought,
she'd want to fuck him. For old time's sake.

He was taking a risk approaching without being certain she
was alone, but he wanted to be south of Richmond by midnight,
with Brooklyn behind him forever.

He wiggled out of the Chabad uniform in the driver's seat;
donned a plain black T-shirt, cargo shorts, and his Dodgers hat. He
knocked twice at apartment eight, and he was raising his arm for a
third rap when the bullet pierced his chest.

CHAPTER THIRTY-EIGHT

August 2014
Atlantic City, New Jersey

A lot of things had changed in her life since the summer Joe the Jew stuck a gun in her mouth, but a lot of things hadn't. She made better choices now, but still woke up every morning wanting to get high. She'd accepted that she always would, which was why she went to church, and why she kept fucking poor Marcus Reeves, with his bad knees and dopey anniversary celebrations. But she was no fool. Henrietta Day in 2014 may not do the same things Hunny Eubanks did in 1992, but she had seen the same things and felt the same pain and learned the same lessons. One of those lessons was that when she was sober, her gut was pretty good at detecting danger. And when she read that reporter's story in the newspaper, she knew shit was gonna come home to roost. If he was still alive, he'd have to try to get rid of her.

So she pulled Roger the night janitorial supervisor aside, and he got her a gun. Gina had one for a little while back when they lived together in Bushwick. A guy she used to see came by late one night and asked her to hold it. He didn't even wanna fuck, just needed to stash the thing. After a week, she sold it for a hundred dollars and they got high. Gina was dead now. Long dead. Like most of the people Hunny used to know. But not Hunny. Not yet.

What did she remember about Joe? He was smart, but not street smart—at least not as much as her. That could have changed by now. Either way, he was always going to be physically stronger. So she couldn't hesitate. She watched from the window, and when the white guy in the ball cap came across the parking lot, she pointed her gun at the door and waited for the knock.

After the first shot, she looked through the peephole. He was down, but not out. She opened the door and took three more shots until she was certain.

There was nothing in the apartment she couldn't replace. She could clean for cash anywhere she could get a reference, and there were still a couple people who would help her: a cousin near Savannah; an old classmate in Jacksonville. She knew they would all look for her—the police, the reporter. And maybe they'd find her. But she wasn't gonna give herself up. If they wanted her, they'd have to work hard, just like she'd done all her fucking life.

CHAPTER THIRTY-NINE

I take a livery cab home from Crown Heights, get in the shower to wash as much of the blood off me as possible, then open my laptop and start writing. I write about seeing Saul's name in DeShawn's file; I write about meeting Ontario and LaToya, and about finding the evidence box with Judge Sanchez. I write about the Pastors Green, Dorothy and Abel, and the lovesick Legal Aid lawyer-turned-real estate agent. I find the place in my notebook where I scribbled notes from that morning's meeting with Daniel and Saul and Naftali, and I add that conversation. I keep writing when Iris comes home, and when I'm done, I e-mail what I've written to Amanda.

Want some context on the latest murders?

About twenty minutes later, Amanda e-mails back.

Can you come over tomorrow?

I'm scheduled to work a 10-6 on the city desk, but I e-mail my cadre of fellow stringers and find someone to cover the shift. Everybody needs an extra $150 these days.

I don't sleep much, so at dawn, I start walking to Amanda's. I don my headphones but don't turn on any music. I feel like I have to listen to what's happening inside me, even though I don't know what it is. Is Joe coming for me next? Did I get those men killed? I still haven't heard from Hunny. The consequences of what I've done are so vast I worry that if I stop walking I'll collapse and never get up. Amanda brings two mugs of coffee outside and we talk on her front porch. She sits, but I can't.

"So how are you?" she asks.

"Okay."

"Have you ever seen bodies like that before?"

"Shot? Sort of," I say, remembering the kids beneath white sheets on the playground in Roseville. "Not that close up."

A few seconds pass.

"I can't publish what you sent me," she says. "I can't give these deaths that much more attention than I give everybody else. You know? That's not fair. But it's amazing. I can't believe how much you found out so fast. This shit happened decades ago. I e-mailed my friend at the *Guardian,* and she wants it, with some minor edits. Will the *Trib* let you do that?"

"As far as they're concerned, I'm off the story. Too close to it."

"Yeah, well, their loss. You're not hiding anything with this, and it needs to be out there. But listen, I've got a question for you. I applied for a grant from the Open Society a few months ago, and I just heard it came through. A hundred thousand dollars to expand the scope of the Project."

"Wow, that's awesome," I say. "What's your plan?"

"I want to hire you."

"Me?"

"I want to be able to write more about the people who die here.

I've got all this data and all these contacts, but I'm not the writer you are. And I'm not as good a reporter, either.

"We can work on the details, but I'm thinking, you pick a murder every week, maybe more, maybe less, and do a deep dive. And you can do issue stories, too. Look for patterns in what's happening. Domestic violence, the iron pipeline, mental illness, gangs. How are people really dying in this city, and why? My friend at the *Guardian* might be interested in partnering up, so your stories could have real reach. Which is what I want. It's hard for people to connect with maps and data. I need shoe leather. And narrative."

I look at her to make sure she's serious.

"What?" she asks. "What are you thinking?"

"I'm thinking with that much money you could hire someone away from *ProPublica,* or *The Times.*"

"Yeah," she says. "But I want you."

Detective Richter calls a few days after the shootings to tell me (off the record) that the gun found on the man shot to death outside Henrietta's Atlantic City apartment was the weapon that killed Isaiah, Naftali, and Daniel.

"The guy didn't have an ID, so we're still confirming he's who we think he is. Joseph Weiss has exactly zero paper trail since 1994."

I ask her about Henrietta, and she says they're still looking.

"We didn't find anything personal in her apartment. Even her boyfriend says he didn't know her real last name. Her prints are in the system, though. Eventually, she'll show up."

Or not.

The Sunday desk assigns Jack Owens to look into Joseph Weiss's background, but the only story he does is about Weiss getting kicked out of the Army in early 1993. Jack tells me at a happy hour a couple weeks later that he tracked down Weiss's former cellmate from military prison, but the *Trib* didn't think it was worth sending him to Indiana where the guy is incarcerated. So far, I haven't seen any reporting on the last twenty years of his life, except that his parents told the Associated Press they got a phone call from him once a year, on Yom Kippur.

The *Trib* and the *Ledger* and half a dozen other city news outlets send reporters up to Aviva's house in New Paltz where she and Saul hole up after the story of the corrupt Jewish cop who covered up for the Jewish murderer goes live. All three cable news networks cover the triple murder in Crown Heights, but Saul's involvement is too "inside baseball" to make waves nationally. Several papers contact Pete Olivetti, retired and living in Sarasota, but the best quote anyone gets is "Katz seemed like a straight shooter to me." Sandra Michaels maintains she is "looking at options" for charging him with something, and the NYPD calls him a "bad apple" at every opportunity, but Saul tells me his lawyer assures him the statute of limitations for anything that he did in 1992 has long expired. And even if DeShawn decides to sue, the lawyer says he'll almost certainly sue the city, or maybe the state, not Saul personally. The Kings County DA's office creates a "task force"—which consists of two people working a couple hours a week—to examine all of Saul's old cases. So far, they haven't found anything.

The people Saul helped lock up over two decades, however, are getting lawyers. And Aviva blames me. I hear nothing from her for weeks after the murders, and then early one Sunday morning she calls.

"All these crazies! Lawyers coming by the house! Letters from prisoners!"

"What?" I had been deep in a dream about my first apartment in Gainsville. The one Iris and I shared with two other girls sophomore year. In the dream we were throwing rocks into the pool from our concrete balcony. It was dusk and the pool light was on. There was something in the water we were trying to kill.

Saul's voice in the background: "Aviva!"

"She should know!"

Saul comes on the line.

"Rebekah, I'm sorry. This is . . . we need to have a discussion."

"What?"

"Your mother is very angry. . . ."

"You are angry, too!" shouts Aviva.

"Aviva, stop it!"

"Are you okay?" I ask. "Is she okay?"

"Yes. This has gone on long enough, Aviva."

"Where are you guys?" I ask.

"We are in Brooklyn. We drove back late last night. Your mother hasn't slept."

I look at the time on my phone: 5:18 A.M.

"We will come to you," he says.

Iris won't be up for hours, so I tell Saul to meet me at a park near my apartment. The sun is just up and the air is lighter, the pavement cool. This early, it's a different population in Park Slope. There are the runners—on their way to or from Prospect Park, smartphones velcroed to biceps, T-shirts commemorating the most recent race; and parents—men and women pushing strollers, wearing sunglasses, flip-flops, and drinking Venti coffee. I pick up my own coffee at a bagel shop. The woman next to me is wearing a baby strapped to her chest. The child is astonishingly blond and chewing on a plastic corn on the cob with the words JOHN DEERE printed across. I smile. If Iris were with me, we'd laugh and add the scene to our list of hipster details. Someday, we're going to write *Legally Blonde: Brooklyn,* get Reese to sign on as a perky pro bono lawyer for senior citizens being gentrified out by people like us, and make a million dollars. It feels like the first time I've smiled in weeks. It's hard not to think that a whole bunch of people would be alive today if it weren't for me. DeShawn is probably going to get out; he has one of the best exoneration attorneys in the country. But my mind keeps going to this: is his life worth three other people's? I know it's completely unanswerable, and the wrong question, and obviously unfair, but I can't stop thinking it. Iris and my therapist and my dad say it's crazy to blame myself. But the Davis murders were a case sitting in a dark room until I switched the light on. Would I have started making calls on DeShawn's letter if I had known how Joe Weiss was going to tie up loose ends? And if the answer is no, does that mean I made the wrong choice?

At seven o'clock I find Saul and Aviva sitting on a bench. She stands up when she sees me. He stands up after her.

"Thank you for coming," says Saul. He's a couple days past a shave, which is unusual.

Before I can even ask *what the fuck?* Aviva steps close to me and says, "I think you did this to Saul to get back at me."

I look at Saul.

"I didn't."

"Would you admit it?" asks Aviva. Her voice is tight and her stare fierce. "I don't think so."

"Saul? Can you get in here, please?"

"I am asking you a question, Rebekah."

"And I answered it, Aviva."

"See! She is so angry!"

"I'm not sure what I'm supposed to say."

"I want you to tell me the truth."

"You want me to tell you the truth, but you don't want me to tell other people the truth."

"This is not about other people."

"No," I say, "it's not about *you*. It's about three dead people in Crown Heights. And a cop who fucked up. And an innocent kid who wasted his life in prison. And a man who's probably been running around murdering people for twenty years."

"And you are so special you get to decide?"

I know she is barely my mother. I know that the connection we have is little more than biological. I know—or, I guess, I am beginning to realize—that my fantasies about a future of tender friendship between us were foolhardy. She doesn't get me. She barely even wants to. Fine. I can accept that. But the way she asks me if I think I'm special pinches at my heart. If my dad were here he'd stand up for me. He'd say, yes, she *is* special. She is one of a kind.

"All I did was tell the truth," I say quietly. "I'm not going to apologize for that."

"Why do you have to make everything so public?"

"Because I don't like secrets, okay! *You* gave me that. You left us with nothing but questions. If we don't fucking *admit* what really happened—if we *pretend*—the world just keeps getting shittier and shittier."

"And it is your job to change the world? Let me tell you something, Rebekah: the world will always be the same. There are bad people and they will do bad things and there is nothing you can do to change that."

"I don't believe that," I say.

"Neither do I, Aviva."

We both look at Saul.

"Rebekah is a reporter for the same reason I was a police officer. We believe we can make a little difference. And we believe it is our duty to try. I think you used to admire that about me."

"Well, look where that has gotten you."

"Aviva," Saul says, sighing. "You have to stop this. I made a mistake. *I* did the wrong thing. Your daughter, Rebekah, she did the right thing. You can yell and scream all you want, but you won't change that. And I can't imagine why you would want to. Look at this young woman you created. *Look* at her. If you don't see something beautiful . . ."

His voice cracks and I know he is thinking of Binyamin. Here we are, mother and daughter, both alive and healthy, pushing each other away like we will always have time to repair the damage we are doing.

Aviva looks at Saul. She sees it, too.

"I only want for things to be . . . easy between us," she says finally. "We have, all of us, been through so much. I just don't see why we should bring more heartache."

I could say that things will never be easy between us. And I could say that she is the one who made it so. I could even say that she doesn't doesn't deserve an easy relationship with me if she can't bring herself to at least attempt to understand what I've devoted my life to. But instead I put my hand on her arm and say, "I know."

CHAPTER FORTY

November 2014
Coxsackie Correctional Facility, Coxsackie, New York

DeShawn was snapping green beans when the CO with the terrible breath and the earring came to bring him upstairs.

"Perkins, you got an emergency call."

It was two days before Thanksgiving, and they were deep in the weeds with prep. His boss, Manny, was grumpy because Charles had, once again, neglected to label the jugs of vegetable oil (*"It's obvious what they are!"* / *"That's not the point!"*), and everyone was on edge waiting for the judge's ruling in DeShawn's case.

"Go ahead," said his boss, Manny. "God bless."

DeShawn took off his apron and squinted, red-faced and teary from the sting of the onion air and the heat of eleven ovens. He had been bringing in the articles for months: the withheld evidence; the dead Jewish killer; the still-missing ex-hooker. But nobody was getting their hopes up. The men on the kitchen staff knew that the system that put them in their cages was designed to keep them there. Prosecutors didn't admit mistakes if they didn't absolutely have to. Judges looked for any reason to reject your appeal. If your motion wasn't just so, if the legal rationale not in exactly the right vernacular: *denied*. Justice had nothing to do with it. It was a game of language and egos, and if you couldn't afford a good lawyer—even a good jailhouse lawyer—you didn't stand a chance.

For more than ten years after his conviction, DeShawn was angry about this. *They gonna lock me up for nothing? I'm gonna make 'em regret it*. He fought over nothing and got locked in the box and got even angrier. And there was a lot to be angry about. He never got a letter, never had a visitor. There was a hundred dollars in his account every month, but nobody could tell him where it came from. Was somebody fucking with him? He spent the money on little things—a sweatshirt, a decent razor, snacks—and hustled a little more cash where he could. But a good hustler was friendly, and DeShawn had turned into a man people tiptoed around. He never shook who he wanted to be, though. He never shook Malcolm. So when Manny chatted him up after DeShawn transferred from Sing Sing to Coxsackie in 2004, he let the lifer from Flatbush draw him out.

"You from Brooklyn, right?" asked Manny one night after dinner. Manny was pushing a seven-foot metal cart of food trays through the dining hall, and DeShawn was dawdling, checking out flyers for jobs in the laundry and the library, notices about upcoming movies, warnings about contraband and HIV.

"Yeah," he answered.

Manny pointed to another tray cart. "Wheel that back for me?"

Manny was a talker. He'd killed two people in a home invasion in 1983 and knew he was going to die behind bars. His kids visited a couple times a year, and he had people he could trust inside. He was part of the Brooklyn crew at Coxsackie, and for as long as anybody could remember, Brooklyn ran the kitchen.

At first, DeShawn just listened. But because they were always talking about cooking, pretty soon he told a story about Sabrina.

"She used to give me and the other kids assignments. She'd be like, here's a recipe, now figure out how to make twice as much. Or half as much. She was trying to teach us math, but, you know, be fun about it. One Christmas we were gonna make this gingerbread house, and I was all excited because I was gonna take it to school. I told everybody. But I did something wrong with the baking soda. Or maybe I used baking soda instead of baking powder. So the walls and shit came out all soft and you couldn't stand 'em up to build the house. I cried and Sabrina was like, it's really hard to be good at baking. She said, 'Cooking is an art. Baking is a science.'"

"That's true," said Manny.

"So that was like a challenge to me, you know? Like, I'm gonna be a *scientist*."

Manny and Charles exchanged a look.

"Charles been wanting to get out of bread and cake. You game?"

DeShawn shrugged.

"I'm getting pretty sick of watching you shrug, DeShawn," said Manny. "You just gonna shrug the next fifty years of your life away? *I don't know.* Shit."

"Fine," said DeShawn. "I'm game."

It was an easy fit. DeShawn loved the bakery. He loved the smells from the oven—sweet in such a sour place. The crunch of sugar in buttery batter and the way the flour tasted in the air. Some guys inside sold drugs, some sold their law knowledge, some sold tattoos— DeShawn sold cakes. Mostly birthdays and parole, but the cakes tasted so good guys started creating occasions: Danny from the Bronx benched a record; Woodstock Steve finally cut his stupid fucking braid. The endeavor gave his brain something to focus on. He could charge more for lettering on the frosting, or carrot cake instead of plain yellow. And the more creative he got, the more people ordered. If he got everything done for the kitchen and they had leftovers— which they always did—Manny was cool with it. The CO's, too, as long as DeShawn dropped everything to whip up something pretty for an almost-forgotten anniversary.

Over the years, he sent his letter and the photocopies of his case file to hundreds of lawyers, hoping somebody would take his case. In 2012, he watched a program on TV about a group of journalism students in Chicago who got people exonerated. So he started sending letters to reporters.

The lady from the *Trib* was the first person who wrote back, and just a few months later the whole world looked different. He had a lawyer with a Manhattan office, and what everybody in the kitchen thought was a damn good chance of eventually getting out. As soon as the shit went down in Crown Heights, he started getting letters himself. LaToya wrote, and Dorothy Norris, and Pastor Green. There were apologies, and explanations, and promises. He wasn't sure what to do with it all. Ontario was the only one who actually came to see him. The nine-year-old DeShawn remembered was now six inches taller and a hundred pounds bigger than his older foster brother, but he cried like a baby in the visiting room. Poor kid didn't know what to think. He blamed himself, sure he must have pointed the finger in some way. DeShawn let him get it out, and when he composed himself they started talking food. Ontario said that he might be able to get him a job at a restaurant. Once that was in the air, DeShawn couldn't help but hope. He'd never really been able to see himself outside again. Where would he fit? In a kitchen, of course.

As he followed the CO up to the phones, DeShawn reminded

himself that even if the judge said no now, it wasn't the end. This was only their first try, his attorney had assured him. There were always other motions and other strategies. With all the new evidence, it was just a matter of time.

He picked up the receiver in the counselor's office. It was his attorney, Harry Blum.

"DeShawn, you ready for some good news?"

"Sure."

"The judge reversed your conviction. And I just got off the phone with Sandra Michaels. Her office isn't going to re-try your case. They sent a messenger to Albany with the judge's order this morning. The paperwork should be at the prison tomorrow. You can spend Thanksgiving with your family."

Ontario, Tammy, and the two girls were waiting in the parking lot. DeShawn felt all kinds of terrible making them battle holiday weekend traffic, and even worse that the situation all but forced them to invite him to Thanksgiving dinner. He started to apologize but Tammy shook her head.

"It's like I told Ontario and the girls. Either you're family or you're not. If you're family, you're family. And Ontario says you're family."

Tammy insisted DeShawn ride up front. She squeezed herself between the carseats in the back of the Maxima, and all three females quickly fell asleep.

They merged onto the Palisades south. It was a clear day, and many of the trees still held their leaves.

"You got a beautiful family," said DeShawn.

"We try," said Ontario. And then a moment later: "I do. I know."

From the George Washington Bridge, DeShawn caught his

first glimpse of the city. The city he'd never left until he left in shackles. The towers downtown were gone, he knew that. But what else was no longer there? And what had replaced it? Cars sped by and DeShawn rolled his shoulders back, straightening his posture to face his new life. He wasn't yet forty. He had living to do.

"Kenya's birthday is tomorrow," said Ontario as they crept onto the Brooklyn Bridge from the FDR. "It always gets lost in Thanksgiving. I'm counting on you to surprise her with a cake."

ACKNOWLEDGMENTS

Thank you to my agent, Stephanie Kip Rostan. Your belief in my abilities and ideas has allowed me to live this dream of being a novelist. Thank you to Gillian Flynn for introducing us, and thank you to the entire team at Levine Greenberg Rostan for your hard work and cheerful attitudes.

Thank you to my editor, Kelley Ragland, for being patient while I learned to be a mom this past year. Thank you to Andy Martin, Elizabeth Lacks, Sarah Melnyk, and the entire Minotaur gang for your constant support and encouragement.

Thank you to my friends and colleagues at CBS News: Erin Donaghue, Graham Kates, Michael Roppolo, Susan Zirinsky, Nancy Lane, Dan Carty, and Paula Cohen.

Thank you to Mordechai Lightstone, Shabaka Shakur, Maurice Possley, Eugene O'Donnell, Michelle Harris, and Shulem Deen for sharing your insight and expertise.

Thank you to all the amazing people with the Jewish Book Council, Jewish Federations, and Hadassah for hosting me in your communities and providing the opportunity to meet with and learn from readers across the country.

Thank you to my Fresno, California, public school teachers: Gordon Funk and Bill Greene at Manchester Elementary; Marty Mazzoni at Edison-Computech Junior High; and especially Robert Jarnagin at Bullard High School who taught me, in the words of Harold Bloom, "how to read, and why."

Thank you, as always, to my family: my father, Bill Dahl, for inspiring me to get interested in the law, but to avoid becoming a lawyer; my mother, Barbara Dahl, for telling me to "bring a book" wherever I go; my sister, Susan Sharer, for being my tireless publicist; my sister-in-law, Lori Bukiewicz, for taking such good care of me and my son while I finished this book; and my husband, Joel Bukiewicz, for everything, but especially for making me laugh every single day. This book is dedicated to my son, Mick, the sweetest soul I know.